# Gangstress

# Gangstress

by

*INDIA*

URBAN
BOOKS

*www.urbanbooks.net*

Urban Books, LLC
300 Farmingdale Road, NY-Route 109
Farmingdale, NY 11735

ISBN 13: 978-1-60162-135-1
ISBN 10: 1-60162-135-3

First Trade Paperback Printing June 2019
Printed in the United States of America

10 9 8 7 6 5 4 3 2 1

*This is a work of fiction. Any references or similarities to actual events, real people, living or dead, or to real locales are intended to give the novel a sense of reality. Any similarity in other names, characters, places, and incidents is entirely coincidental.*

Distributed by Kensington Publishing Corp.
Submit Orders to:
Customer Service
400 Hahn Road
Westminster, MD 21157-4627
Phone: 1-800-733-3000
Fax: 1-800-659-2436

# Gangstress

by

*INDIA*

# Prologue

## *The Verdict*

I was nervous as a muthafucka sitting in the courtroom, awaiting the verdict on running a continual criminal enterprise. Shit was going in slow motion, and I couldn't hear anything because my damn heartbeat was pounding loud as hell through my eardrums. I glanced at the jury, which consisted of twelve of my peers. They were men and women from all walks of life. Some were brown while others were pale. A few of them were big, and some were small. Although they had several differences among them, the one thing they all had in common was that I couldn't read their expressions.

Swallowing hard, I redirected my attention toward my lawyer, who was the best attorney money could buy. However, I soon shifted my gaze again because I couldn't read him either. His Italian ass was sitting here sugar sharp with money I had shelled out for him to get me out of this mess, and his nonchalant demeanor had me up in arms. His expression told me either he had this case in the bag and I would be out of here before lunch, or his ass knew I was going up the creek without a paddle. If that was the case, he would surely attempt to use the $4 million I had given him to get the fuck out of dodge. What he didn't know was I had already sent someone to get to know his family in the worst way if shit went sideways, if you get my drift.

By the way, my name is Janelle Renee Doesher, but the world has come to know me as Jane Doe. I'm the boss of America's first publicly known All Female Mafia, or AFM for short. If you don't know about me or my pedigree, all you have to do is pick up any current newspaper article or the latest issue of any hood magazine. If that fails, then just ask a muthafucka about me, because my name rings bells for the shit that I've orchestrated and executed with perfection. I ain't one to brag nor boast, but what I will do is recommend you go and do your research, because my reputation speaks for itself. I'm not new to this. I'm true to this. Always have been and always will be. My daddy was gangsta, and from birth, I was destined to follow in his footsteps.

This wasn't my first time in a courtroom. Truth be told, this was my third time at the defendant's table. The first two times I was there as a kid on some juvenile shit like trespassing and running away from my grandmother's home. Lucky for me I got off easy and had it expunged from my record. I vowed never to fuck up again, and by "fuck up" I mean to get caught. Hell, my ass wouldn't have ever stepped foot back into a place like this had it not been for some snitch who saw fit to throw my ass in front of the bus because they couldn't handle the pressure of going upstate to do a bid.

The more I thought about it, the madder I got. I began to chew on the inside of my jaw until I felt the tissue separate and I tasted blood, which I swallowed. It's funny how everybody rolls with you when the times are good and your paper is long. They swear to ride or die with you until they find themselves in a predicament that nobody but God could get them out of. Once they find out they're facing hard time, they'll start singing like a canary. The killer part is if they ass never would have said anything in the first place, everybody would've been home scot-free and back to getting money. But now my ass was facing a minimum of twenty years with a maximum life sentence behind bars because some weak-ass snitch didn't want to do a measly three years.

As my thoughts wrapped around my life and the current situation someone had put me in, I unconsciously glanced up at the clock on the wall, knowing that if I were to be found guilty, all hell would break loose. The remaining members of my crew who were still out in the streets would bring death to the doorstep of the person who put me here. It was a harsh reality, but it was what it was at this point.

"Come on, Jane. It's show time," my attorney, Richard Lennigan, whispered. He fastened the middle button on his tailor-made Italian suit then stood, so I followed suit.

"Men and women of the jury, how do you find the defendant, Ms. Janelle Renee Doesher?" the black middle-aged judge named Joseph B. Hemsly asked the nervous group of jurors. A heavy-set African American lady with full lips and a burgundy Afro, giving off an Angela Davis vibe, offered a sympathetic glance my way. I knew what she was about to say before she even spoke the words from her lips into the atmosphere.

"We, the jury, find the defendant, Janelle Renee Doesher . . ."

At this point, I blacked out and heard nothing else as images of my life flashed before my eyes. I saw instant replays of highlights and even a few low points in my life. There were also a few vivid images of my parents, and I began to cry. For it was the very day they left this earth that my life took a turn for the worse. Overnight I became a woman and a menace to society at the same damn time.

Here's my story from the beginning.

# Chapter One

## *Fourteen Years Ago*

"Happy birthday, baby girl!" my daddy said upon entering the kitchen. "Today is your day, and you can have whatever you like." He planted a kiss on my cheek.

"I can have anything, Daddy?" I smiled, and he nodded. My mother, Monica, tried to conceal her smile while shaking her head in a disapproving manner.

"Julius, if Janie gets one more thing, we will need to buy a bigger house," my mother added.

"Then I guess we just need to call the real estate agent right now, because there ain't nothing in this world that my daughter can't have." He playfully slapped my mom's big, round butt, and she giggled like a schoolgirl. I loved to watch the two of them interact with each other. They had been together for eighteen years, yet they still treated each other like they'd just met.

"That girl is spoiled."

"Well, that makes two of us," I added from my seat at the kitchen table, and everyone laughed. My father was the best provider a girl could ask for. We lived in the lap of luxury and were spoiled with everything afforded to rich people. The way we lived our lives most normal people could only dream about.

"So how old are you, eleven?" he teased.

"Daddy, you know I'm sixteen." I smacked my lips.

"Sixteen!" He grabbed his chest and pretended to have a heart attack. "Where did the time go?" he asked my mother while glancing at his Cartier wristwatch.

"I know, our little girl is growing up." She smiled.

"In my mind, you will always be my little girl." My daddy planted another kiss on my cheek.

"In a minute she'll be dating, then marriage and kids." My mother wiped a tear.

"Fuck that! Ain't no nigga good enough for my daughter." My father shook his head as the doorbell rang.

"Daddy." I laughed while scurrying into the foyer to see which of my party guests had arrived. When I reached the oversized door, I could see Ace, my godbrother, through the glass panes. He was standing there in a Black Label long-sleeved shirt with the matching jeans, carrying a card and a teddy bear and holding a balloon that read "Happy Birthday."

"What's up, fam?" He hugged me, and I tried not to shudder. The scent of his Issey Miyake cologne had me dizzy.

"Hey, Ace. Thank you for the card." I snatched it and headed back into the kitchen with him on my tail.

"What's up, pops." He bumped knuckles with my dad and kissed my mother on the cheek. Next, he went into the fridge and searched for something to eat. Ace was practically family, so no one paid him any attention.

"I'm for real, Janie." My father picked the conversation back up where he had left off. "If a nigga can't love you, respect you, and take care of you the way I love, respect, and take care of you, then fuck him!" My father was as serious as a heart attack, and I felt one of his speeches coming on.

Ace peered at me while smashing a piece of cold chicken, and I looked away. Over the years we'd played this game of cat and mouse, but we both knew it wouldn't lead to anything serious out of respect for my father.

"Janelle, pay attention," my father continued. "These little girls get with these knucklehead boys and lose their minds. Half of these niggas are selling wooden nickels anyway. They don't have a pot to piss in or a window to throw it out of, but somehow they manage to talk these girls out of their panties and common sense."

"Julius!" my mother interjected, and Ace and I burst out laughing. Although my father was in his thirties, he had the soul of an old nigga and would drop lines straight from the seventies. What in the hell was he talking about wooden nickels for anyway?

"What, Monica? I'm speaking the truth." My father kept it one hundred all the time whether you liked it or not. He never sugarcoated anything, and I admired that about him.

"Janie ain't trying to hear no lectures on her birthday. Save that conversation for another day."

"I just want her to know that she don't have to fall for the first nigga who shows interest in her." He turned his attention back to me. "All these dudes want is some pussy, and you're more than a piece of ass! The world is yours, baby, and you're worth waiting for, believe that!" he said while gazing at me with loving eyes.

"I know, Daddy." I smiled.

"Anyway, I ain't gon' ruin your birthday with one of my rants, so I'll zip it for now." He pretended to lock his lips up and throw away the imaginary key.

"Open the card, girl," Ace instructed me.

"I was going to wait until the party, but since you're rushing me, I guess I have no choice." I slid my acrylic fingernail across the pink envelope and pulled out the card. Before I could even read the words, two $100 bills caught my attention.

"Aw, thanks, Ace!" I wanted to hug him again but didn't want to make my parents suspicious.

"No problem, fam. Don't spend it all in one place." He tossed the naked chicken bone into the trash.

"That's so sweet," my mother gushed.

"Good looking out for your sister. That's what big brothers are supposed to do." My father patted Ace on the shoulder. "If anything ever happens to me, you better protect my two ladies like your life depends on it."

"Julius, stop talking that nonsense. You ain't going nowhere." My mother hated to speak about death, but my father knew it was always lurking around the shadows. In the dope game, he was the man. Therefore, he had more enemies than friends and never knew when someone would try to come for the king.

"Pop, you know I got you, but like Monica said, you ain't going nowhere." His cell phone buzzed.

"Yeah, I know you got me, young'un, because I trained you well." My father was proud of his protégé, as if he were his own son.

"I hate to break up this family moment, but that was money calling." Ace placed the phone into his pocket.

"Go get that money, son. I'll get with you later." My father once again bumped knuckles with Ace and walked him to the door.

"I think a certain someone has a crush on another certain someone." My mother smiled, exposing both of her deep dimples.

"I do not have a crush on Ace." I rolled my eyes, trying my best not to tell on myself.

"I wasn't even referring to you. I was gonna say it's the other way around." She giggled.

"What's so funny?" My father reentered the kitchen.

"Nothing. Janie and I were talking about something we saw at the mall yesterday." My mother winked at me.

Just then there was another knock at the door. I jumped up because I knew it was either my best friend, Alicia, from down the street or another friend here for my big party.

Swinging the front door wide open, I frowned at the sight of the short, chubby woman standing before me with a matted Afro. It was Pauletta, my grandmother. "Well, hello to you too," she said to my back as I turned and headed back to the kitchen table.

Don't get me wrong, I loved my grandmother because I had to, but I didn't like her very much. Whenever she came to visit us, she would almost always manage to make my mother cry or piss my father off. Pauletta frowned and turned her nose up at the way we were living, but for the life of me, I couldn't understand why. My father was her son, and I thought she should be proud of the lifestyle he provided for his family. We lived in a prominent upscale community north of Detroit. Our home was immaculate, to say the least. It measured 4,000 square feet and sat on a large plot of land in a fairly new neighborhood. We had two living rooms, a dining room, five bedrooms, four bathrooms, a media room, a playroom, a barber/beauty shop, and a country-style kitchen with marble flooring and granite countertops.

"What brings you by, Mama?" my daddy asked after giving her a brief hug.

She removed her old, worn trench coat and held up a gift bag. "I came for the birthday girl." She shook the present like it contained a million dollars, and I smiled, although I knew better. My grandmother was very frugal. Last year she got me a sweater from the Goodwill, and the year before that she purchased me a $5 gift card to Walmart. "Well, aren't you going to open it?"

"Yes, ma'am." I smiled and removed the pink and purple gift bag from her hand. After I pulled out the metallic tissue paper, my gift was revealed. It was a Lisa Frank diary accompanied by a pack of colored pens.

"All young girls like diaries, right?" she asked.

I nodded to play along, and then I gave her a hug. "Thank you, Gran," I said with more excitement than I actually felt. For one thing, I was sixteen, and Lisa Frank was so four years ago. I also didn't know what to do with it because my father had often warned me never to write important things down on paper. I didn't exactly know what he meant by that, but I always followed his instructions.

"You're welcome, sweetheart. I know it's not what you're used to, but it's all we hardworking, nine-to-five folks can afford." My grandmother placed her black purse down on the cherry wood table and took a seat. Her comment was meant as a jab, and it struck a chord with my mother. I watched as she rolled her eyes and excused herself from the room. She quickly retreated down to the basement where the party was to be held. Her excuse was to finish decorating, but we all knew what the deal was.

"Mama, why are you always starting some shit?" I knew my dad was furious by the way the vein bulged from his dark forehead. Staring in his direction, I noted that he was a handsome man even when he was angry. His ebony skin was flawless, which accented the whites in his eyes and his pearly white teeth. His hair was black and wavy. His eyelashes were long, and the goatee around his mouth gave the dimple in his chin definition. My daddy wasn't very tall, probably five feet nine inches at best, but he spent a lot of time in the gym. What he lacked in height he made up for in muscles.

"Julius, you better watch how you speak to me," Gran warned with the wag of her finger.

"I'm sorry for disrespecting you, Mama, but every time you come here you make these rude-ass comments, and I don't know why."

"I'm just speaking the truth, son. Y'all over here living like the Kennedys when everybody around you lives in a recession."

"Damn, it's like you mad that we have moved up in our lives. I offered you this life. You refused it!" he said through clenched teeth.

"You are damn right I refused it!" Gran yelled. "You people call this the glamorous life, but ain't a damn thing glamorous about constantly looking over your shoulder." She huffed. "Julius, I raised you better than this! I worked three jobs to provide a good life for you. I kept you in church and kept your head in them schoolbooks. You should've gone to school and made something of yourself," she continued to fuss.

"Mama, in case you haven't noticed, I have made it!" My father pointed at himself. "How many niggas do you know of in the hood who are living this good?" He hit the table, and my grandmother's purse fell to the floor.

"Yes, you made it, son, but you made it with other people's blood on the money you spend every day."

Gran was overweight by a good hundred or so pounds. I knew getting her purse off the floor was much too difficult a task, so I snatched it up and handed it back to her.

"Mama, I don't give a damn whose blood is on it. As long as I can provide for my family and satisfy their needs, I'm good. When I go to sleep at night, my conscience is clear."

"You should be setting a better example for Janelle. You think she'd be proud of the occupation you have?"

At the mention of my name, I decided to vacate the premises. I needed to go and check on my mother anyway, but before I was even at the basement door, I heard my father speak again.

"My daughter ain't stupid. She knows the truth! I'm a hustler, and I'm going to hustle until the day I die! Why can't you understand that, Mama?"

"Listen, son, all that killing, stealing, and drug dealin' ain't what the Lord intended for the world, and it pisses Him off. No matter how tough you are on those streets, you ain't no match for the Creator. Your arms are too short to box with God, son, and soon your time will be up," Gran warned.

"Well, until the good Lord calls me home, I'm gonna ball until I fall! The legacy I plan to leave for my daughter will be epic!"

Those words are forever etched into my mind because that was one of the last things I heard my daddy say.

# Chapter Two

A crash through the kitchen window grabbed everyone's attention. Items flew into the house like grenades. There appeared to be several small cans with smoke spilling out. Before my daddy had time to react, someone or something tried to force its way into the back door. "Janie, take Gran to the safe room and tell your mama to lock up," he yelled, and I reached for my grandmother's hand as she waddled toward me.

"Daddy, come on," I screamed.

"I'll be down there in one moment, sweetie." He winked to reassure me, but I knew he wasn't coming. As soon as we made it down into the basement, my mother waved us over to the safe room.

"Hurry up!" she urged, having already heard the commotion going on upstairs.

We entered the small, vaulted room and locked the door behind us. My mother flipped on the security cameras to get a bird's-eye view of the situation. There were a total of nine twelve-inch monitors linked to hidden surveillance cameras strategically placed throughout the house. Previously, my daddy said he wanted to be aware of every move being made throughout the house in his absence. I thought he was just being paranoid, but today the security footage was very helpful.

Monitor six displayed the kitchen, and I could see my daddy covering his mouth from the gas. He was backed into a corner, holding one of the pistols he kept in the kitchen pantry. The smoke was a greenish gray color, and it was so thick that it was becoming difficult to see anything. I couldn't tell what was going on upstairs, but I could hear things being shattered. The safe room was soundproof but allowed the sound from the outside to come in.

I squeezed my mom's left hand nervously, and she patted my back with her free hand. Although I could tell she was a nervous wreck on the inside, her facial expression was calm, cool, and collected. "It's okay, baby," she reassured me while studying the monitors. Her big brown eyes squinted, trying to see what the hell was going on. Out of habit, she began to chew on her full lips. My mother was a dime, if I said so myself, and I was glad that I favored her. In my opinion, she resembled a thicker version of the rapper Charli Baltimore, with light skin and similar facial features like those pouty lips and slanted eyes. The two women even shared the same body type, height and all. The only noticeable difference was that my mother's hair was honey blond instead of red. "Daddy will be okay," she added, still holding her emotions in check for my sake.

"Why are they doing this?" I cried.

"That's the game, baby," she responded like this home invasion was nothing. I had never been involved in anything like this, so I was scared.

Bang. Bang. We heard shots pop off upstairs, and that's when my mother lost her cool and went ballistic. She immediately hit the key code on the safe and reached inside to retrieve two Desert Eagles. With one gun in each hand, she turned to me. "Janie, Mommy loves you so much, and I'm so proud of the woman you've become!"

"Where are you going?" I panicked.

"Daddy needs my help, baby." She kissed my cheek.

"Mom, don't leave me please," I begged. We heard it again: pop, pop, pop.

"Gran will be here with you, and everything will be okay. Don't be scared, baby girl." My mother kissed me one last time and headed out of the safe room. That was the very moment that I learned firsthand what a down-ass bitch was. Many people talk about that shit, but my mother was a real one. Without a second thought, she risked her life to save his.

A few moments after she left, I wiped my tears and turned my attention to the television monitors. Frantically, I searched for a visual of her and held my breath until she appeared on the screen. As I watched, things seemed to move in slow motion as she crept up the stairs and into the formal living room. I figured her plan was to go through the living area, into the dining room, then into the kitchen to sneak up on the attackers. But just as the smoke began to clear, I saw a masked gunman creep up behind her. This was like a scary movie, and I wished I could've turned the channel.

"Mommy!" I screamed as if she could hear me, but it was useless. My ears started ringing, but I didn't hear the shot that sent my mother to the floor. However, I did see her stomach explode as the bullet pierced her skin and penetrated her body.

"'Yea, though I walk through the valley of the shadow of death . . .'" My grandmother had begun to pray while I frantically searched for life in my mother. "This was not supposed to happen this way," Gran kept screaming and shaking her head. My mother hadn't moved, but where was my father?

Finally, on monitor two, I saw my daddy crawling toward the front door. He was wounded but still alive. In an instant and without hesitation, I reached for one of the weapons inside of the open safe. I wasn't sure what type of gun it was, but I vaguely remembered my father calling it Nina.

"Janelle, what are you doing? They'll kill you!" Gran warned.

I didn't bother to reply. In my mind, I was already dead without my mother and father. If they killed me, at least we would all be together again.

I hit the stairs three at a time and gripped the gun like my life depended on it. On several occasions, my daddy had taken my mom and me to the gun range, so I was well educated with how to pull the trigger. As I made it to the top of the stairs, I paused to listen but heard nothing except the sound of police sirens. Figuring the worst was over, I headed over to my father, because trying to save my mother was no longer an option. I knew with a hole the size of Texas in her stomach, she was already on her way to the afterlife. When I reached my father, I noticed he was hurt pretty bad and bleeding from everywhere.

"Janelle." He tried to speak but went into shock and started gasping for air.

"Daddy, who did this to you?" I cried and dropped my head onto his bloody shoulder, holding on to him for dear life. I desperately needed my daddy to get up. He couldn't die. Not today, on my birthday. "Daddy, who did this?"

"Family," I heard him whisper, then he gurgled up blood. I didn't know what he meant that day, but in the years to come, it would hit me like a ton of bricks.

# Chapter Three

The death of my parents was devastating, to say the least. The memory of our last day together is forever at the forefront of my mind. I often wondered who was responsible for the heinous crime, and I vowed daily to get answers one way or another. I wanted so badly to seek vengeance on the culprits. The shit they caused had a domino effect on my life, because things just kept getting worse.

With both my parents gone and no other family to claim me, I had two options: become a ward of the state or live with Gran. Neither option was ideal, but I reasoned with myself that Gran's house had to be better than living in the system. Boy, was I wrong!

The first sign that Gran was on that bullshit was while planning my parents' funeral. With all the money my father had, everyone expected him and my mom to be laid out in style. I'm talking tailor-made suits, custom caskets, the whole nine. Instead, Gran had them cremated before having a simple memorial service at her church. I questioned her about her choice of funeral arrangements. Her excuse was there was no need to send them to hell in style. It really pissed me off, but what could I do?

Her second strike occurred when she donated all the money that my parents' friends had given her out of respect for my father to the muthafuckin' church. Her pastor praised her for being a saint, but I thought the old bitch was crazy. Didn't she notice that her beloved pastor had upgraded from a Lincoln Town Car to a Lincoln Navigator while she still drove a Ford Escort? When the pastor and his family went home to a mini mansion in Bloomfield Hills, we went home to a raggedy, run-down apartment on Woodward.

Gran's third strike came when she changed my school and stripped me of everything I owned. I went from riches to rags, so to speak. She made me donate all of my Michael Kors, Alexander McQueen, Coach, and other designers to the homeless shelters in her neighborhood. Then she took me shopping at Kmart. Ain't that some shit? While I walked around looking like a bum, the bums walked around fresh to def. I was tired of Gran, her rules, and her way of living. Night after night I prayed to wake up from this nightmare, but day after day I awoke to the same shit. It was time to make a move and get the fuck out of dodge. I'd been here ten months and twelve days. Today would be my last.

"Ain't you gon' say good morning?" Gran spoke from the corduroy sofa that had seen better days.

*Damn, you didn't even give me a chance!* I thought, but I said, "Good morning."

"You better hurry up before you miss that bus for school." She gave me the once-over with her eyes. "Why are those pants so tight? And why are your bra straps showing?"

"It's the style, Gran." I sighed and grabbed an apple from the kitchen. I started to grab two since I knew it might be a minute before my next meal. I didn't know where I was going, but I was hell-bent on leaving here.

"Girl, you better fix them clothes before somebody mistake you for a streetwalker."

"Yes, ma'am." I bit the apple and pulled my top over my shoulders. "See ya later," I lied.

"You're forgetting something."

"No, I have everything," I lied again.

"What about that book bag?" She pointed a finger in need of a manicure to the red backpack on the floor.

"I don't need it anymore."

"And why not?"

"Because today is the last day of school and then we're out for summer vacation." I hadn't lied about that part. Today was the last day of school, which made my getaway that much smoother. Teachers were not taking attendance. They couldn't care less if I showed up for class. Therefore, the truancy line wouldn't call and alert Gran of my absence.

"All right, I guess." She looked skeptical. "Well, come straight home, because tonight we have a meeting at the church," she reminded me on my way out the door. I rolled my eyes because the only meeting I had today was with the next thing smoking away from here.

# Chapter Four

After five long hours and three bus transfers, I was back in my old neighborhood. My parents' property had been seized by the FBI. Therefore, I couldn't go home, but I did feel good being back on the old block. Everything appeared to be the same, minus the FOR SALE sign in our front yard. I started to go kick the sign down but decided to keep walking toward Alicia's house instead. The school she went to was already on summer vacation, so I knew she would be home.

Just as I rounded the corner, my best friend Alicia Malone came out on to her porch with a magazine and her cell phone. "What's up, girl?" I called out while walking down the street. She squinted from the sun and smiled wide when she figured out who I was.

"Damn, bitch, you can't call nobody." She ran off the porch toward the sidewalk to greet me.

"I've been on lockdown," I explained.

"Girl, I've been missing you so much." She smiled again. "I didn't get a chance to make sure you were okay after what happened." She put her hand on her curvy hips.

The top of her body was small, but from the hips down she was at least a size twelve. Alicia was brown skinned with high cheekbones and a big smile that was very contagious. We'd been best friends since kindergarten, and nothing would ever change that. Both of our daddies had hustled and lost their lives in the game. It just so happened that my father and her father were also best friends. She was practically my sister, and I was happy to be back in her presence.

"Girl, did you hear me?" Ali snapped her fingers.

"Yeah, I heard you," I lied. I couldn't recall a thing she had said.

"Anyway, I can't believe your grandma let you out."

"She didn't. I ran away." I walked up to her porch and took a seat. After a tiresome day and walking several blocks, I was beat. The Kmart gym shoes did nothing to comfort my aching feet, so I removed them and began to massage my toes.

"You ran away?" Ali repeated. "Where are you going to go?" she asked out of genuine concern.

"I'm down to go anywhere except back to that bitch's house." I was dead serious, and Alicia could tell.

"Well, you know you're always welcome over here," she offered, but I hesitated. Her stepfather, Tyrone, was abusive and had kicked Alicia's and her mother's asses every time he felt like it. I'd kill the nigga dead or return to Gran's house before I let him put his hands on me.

"I'll think about it." I smiled. Truthfully, I really didn't have anywhere else to go, but I needed to see how things were lying with Tyrone before I agreed to stay here.

"Are you hungry?"

"Yeah. What do you have?" My stomach rumbled on cue.

"I have some leftover pizza from last night. Let me go heat you up a plate." She went inside the house, and I stayed on the porch.

After a few minutes of waiting, I grabbed a *Jet* magazine and began to thumb through it when I spotted a familiar car speeding down the block. It was Ace, my father's protégé.

"I know that's not who I think it is," he called from the window.

"It depends on who you think it is." I smiled. I hadn't seen Ace since the afternoon my parents were killed. My stomach fluttered, as I had often thought of him and wondered what he was up to. Had he moved on in life, was he locked up, or did he even remember me, let alone his vow to look after me? Most people didn't honor promises like that, but I knew Ace was different.

As I approached the idling car, my mind traveled back to the day my daddy had brought him home. It was New Year's Eve when my father found him at McDonald's begging for money and food about five years ago. Ace was only thirteen at the time, so naturally, my father was curious as to where his mother or father were. He confided in my father and told him that he and his mom were on the run from her pimp back in Atlanta. The very day they arrived in Detroit, their rental car was hit head-on by a driver who had been texting. His mother, Elaine, died on impact, and he was rushed to Children's Hospital after suffering a broken arm. Once the medical staff found out he had no other family members, they alerted child protective services, and you know how the story goes.

Ace was in the system for exactly two weeks and had already endured beatings, starvation, and molestation. He decided enough was enough and left with the clothes on his back. My father felt for the young man, so he brought him home and cleaned him up. My parents couldn't enroll him in school without paperwork, so my father gave Ace a job and started to teach him the ropes of the dope game. He treated Ace like a son and was grooming him to take over the family business for that fateful day when he was to retire. Unfortunately, my father was killed before Ace's training was complete. Therefore, my father's right-hand man, Chucky, took over the hustle. I wasn't sure where that had left Ace, but I sure hoped he was still employed in the family business.

"What's up, ma?" Ace pulled to a stop in front of Alicia's mailbox. "What's good, family?" His smile was as wide as a fat woman's ass, and his dimples were sexy and deep. Anthony "Ace" Valquez was African American and Puerto Rican. I couldn't remember which parent was of which ethnicity, but the boy had pulled the best genes from both of them. His caramel skin, long, black eyelashes, hazel-green eyes, full lips, and strong bone structure made him the crème de la crème to women.

"Hey, you, long time no see." I walked toward the black and red Dodge Charger with white racing stripes. He was in the car with some chick who was all frowned up.

"Girl, I thought you had fallen off the face of the earth." He looked me over from head to toe. Inwardly, I felt embarrassed about my low-budget attire, which consisted of an oversized Hanes T-shirt, black stretch pants, and white knock-off Sketchers. However, there was nothing I could do about it now, so I played it cool. "You look good." He smiled again.

"Stop lying, nigga." I rolled my eyes, and his passenger smirked. Was this bitch laughing at me?

"I ain't lying, fam." He raised his right hand in defense.

"Whatever!" I snapped.

"Stop trippin', girl. Don't nobody give a fuck about what you wearing. I'm saying you look better than I expected you to look after losing your peoples, that's all."

"Oh." I looked away awkwardly. "Yeah, I'm doing as well as can be expected, I guess."

"I tried several times to get at you, but your grandmother wasn't playing that shit." He laughed.

"Yeah, Gran is definitely something else." I laughed too. "How have you been doing?" I knew how much he loved my father, and I could still see the pain in his face.

"I'm cool, I guess, just a little fucked up." He sighed. "I still can't believe that nigga gone."

"Me either."

"I beat myself up every day, fam." His jaw muscles flexed. "Had I still been there, maybe shit would've been different."

"Hey, ain't no sense in crying over spilled milk. We just got to pick up the pieces and keep pushing." I too had wondered what if Ace had been there during the ambush, but I shook it off because I would've probably had three deaths to deal with instead of two.

"What are you about to get into?" He started the car back up, which pleased his date, who appeared to care less about our conversation.

"Nothing for real." I shrugged. "I'm just going to post up here until I can come up with my next move."

"Come take a ride with your boy." He unlocked the car.

"I thought we were going to the movies, Ace!" his chick snapped.

"That was until I saw my sister. Now you can ride with us, or I can take you home." He gave her a stone-cold stare that meant business.

"I thought it was going to be just me and you," she tried to whisper in a seductive tone. "Wouldn't you rather be doing grown folk things than to be bothered with some kid?"

I was about to dog check this ho, but Ace cut to the chase before I had time to vocalize my thoughts.

"I guess you didn't hear me, Bianca. That's my sister. She comes before any pussy, point blank period. I tried to be nice and ask you to roll with us, but now I changed my mind. Just get the fuck out." He spoke firmly yet softly.

"Are you being for real, nigga? You just gon' put me out and make me walk home?"

"Your house is around the corner. You'll be fine." He shooed her away, and I laughed. "Come on, sis, let's ride."

"Where are we going?" Alicia walked up to the car and joined the conversation. "Hey, Ace." She smiled like a lovesick puppy. Ace waved and smiled, and I shook my head. Ever since I could remember, Alicia had had a huge crush on Ace. He didn't share the same feelings, but he always remained polite with her.

"What's up, Alicia." He nodded. "I was just about to take Janie for a ride. Would you like to roll too?"

"And you know this, man." She imitated Chris Tucker while handing me the paper plate of leftover pizza she had warmed up for me.

"Where are you taking me?" I sat in the passenger seat and fastened my seat belt.

"You'll see." He cranked up the music and sped off toward our destination.

# Chapter Five

"Ace, you really didn't have to do all of this." I held up the shopping bags filled to the brim with clothing from Gucci, BCBG, Bebe, Burberry, Juicy Couture, and many others.

"We're family, and besides, I owe your father everything. If it weren't for him, I'd probably be dead." He tossed a cup of frozen yogurt into the trash can.

"I really appreciate you." My words were sincere, and I was grateful to have him.

After leaving Shoe Maniac and Express, I went into the nearest restroom and discarded my pink cotton T-shirt, denim jeggings, and white Kmart knock-off shoes. My new gear consisted of a sheer canary yellow button-up, white linen shorts, and a pair of white wedge heels. Alicia pulled my long hair up into a bun as I admired the two-carat studs Ace had purchased for me from Zales. "My father always said that when you're dressed well, you feel good, and I feel better than I've felt in months," I told Alicia.

"You look gorgeous." She grabbed her bags and waited for me to grab mine.

"I can't believe he cashed out like this." My retail bill alone was well over five racks. He'd even bought me panties and bras from Victoria's Secret, body lotion from Bath & Body Works, and a new purse and matching wallet from Michel Kors.

"Ace is just sweet like that." Alicia exited the restroom, and I followed her. "I'm surprised he ain't wifed nobody up yet."

"He is a playa." I shook my head. For as long as I'd known Ace, he changed woman like he changed underwear.

"I don't think so. Maybe if he found the right girl, things would be different." She nudged me.

"I guess." I shrugged as we headed back into the mall.

"It's about time!" Ace stood from his seat at the food court. "I thought y'all would be in there another hour."

"You can't rush perfection," I teased.

"Come on, let's roll." He grabbed his cell phone and keys off the table. As we left Somerset Mall, I thanked Ace again for the kind gesture. In Detroit, all of the people with money shopped here, and I must admit it felt pretty damn good to have a few labels back in my life.

"Where to now?" Ali asked while flexing the new Movado timepiece Ace had bought her.

"Just sit back and enjoy the ride." He turned up the music, and we headed downtown.

The first spot we pulled up on was off of McDougal. It belonged to this old head named Larry. Larry was a numbers man who had more money coming through his place than the Michigan Lottery commission itself. "What are we doing here?" I asked. I knew my father offered Larry protection in exchange for a hefty fee, but that didn't have anything to do with me.

"We're here to collect Julius's money."

"My daddy has been dead almost a year. Larry ain't gon' pay me." I shook my head.

"Your father was well respected out here in these streets. Even though he's gone, his legacy lives. Larry is a stand-up guy, and he'll do right by you." As Ace put the car in park, I reached for the door handle. "Chill, shorty.

You can't just be rolling up unannounced. Let me call him first." Ace pulled out his phone and dialed Larry.

After a minute or two, the old man emerged from the well-kept house, smoking a cigarette while pulling an oxygen tank. "What's going on, young blood?" He leaned down into the window.

"I can't call it, fam." Ace leaned over and dapped him up. I watched as their knuckles collided with one another.

"Who this you got with you?" Larry leaned in and tried to get a better look at Alicia and me. "These are some thoroughbreds you got here, young'un." He licked his lips, and I almost gagged.

"This is Julius's daughter." Ace pointed at me, and the old man choked on his cancer stick.

"Aw, shit! Why didn't you say something sooner?" he scolded Ace. "I'm sorry, young lady, please forgive me and accept my condolences for what happened to your old man." He truly appeared embarrassed. I smiled and nodded my forgiveness.

Ace cut to the chase. "Look here, old timer, we came through 'bout some business. Janie is here to collect on her father's last payment."

Without hesitation, Larry reached into his pocket and handed me a wad of crisp bills. "I only owed him five, but I put another grand in there to apologize for my behavior." Larry flicked out his cigarette and smiled.

"We sure do appreciate it, old timer." Ace started the car.

"Hey, Julius was a good man. It's only fitting that I do right by his daughter." Larry put the brown wallet back into his pocket. "Wish these new ones was like him."

"Thanks again," I said before we pulled off toward our next destination.

# Chapter Six

By now, we had been riding around the city for the better part of the day, and I was tired. After about seven locations, I was $16,000 richer, but who knew how draining collecting money could be? Don't get it twisted, I was very grateful, but everyone wanted to talk and share fond memories about my father, which only made me sadder as the day progressed. My parents were well known throughout the inner cities of Michigan, but I had no idea how much they were loved. Thankfully, we were pulling up to our last stop.

"I got this. Just keep the car running," I instructed Ace. This spot belonged to Gudda, one of my father's homies from way back. He was like family, so I felt comfortable approaching the home alone.

"This is a trap house," Ace announced like I was a moron.

"Duh!" I rolled my eyes. I was tired of him thinking I was some punk-ass little girl. Alicia laughed at my antics, but Ace wasn't amused.

"All right, big shot." He smirked. "You better take the strap." He reached into his waistband and handed me a .38-caliber hand gun. I didn't know what the hell he expected to go down inside of Gudda's spot, but I took it and tucked it behind my back in the waist on my shorts.

As I stepped from the car, my heart began to pound. For some reason, I was nervous, but I shook it off and approached the side door. This house on Promenade was in a bad area on the east side, but like I said, Gudda was my daddy's people.

Tap. Tap. I knocked hard enough to be heard but light enough not to be mistaken for the police. "Who the fuck is that?" some man with a heavy voice asked without opening the door.

"It's Julius's daughter, Janie," I spoke to the door.

"What the fuck you doing around here?" The man still hadn't opened the door.

"I'm looking for Gudda!" I snapped. It was getting dark out here, and I was getting paranoid. "Are you going to let me in, or are we going to keep talking through this punk-ass door?" I looked at the car and Ace was looking back at me. I held my finger up to indicate to give me a few more minutes.

"This ain't no place for little girls." The man finally opened the door and let me in.

"I just need to talk to Gudda for a minute. Is he here?" From my position at the side door, I could see straight into the basement where some dopefiend was giving head to two men at the same damn time. The woman was buck-naked and on her knees crawling from one lap to the other. I couldn't see the men's faces, but I could see they both were working with small units.

"I said he upstairs!" The man put his hand in front of my eyes and snapped me out of my daze. "Go through the kitchen and turn left. He's in the first room on the right."

As instructed, I walked through the kitchen and tried not to stare at the woman standing at the stove stirring a boiling pot of something while wearing rubber gloves and a painter's mask. Once in the living room, I was caught off guard by the man leaning against the wall. He had fallen asleep while standing. I thought he was going to fall over on me, so I ran past him and up the stairs. Naiveté is a funny thing. At the time, I didn't know the woman in the kitchen was actually cooking crack, and the man in the living room was as high as a kite on what is called a dopefiend nod. Later on in life, I eventually learned firsthand how a trap house operated.

"Come in," Gudda yelled after I knocked on the bedroom door.

"Long time no see." I stepped inside to find him on a leather sectional playing the Xbox.

"Well, look at what the wind blew in." He paused the game. "You are looking good, girl. Come take a seat next to cousin Gudda." He patted the seat next to him. The look in his eyes made me uncomfortable, so I remained standing. "Damn, Janelle, you came all this way and you won't even take a seat."

"It ain't like that." I didn't want to offend him. "I just came through to pick up the money you owed my father." I swallowed hard because Gudda was looking at me sideways.

"What money?"

"My father's cut is forty percent of your operation. He usually collects on the first and the fifteenth of the month, but he died on the thirty-first." I tried to sound like I wasn't to be fucked with, but my poker face needed work. "I'm just here to get what you would've paid him on the first had he not been killed."

"In case you haven't heard, I don't owe no dead nigga shit."

"He ain't just no dead nigga. That's your friend." I couldn't believe how reckless this fool was talking about my father.

"Let me school you real fast." He spoke while grabbing the remote to turn the channel on the wall-mounted sixty-inch television. A surveillance video from downstairs came on the big screen. "Ain't no friends in this game," he continued.

"So you saying fuck my father?" My nostrils flared.

"That's exactly what I'm saying." He grabbed a small glass off the coffee table beside him and took a deep gulp of the brown liquid inside.

"Fuck you, Gudda!" I shook my head. "After everything my father was to you, you should be ashamed."

"No hard feelings, Janelle. That's just the game." He shrugged. "Now let me walk you out." He stood from the couch and lunged toward me.

"What are you doing?" I tried to dodge him, but somehow I got caught up against the door.

"You up in here looking like a bag of candy, and I got to get me a taste." With one hand on my throat, Gudda used his other hand to unfasten my shorts.

"Stop!" I tried to yell, but it was useless because my air supply was limited.

"Who gon' stop me? Yo' daddy?" He laughed.

This nigga was crazy if he thought I was about to let him violate me. Without a second thought, I reached behind my back and grabbed Ace's gun. Pop! Pop! I sent two shots to Gudda's gut. My father always told me to never pull a gun unless you were going to use it, so that's exactly what I did.

"Fuck!" He let me go and grabbed the two holes I'd just put into his body. Almost on cue, I heard footsteps leading upstairs, and I began to panic. I had totally forgotten that Gudda had his goons downstairs waiting and ready to handle me.

"Shit!" I looked around the room for an exit strategy, and that's when I almost fainted. Right there on the surveillance cameras was a room full of the boys in blue. I must've had the worst luck in the world to shoot a dope dealer at the same time his joint was being raided.

"You're surrounded by the Detroit Police! Come out with your hands up," I heard on the other side of the door.

Sweat gathered on my forehead, and I wasn't sure what was pounding loudest: my heart or my head. "I repeat, you are surrounded, come out with your hands up!"

"Fuck it," I said to myself and headed out of the window. The jump was two stories high, but with no other options, I did what I had to do.

# Chapter Seven

"Ahh." I fell on top of the hood of a parked Lincoln Navigator and came down hard on my ass. I looked from right to left and knew that making it to Ace's car was no longer an option. I could see the flashing blue and red lights coming from the front of the house. I was already in the backyard, so I headed for the alley.

"The shooter took the window," I heard behind me. "There she is, Mack."

"I got her."

I heard the man running behind me, but I didn't turn around to see how close he was. Woof! Woof! Woof! A big-ass pit bull barked from a neighbor's yard. Fear of the vicious animal was nothing compared to the fear of getting caught by the cops, so I kept pushing.

"Freeze!" I heard as I hopped over a fence and dodged two stray cats. I swear on my parents, I was moving like a track star, but the police officer was on my ass.

"Put your gotdamn hands up or I'll shoot you," he warned.

Quickly, I contemplated his threat and weighed my options. If he killed me, at least I would be with my parents, so I kept running until I hit a dead end.

"Fuck!" I kicked a cardboard box. There was nowhere else to run and nowhere to hide.

"Drop the weapon and place your hands behind your head." The officer was out of breath, and so was I. Having no other choice, I did as I was told and the officer arrested me.

"What are you doing out here in these streets?" The young black cop pulled me up from the ground by my wrists.

"I got the right to remain silent, right?" I looked at him, and he smirked.

"I guess you do." He stopped walking and looked at me. "What's your name, little girl?"

"I want a lawyer." I had watched too many episodes of *Law & Order*.

"Suit yourself. I was just asking because you looked familiar, that's all." He started walking again.

"My name is Janelle. Janelle Doesher."

"Are your parents Julius and Monica?" He stopped walking again. I didn't know how to respond. For all I knew, this cop could've had a grudge with my parents. "It's a simple question, baby girl."

"What happens if I say no?"

"Then I take you to jail," he responded nonchalantly.

I looked him over and decided to be honest. After all, I was already going to jail anyway. "Yes, those are my parents." I sighed. "How did you know?"

He stared at me for a minute and unlocked my handcuffs. "You look just like Monica." He stared off into the distance. "Me and your folks was cool. I really miss them."

"I don't remember my father having cops for friends," I half joked.

"If I weren't a friend, why would I uncuff you?"

Dude had a point.

"Anyway, why were you in the trap house and why did you shoot Gudda?"

I wanted to ask him why he was being so nosy, but I decided that he was only trying to help me, so I controlled my tongue. "Real talk, Officer Bryant." I peeped the gold name tag. "I fell on hard times and came to see Gudda because he owed my daddy some money."

"So you thought you was bad enough to roll up in the spot and take what you thought was yours?" He was amused.

"First of all, I didn't roll up acting like a Billy bad ass. I politely asked the nigga for my father's money, and one thing led to another." As I talked, a call came over Bryant's walkie-talkie asking him if he needed assistance.

"No, I'm on my way back empty-handed. The suspect got away." He spoke while looking at me. "You better get lost before my squad catches you here."

"Thanks for the lookout."

"Take my card in case you find yourself in any more shit." He reached into his uniform pants and produced a white card with blue writing.

"Would it be too much to ask for my gun back?" I smiled innocently, although I wasn't dumb enough to let this nigga walk away with evidence that could put me away for a very long time.

"You Doeshers are a trip." He shook his head. "Take it and get lost! I better not catch you nowhere near the trap again."

"Roger that!" I turned around and once again ran off into the distance.

# Chapter Eight

After getting my free pass from Officer Bryant, I ran off into the darkness of night and didn't stop until I was at least thirty blocks away from the crime scene. Having no idea what had happened to Ace and Alicia, I approached a lady at the gas station and asked to use her phone. After a minute of staring me down and concluding that I wasn't shady, she handed over a smart phone covered by a studded Hello Kitty case. The 40-something woman was too damn old to be rocking with Hello Kitty, but I didn't even have a phone, so who was I to judge?

"Who dis?" Ace answered on the second ring.

"It's Janelle."

"Where the hell you at, shorty?" He was concerned.

"I'm on the corner of Gratiot and Connors at the gas station."

"I'm on the way. Sit tight." We ended the call, and I was relieved that they hadn't been arrested for sitting in front of the dope spot.

"Thank you, ma'am." I smiled and handed her back the phone along with a $20 bill from my pocket.

Within five minutes, Ace was pulling up on two wheels.

"Janelle, I'm so glad to see you!" Alicia got out of the car and hugged me like she hadn't seen me in years. "Girl, I thought you was going to jail for sure."

"Me too!" I squeezed her back.

"How did you get out of there?" Ace puffed on a Newport. I could tell that his nerves were all shot to hell by the expression on his color-drained face. He took his god-brother role very seriously and was really overprotective when it came to me.

"Some officer named Bryant let me off the hook, and he even gave me the gun back." I fastened my seat belt.

"I know Bryant. Your father had him on payroll." Ace pulled off slowly.

"How did y'all get away?" I asked.

"I spotted the SWAT van idling on the corner, so I pulled off and sat three blocks over. I didn't want to leave you, but I knew it would've been bad if we got flicked." Ace rolled his window down and flicked his cigarette.

"Janelle, I heard gunshots right after we pulled off. What the fuck was that all about?" Alicia quizzed me.

"Man, Gudda got stupid, and I shot that fool." I sighed.

"Did you kill that nigga?" Ace looked at me with his left brow raised.

"I don't think so." I shook my head, and Ace stopped the car.

"What did you stop for?" we asked at the same time as Ace slammed on the brakes.

"Next time you shoot a nigga you better kill 'em."

"Why?" Alicia asked.

"No witnesses and no evidence!" he reminded her. "Ain't nothing we can do about Gudda right now anyway, but we can get rid of the evidence. Open the door and drop the burner into the sewer," he instructed. "The water will wash all the fingerprints away, and by tomorrow that bitch will have floated all the way into the Detroit River."

I did as I was told, and we headed back to Alicia's house in silence.

# Chapter Nine

We said our goodbyes to Alicia and watched her until she was safely inside her house. "Are you sure it's cool that I post up at your crib?"

"Yeah, I told you, *mi casa es su casa*." He pulled off and headed to the two-bedroom flat he shared with his best friend, Damien.

He and Damien ran several traps for Uncle Chucky, and from what I could tell, Ace had become the man on the west side of the city. His phone stayed off the hook with order requests, and it reminded me of how my father used to get down. Speaking of my father, during the ride to Ace's house, I realized this was the first time we had been alone in all the years we'd known each other. For some odd reason, I began to feel nervous. There was always an invisible line we never crossed because of my father, and now that he was nowhere in the picture, I wondered what would happen between us.

"Home sweet home." Ace pulled into the driveway, cut the engine, and helped me retrieve all of my shopping bags. The place was nothing major, but I was thankful not to be going back to Gran's house, so I dared not complain.

"There go my nigga right there," someone yelled as we stepped through the front door. "Come get down on this *Madden* with ya boy."

"What up, D." Ace spoke to his homeboy and nodded a "what's up" to the others. The living room was currently

being used for a smoking session. There were three men
and one girl playing the Xbox while passing around not
one but two blunts. The stereo system was bumping
Jeezy so loud that the walls were vibrating and my teeth
rattled.

"Yo, cuz, who dat?" Damien paused the game and
turned the volume down on the music.

"This is my godsister, Janelle," Ace introduced us.

Damien hopped to his feet and made his way over to
me. "Damn, Janelle baby, where you been all my life?"
He kissed the back of my hand. I didn't know what to say,
so I smiled politely.

"Don't mind this nigga. Come on and let me show you
my room." Ace nodded for me to follow him down a small
hallway.

"Naw, bro, show her fine ass to my room," Damien
teased, and his audience cracked up laughing. "That
bitch is fine as a muthafucka!" He spoke in a hushed tone,
but I could still hear him.

"That fool is crazy. Don't pay him any attention. He's
harmless." Ace removed the red and white Adidas from
his big feet and placed them back into the box on his
closet shelf.

"It's all good." I plopped down on the king-sized bed
and rested up against the headboard. "I just appreciate
having a place to crash until I get right."

"So what's the plan?" Ace removed his red Adidas
shirt and hung it up. I tried to ignore the defined chest
muscles peeking from behind his white undershirt, but I
did sneak a few peeks when he wasn't looking.

"Honestly, I don't know what my next move is." I
sighed. "I can't go back to my grandmother's house for
sure."

"I already told you that you can chill here for however
long you need." He took a seat on the floor across from
the bed.

"Ace, that's really kind of you but—" Before I could finish, there was a knock on the bedroom door.

"What?" Ace yelled over the loud music that had started back up.

"You got a situation out here, bro." Damien was trying to be discreet, but I could tell the word "situation" was a code word for "female."

Ace looked at me apologetically, and I smiled. "You go ahead and handle your business. Just tell me where the shower is." I was too tired to be concerned about his "situation."

"The bathroom is right there." He pointed to the attached facility.

"Where am I sleeping?" I rummaged through my shopping bags in search of nightclothes.

"You can take the bed, and I'll sleep in the living room." He stood and went to the door.

"Are the sheets clean?" I didn't want to be lying in some bitch's nasty juices.

"Just changed them this morning." He laughed and left me to get ready for bed.

# Chapter Ten

After retrieving my things from Bath & Body Works and Victoria's Secret, I eagerly headed into the bathroom. Surprisingly, it was more spacious and cleaner than I anticipated. There wasn't much to the space besides white walls, a black rug with the matching shower curtain, and a *Scarface* movie poster hanging from the wall. I didn't care what it looked like though. All I wanted to do was peel off my clothes and relax in a hot bubble bath. Gran was so strict about her water bill that I was only allotted one twelve-minute shower per day. Therefore, I was long overdue for a bath.

I turned the water on full blast and poured in my favorite scent. Immediately, the bathroom smelled of sweet pea and I watched the bubbles form. After a few minutes, the hot water began to steam up the mirror. I anticipated how good my muscles would feel after a long soak. Jumping from that two-story window had done a number on me.

Before stepping into the bathtub, I wrapped my hair and removed my new jewelry. Just when I decided to step into the bathtub, I remembered I didn't have a washcloth. Of course! I smacked my lips and headed back into Ace's bedroom. Freely, I walked through the room naked to retrieve my towel with no worries because he was out in the living room entertaining his company.

"You better chill that shit out!" I heard yelling over the music. I listened closely and even placed my ear to the door. Someone was not a happy camper.

"Fuck you, Ace! I came over here to chill with you, and you got another bitch in the back."

At the mention of me, my eyes widened, and I laughed. Ace was such a playboy. Although he and I weren't an item, I would've paid to see him talk himself out of this one.

"I told you that's my sister! I ain't gon' keep repeating myself." Ace hollered back. By now, Damien had turned the music down so he and his guests could get an earful. I shook my head and turned back toward the bathroom when the bedroom door opened and someone attacked me from behind.

"Bitch, I knew you was fuckin' my man." She was damn near on my back with a death grip on my face. I shook wildly like one of those people covered in flames.

"What are you doing?" I yelled while Ace tried to pry the girl off of me.

"You skank bitch! Why can't you just find your own man?" She hauled off and slapped the shit out me. I had been blindsided, and I felt defenseless because I didn't know whether to throw a blow or cover my assets, literally.

After she tried to strike me again, I said fuck it, and we got to bangin'. There was nothing Ace could do at this point because we were all over that room tearing shit up! I gave old girl a one-two combo and hit her with a few jabs to the gut. Of course, hair was pulled, and lips were busted, too. She came hard for me, but in the end, I walked away the victor. The whole incident lasted probably fifteen minutes. By the time it was over, Ace's room was a mess, and we had an audience in the doorway. I wasn't sure if they were there to see the cat fight or my vagina, but either way, it irritated me and I was ready to leave.

# Chapter Eleven

After the brawl, Ace put his female companion out and apologized profusely. I told him that I wasn't mad at him, but I requested that he drop me back off with Alicia. My hand was swollen, my arms were bruised, and my scalp was sore from that bitch pulling my hair. Ace insisted that I stay, but I told him his house was not the place to be. I wouldn't be able to face him or his roommate again after they saw my birthday suit, and I damn sure didn't want any more run-ins with his chickenheads.

"I thought your pimp hand was strong. You better get them hoes in check." I laughed as we pulled into Alicia's driveway. I'd called her when we rounded the corner, so she was waiting for me in the doorway.

"I ain't no pimp. Stop saying that." He licked his lips.

"Anyway." I rolled my eyes and retrieved my bags.

"Are you sure you don't just want me to get you a hotel room?" he offered for the second time tonight. He was fully aware of the issues Alicia had with her stepfather, and he didn't want no shit.

"Yeah, I'm sure. You've done so much for me, and it's already been a long day. I'll just crash here and call you in the morning." I gave him a hug, and we said our goodbyes.

"I'll slide through here tomorrow and check on you, all right?" he called from the driver's window as he backed out.

"Okay. See ya tomorrow." I smiled and followed Alicia into her home to call it a night.

Upon my entrance, all I could hear was Marvin Gaye playing loudly and arguing coming from upstairs. "Is everything okay?" Immediately I was concerned.

"Just ignore it." Alicia waved off the loud tones and harsh words like everything was peaches and cream. Over the years, she'd gotten used to the fussing and fighting, but I didn't like it. "Once you get into the basement the sound will go away."

She locked the door behind us, and we proceeded downstairs into her bedroom. The large space was a little too messy for my taste, but once again I had no complaints because anything was a major come up from Gran's apartment. Speaking of Gran, I knew she was probably worried sick about me, so I picked up the phone and called her before she called the police and reported me missing.

"Hello." She sounded calm but worried.

"Hi, Gran." I cleared my throat. "It's me, Janelle. I just wanted to let you know that I'm okay."

"Where are you?" Now she sounded pissed yet relieved.

"I'm with one of my friends." I didn't want to give my exact whereabouts away. "Her mom said it was cool for me to spend a few nights over," I lied.

"Janelle, do you know how worried I've been? You were supposed to have your tail back in this house since three o'clock this afternoon."

"Yes, ma'am. I know you were worried and I'm sorry. I just needed some time to clear my head." I looked over at Alicia, who was giving me the "you're in trouble" face.

"Clear your head about what, Janelle?" she snapped. "Tell me what in the world a sixteen-year-old could possibly have to clear her head about?"

"I need to clear my head about everything!" I tried to remain calm, but she was pressing my buttons. Gran wanted me to go on living life like I hadn't lost my parents nearly a year ago. She had never given me the opportunity to grieve, and I was like a volcano that was ready to erupt.

"First thing in the morning, I'm coming to get you," she threatened. "What's the address?"

Click. I hung up in her face and handed the phone back to Alicia. "That woman gets on my nerves." I fell back onto the full-sized bed.

"She's just worried like any grandma would be," Alicia said, trying to play devil's advocate.

"There is nothing wrong with being concerned, but she's flat-out evil. She ain't right in the head, Ali, I swear." We both laughed.

"What are you going to do with all this money?" She patted the Gucci book bag Ace had given me to carry all of the money that was collected earlier today.

"I want to find us an apartment and then find another way to make more money." I slid the book bag beneath her bed.

"Who do you think will give two teenagers an apartment?" Alicia looked skeptical.

"You better believe money talks." I slapped her a high five. "Plus my daddy had some good connections."

"Okay, let's say we get this apartment. How in the hell will we pay for it month after month?"

"I'm a hustler's daughter. I will always find a way to get money." I winked. "I might even join the dope game and reclaim my father's throne." It was just an idea, but as usual, my best friend was down.

"Whatever you choose to do, I'm riding shotgun." She gave me a high five, and we talked for a few more hours until we both fell asleep.

# Chapter Twelve

"Alicia, there is someone here named Anthony," Joanne called down the stairs, and I jumped up.

"Ace is here. Get up." I tapped Ali.

"Oh, shit! I have to go brush my teeth and get my face together." She jumped out of bed and beat me up the stairs.

"Good morning, Aunt Joanne." I hugged my friend's mom. "Tyrone." I bypassed him.

"Alicia didn't tell me you were coming over. How have you been, baby?" Alicia's full-figured mother asked while retrieving orange juice from the refrigerator.

"I'm good."

"Well, breakfast will be done in a few minutes, okay?" Joanne placed the OJ in front of her husband and turned back toward the stove. Tyrone just glared at me.

"Hey, Ace. You're here awfully early." I noted that the time on the cable box read eight thirty-two.

"It dawned on me that I forget to buy you the essentials." He handed me a Walmart bag. "Figured you might need this in order to start your day."

Inside of the bag was a toothbrush, toothpaste, mouthwash, deodorant, pads, tampons, and panty liners. Laughing hysterically, I held up the tampons. "Really?"

"I didn't want you to get caught slippin' just in case your friend showed up." He laughed, and I punched him in the shoulder.

"Only you would think to buy something like this."

"Oh, yeah, I got you a cell phone." He handed me the Android.

"Thanks, bro."

"No problem." He stood from the sofa. "Call me later if you need me." He glared at Tyrone, who was still staring.

"Will do." I walked him to the door then closed and locked it.

"Aw, man, did I miss him?" Alicia ran down the stairs all made up with makeup like she was going somewhere this early in the morning. I just laughed and headed back into the kitchen.

"So, Janelle, how long are you with us?" Joanne placed four slices of bacon onto Tyrone's plate.

"Just a few nights if that's okay with you."

"Of course it is, sweetheart." She rubbed my back. "We miss you around here."

"All I want to know is why you asking her if it's okay for you to stay here when you should've been asking me?" Tyrone added his two cents, and the room fell silent.

"I just figured since this is her house, the proper thing to do was to ask her." I politely tried to put that nigga in check. Alicia's father had paid for this house. All this nigga was doing was freeloading.

"This is my muthafuckin' house!" He pointed at his chest.

"Tyrone, don't talk to her like that, baby. Just eat your breakfast." Joanne tried to defuse the situation, but Tyrone was too turned up.

"You little bitch, did you hear me? This is my muthafuckin' house. When you're here, you better show some gotdamn respect."

"Bitch?" I stood from the table, and he did too. "I don't know who pissed in your grits, but you better leave me the fuck alone." I was dead-ass serious.

"You think since you're a Doesher that I'm scared of you?" He leaned across the table and swung. The fool was obviously intoxicated, because he missed me and knocked the orange juice container over.

"Tyrone, stop it!" Alicia yelled, but then he turned on her.

"Make me." He swung and caught her with a right hook. Joanne tried to pull him off of her daughter and ended up catching a backhand, which busted her lip. By now I was up in arms and about to whip his ass. I grabbed the butcher knife and went straight for his neck. Hemming him up against the refrigerator, I gritted my teeth.

"If you touch either one of them again, I swear on my mother I will kill you dead."

"You think you tough enough to threaten me?" He squinted through red eyes.

"I'm not threatening you, Tyrone. This is a warning."

"Joanne, are you going to let this happen?" He looked at his wife, who was shaking uncontrollably. "Tell her to leave!"

"Please let him go, Janelle." Joanne tried to wipe the blood that was running down her chin.

"I said tell her to leave!" he yelled, and she jumped.

"Janelle, I love you, and I thank you for looking out for Alicia, but I think it's time for you to go home, wherever that might be." She looked down at the wooden floor. I wanted to ask what type of monkey shit this was, but I decided to leave well enough alone and respect her wishes.

"Mama, if Janelle leaves, then I'm leaving too." Alicia tried to reason with her mom, but when a woman is weak and docile, there is nothing you can do to change that.

"Well, if that's how you feel, then you can leave too." Joanne wiped a tear away and ran up the stairs into her

bedroom. I stood there stunned and feeling horrible for
Alicia. I couldn't imagine how it must feel to have your
mother pick some nigga over you.

"Call Ace then and let me grab my shit."

# Chapter Thirteen

After getting Alicia put out of her mother's house, I felt terrible. She said it was cool, but deep down inside, I knew I needed to make things up to her. After two weeks of staying at the Courtyard by Marriott on Ace's dime, Alicia and I decided we were done being a burden. It was time to make shit happen, and I knew exactly who I needed to talk to.

I walked into the small bar on James Couzens and nodded at the bartender. The place was filled with a few regulars, and soft music played over the sound system.

"What's happening, shortstop?" Mitch, the owner, spoke from a booth he and a female companion were occupying.

"Nothing much, just looking for Charles." I went over to the table and hugged the Creole gentleman.

"You know that old fool is doing what he does best." Mitch laughed. Normally he wouldn't let someone my age in, but for years his establishment had served as my father's meeting facility. Therefore, Mitch and I were cool, and I was shown favor. "Head on back, shortstop."

As usual, my play uncle was in the back room, shooting dice. "Well, if you ain't a sight for sore eyes." He gave me the once-over before rolling the dice. Uncle Chucky was my father's right-hand man from start to finish. My daddy used to say that Chuck was a stand-up guy, so I knew if anyone was to be trusted, it was him. "What brings you by, young'un?" He looked up from the game for just a split second.

"I wanted to know if I could holla at you about some business." I shifted nervously from one foot to the other. The back room was filled with about four other hustlers in on the dice game. They were all clutching fists full of money and yelling obscenities at one another.

"Speak on it, young'un," he urged without even looking up at me.

"I was kind of hoping to have this conversation alone," I leaned in and whispered into his ear. He looked at me and then back at the pile of money on the floor. I could tell he didn't want to leave the game and was weighing his options. After a few seconds of awkward silence between us, he finally stood up.

"Aye, I'll be back. Give me five minutes." He folded a wad of money and placed it into the pocket of his linen pantsuit. Uncle Chucky was an old-school playa for real. He even had on a Kangol hat with a pair of pointed Stacy Adams snakeskin loafers.

"Come on, Chuck!" one man shouted, obviously disappointed that the game was on pause.

"Nigga, I said give me five minutes. Gotdamn, I ain't never seen a nigga so anxious to lose his dough," he replied, pulling me toward an exit door. "So what's up, niece? How have you been holding up?" He lit a Newport cigarette and took a seat on a blue milk crate.

"I really haven't been doing well at all. In fact, that's why I'm here." I sighed. "I need some fast money, Uncle Chucky."

"Explain what you mean by fast money." He blew out a smoke ring and leaned his back up against the brick exterior of the building.

"I'm talking about hustling. I need you to put me on." I averted his deep gaze.

"You in trouble or something?" He was concerned.

"No."

"So tell me why you wanna be a hustla?" He looked at me sideways.

"I just told you. I need some fast money. I'm tired of being broke." I kicked a rock across the vacant lot.

"If you need money, I got you, believe that." He went into his pocket for some greenbacks, but I stopped him.

"I don't want your money. I want my own!"

"Get a job." He smirked. I didn't.

"Uncle Chucky, I'm serious. I can't do nothing with minimum wage. I need that big money." I laughed.

"Big money comes with big problems. You know that, right?" He flicked his cancer stick.

"I'm a big girl. I can handle it," I retorted. Honestly, this conversation had gone a lot smoother in my head this morning. I didn't think Chucky would play me like a chump. Didn't he know that I learned from the best? As a matter of fact, I learned my game from the same nigga who taught him his game.

"That's just it!" He tossed the butt of his cigarette to the ground and stomped it out. "Janie, no matter how big you are, the hustle game has no room for girls." He stood, indicating that my time was up. "Here's a few dollars. Come holla at me any time you need something, and I got you." He peeled off a few bills and stuck them into the pocket of my jeans.

"For real it's like that?" I blinked back some tears. Now was not the time to be crying like some bitch, but truthfully my feelings were hurt.

"What do you want me to do?" He walked up into my face. "What the fuck do I look like putting my partner's daughter in the dope game? How do you think Julius would feel about that, huh?"

"If he were alive, I guess we could ask him!" I snapped. "Fuck it then. I came to you first because I thought we were family. But one monkey don't stop no show. If you won't put me in the game, trust and believe I know ten muthafuckas who will!" I was done with this nigga, so I stormed past him and back into the building.

Just as I made my way to the door to reenter the main bar, Chucky called my name. I almost kept walking, but then I reluctantly turned to face him.

"Look, let's be clear, I don't give a fuck about no temper tantrums. You said you were a big girl, so act like it!" he barked. "You ain't fit for narcotics."

"But—" I started to oppose, and he cut me off.

"Just shut the fuck up and listen. You ain't fit for narcotics, but a friend of mine is in need of a few good hands for his chop-shop operation. His name is Bobby, and he's over on Mount Elliott." He grabbed a napkin and wrote down the address along with a few other details. "Be there tomorrow at ten in the morning and tell him I sent you." He handed me the napkin.

"Thanks, Uncle Chucky!" I smiled.

"Now g'on ahead and get up out of here. I'll check on you later." He winked and returned to the game.

# Chapter Fourteen

The following morning, Ace dropped Ali and me off at the chop shop and told us to call if we needed him. Upon first inspection, the place appeared to be an auto detail shop, but as soon as the back door opened, we instantly knew otherwise. There were at least ten luxury cars being demolished by men in gray jumpsuits.

A balding Italian man approached us. "Which one of you is Janelle?"

"That's me," I answered, not taking my eyes off of the Lexus with no doors, airbag, hood, or tires.

"So who's the other broad?" His brows furrowed.

"This is my friend Alicia. I heard you needed a few hands on deck, so she's here to help too." I replied as the man pulled a cell phone from the clip on his belt. "Is there a problem?" I wanted to know what the issue was, but Bobby held up his index finger.

"Yo, Chucky, it's Bobby," he spoke into the phone. "Is this some sort of joke? I asked for workers, and you send me not one chick but two." He turned his back to us. The call was on speakerphone, so I could hear the conversation. Alicia looked nervously at me, but I knew Uncle Chucky would work this out, so I was as cool as a cucumber.

"Bobby, workers are workers as long as the job gets done, right?" Chucky spoke in his usual calm tone.

"Look this ain't no fuckin' daycare center. They don't look old enough to have even had their cherries popped," Bobby joked.

"Watch what you sayin', fam. I told you that was my niece!" Uncle Chucky warned.

"Niece or not, these broads better put in some serious work or I'm bustin' your balls the next time I see you."

"Janelle is Julius's daughter. This shit is in her blood."

"All right then, enough said." He ended the call and turned back to face us. "My man Chucky say you two are legit, so welcome to the team." He held out a chubby hand, and I shook it. "You ever stole a car before?"

"No," we replied in unison.

"No worries, my guy will show you what to do." He gave a half smile. "Aye, J.R., come over here," he called out.

"What's up, boss?" A young Hispanic male hustled over to where we were standing.

"This is Janelle and Alicia. They just joined the team. Show them the ropes." He patted J.R. on the back and left us to chop it up.

"First thing first, we need to get y'all some nicknames. In this field, nobody needs to know your government name." He ushered us over to a small makeshift office space.

"Well, people call me Ali," Alicia responded.

"That's cool." J.R. took a seat, and we followed suit. "What about you, red?" He referenced my skin tone. Most light-skinned women were called redbones.

"My family calls me Janie." I shrugged, and he frowned.

"What about Jane?"

"That's fine, I guess."

"Okay, cool. Let's move on to the next order of business." He pointed to several different objects on top of the table. "This is a slim jim. You slide this between the car window and the car frame to open the lock." He demonstrated how the utensil worked and then moved on to the next item. "This is called a RFID. It's used for the newer cars with keyless entry because they have weak cryptographic protection." He smiled like a passionate teacher as he schooled us about grand theft auto. Truth be told, this lecture was sort of boring and I could give two fucks about the shit he was spitting. I couldn't wait to get out there in the field for some live action.

After about three hours of lectures and demonstrations, we were finally handed our assignments and given the rules. Rule number one: Bobby only wanted top-notch quality vehicles, and I was cool with that. The newer the whip, the more you were paid. Rule number two: everybody worked on an individual basis. That way if you get pinched by the police, he would only lose one worker, not a team of workers. Rule number three: no snitching. That shit was self-explanatory.

# Chapter Fifteen

"That shit was dope! I can't wait to jack my first car." Alicia paced the hotel room, still pumped up about her new job.

"Calm down, killa. That shit ain't for shits and giggles." Ace lay across the bed, text messaging some scallywag.

"I know it's serious business. I'm just excited, that's all." Alicia sounded as if her ego had been deflated.

"I told y'all I had y'all covered. Y'all didn't have to sign on with Bobby." Ace put his phone down and grabbed a few of the chili-cheese fries from the carryout box I had in my lap.

"We really appreciate your help and all, but you know it was just a matter of time before that shit got old. Plus, I'm way too independent to let a nigga take care of me." I bit down on my patty melt then tried to catch the gooey Swiss and American cheese from dripping on my shirt. I swear food from L. George's Coney Island was the best. It was the closest thing I'd had to a home-cooked meal since leaving Gran's crib.

"Okay, I get that independent shit, but why y'all niggas couldn't just get nine-to-fives?"

"First of all," Alicia started after pushing her Coney dog aside, "this is Detroit, and you know like I know that all the good jobs are taken."

"All I'm saying is, the grand theft industry is no place for chicks. Both of y'all will be seniors soon. The malls are always hiring high school kids. Y'all could've applied at the Gap when we were there the other day and stacked y'all bread until it's time to head off to college."

I rolled my eyes at Ace and hit him with the pillow. "Niggas like you kill me. Always hootin' and hollering about chicks can't do this and they can't do that. I bet you a rack that I can hustle better than you."

"I know that's right, boo!" Ali gave me a high five.

"One day I'll have my own all-female empire just to shit on you niggas who doubted us." I fell back onto the bed and daydreamed about my future success. Although I was only trash talking with Ace, in the back of my mind, I knew I would one day run the hustle. When other kids spoke of being doctors and lawyers, I spoke of being a gangster. Maybe it was my father's lifestyle or my crazy fascination with mafia movies, but I was addicted to the underworld. Today, it was stealing cars, but who knew where tomorrow would lead me?

# Chapter Sixteen

Today was the day, and it was game time! Alicia and I stepped off the bus at the mall terminal like two women on a mission. Today's location was Northland, a decent mall in a middle-class neighborhood. We could've gone back out to Somerset where the rich people shopped, but their parking lot was under high surveillance and heavily guarded. We needed a place we were familiar with and close to the freeway in case we needed to hightail it out of dodge. I wasn't trying to get caught my first day on the job.

"You ready?" Ali smiled nervously as we headed toward the mall like every other passenger who had just gotten off the bus.

"Ain't no turning back now." I tied the black bandana around my head and tossed on a pair of shades. It was eighty-eight degrees today. Otherwise, I would've worn a hoodie. Alicia sported sunglasses and a wig, which made her appear as though she was an average shopper. We both carried big purses, which housed our tools. Although Bobby said he didn't want any teams, me and my girl threw caution to the wind and said fuck it.

"I'll start over here, and you start over there." I showed her where to go. "And remember: only high-end shit."

Alicia smiled. "I'll see you on the other side."

"See you on the other side," I replied. Without another word, she went off to find her whip while I did the same.

Row by row, I walked the semi-full parking lot looking for something fly to steal, but there were only medi-
ocre cars in the lot. I hadn't heard from Ali, but I was
sure her luck was running about the same. Stealing
cars wasn't all it was cracked up to be, and I was burning up in the summer sun. After an hour of searching, I
was going to call it quits and take a break. As soon as
I was about to step inside the mall, the chrome on this
cocaine white 2012 BMW caught my attention. Like
a hawk, I watched the driver whip into an empty spot.
Casually, I headed toward the car and tried my best to
appear normal. Nonetheless, the owner was too busy on
his cell phone to pay me any attention.

"Yeah, that bitch fucking crazy if she thought I was just
gonna let her take my son to Texas!" he barked into his
mobile phone. "I put an end to that shit, son! That ho
ain't ever gonna bother me and my seed again."

I skimmed him over from head to toe and came to the
conclusion that baby boy was a trap star. The oversized
white tee, baggy jeans, crisp Nike gym shoes, and diamonds around his neck and in his ears told it all.

Chirp. Chirp. He hit the lock on his whip and hustled
into the mall.

The minute homeboy was out of sight, I went into
action. After glancing from left to right, I pulled out my
slim jim and jimmied the lock. Instantly, the alarm on
the Beemer started blaring, so I knew I needed to move
faster. Dropping to the floor of the luxury vehicle, I first
cut the wire belonging to the horn. Next, I cut red and
yellow wires and rubbed the exposed electrical devices
together.

"Come on!" I said to no one in particular as my cell
phone began to ring. I knew by the ring tone that it was
Ali, but my hands were tied at the moment. "Come on.
Come on!" I rubbed the wires across each other again

and was shocked by a spark. "Damn it!" I licked my burned fingertips and reluctantly tried again. I had come too far to turn back. The third time worked like a charm. The car's engine revved, and I hopped into the driver's seat without hesitation. "Yes!" I shouted while taking off like a bat out of hell.

On the way to the shop, I drove fast yet cautiously because I didn't need to get pulled over and I didn't want to damage the car. I heard things being tossed around inside the trunk, but I paid it no attention. The only thing on my mind was how easy this payoff was going to be.

"That's a beaut!" Bobby whistled after I pulled into the garage.

"It's fully loaded." I stepped from the car with a huge grin on my face. Snatching a Beemer on my first time out was nearly impossible.

"Good job, Jane. Go see J.R. for your payout." Bobby popped the trunk, and both of our mouths dropped.

# Chapter Seventeen

"What the fuck is this?" Lying in the trunk was a woman who had been handcuffed, gagged, and beaten. "Oh, shit!" I was totally caught off guard and pissed my pants a little out of fear. "I swear I didn't know she was in there." I shook my head in disbelief.

"J.R., get me some water." Bobby puffed on a cigar and continued to stare at the body. The woman was so still that I just knew she was dead. *What type of nigga would stop at the mall when he has a dead body in the trunk?*

After retrieving the water, J.R. was instructed to splash it into the woman's face. I held my breath for several seconds, and to my relief, she moved slightly, and her eyes popped open. J.R. removed the gag from her mouth but let the handcuffs be. "Who did this to you?" Bobby asked.

"My baby daddy, Jamison." She coughed. "He's crazy. I tried to get away from him but he abducted me and my baby from the Greyhound station," she explained, which jogged my memory about overhearing the man say something about someone taking his son to Texas. "Where is my son? Is he okay?" She appeared frantic, and Bobby looked at me.

"Nobody else was in the car. I'm sorry." I felt horrible.

"Can someone uncuff me?" She was trying to sit up. "I need to get my son."

"Sure, baby girl." Bobby smiled. "We'll be right back." He pulled me toward the office. "It looks like we've got a situation, Janelle."

"I swear on my mother that I didn't know she was back there." I raised my right hand as if I were under oath.

"I believe you, kid, but this still needs to be handled."
He opened the jacket of his Sean Jean sweat suit and
retrieved a 9 mm hand gun. "Head shots are the best."

"Wait! What?" I backed up.

"You brought her in here. Now you've got to take her
out." He blew a smoke ring out into the air.

Instantly, I felt sick to my stomach and weak in the
knees. I had only signed up for stealing cars, not killing
people.

"It has to be done, kid. If we let her out of here, she
becomes a liability, and I won't be able to sleep at night
due to wondering if she'll call the police or not."

"Bobby, I'm not a killer." I shook my head and tried to
keep the vomit I felt rising from escaping my mouth.

"Jane, in the underworld it's kill or be killed, plain and
simple." He was trying to drop me a hint, and I got the
message loud and clear. If I didn't kill her, then I would
be killed.

Swallowing hard, I removed the pistol from his palm
and approached the vehicle.

"Are you going to uncuff me?" the woman asked with
pleading eyes. "I need to find my baby."

Without a single word, I cocked the gun and lit her
body up like a firework display on the Fourth of July.
Truthfully, one or two shots would have been sufficient,
but I can't explain how invigorating pulling the trigger
was. I walked up to the trunk and took one last look
at my victim. Her face and body had been ripped to
shreds, blood was everywhere, and so was brain matter.
Although I had shot Gudda, it hadn't been confirmed if
he died, so technically I wasn't a confirmed killer until
today. I never thought I was capable of taking a life, but
in the years to come, she was the first of many. For it
was on that day and at that moment that I learned the
importance of cleaning up my own messes.

# Chapter Eighteen

"Girl, what in the hell is wrong with you?" Alicia asked one day while we were lounging at the pool. It had been almost a month since I murdered the woman in the trunk and I still couldn't get right.

"Nothing's wrong, just missing my parents, that's all," I lied. Ali was my bitch until the world blew up, but some things were better left unshared.

"I hear that." She patted my thigh and walked toward the Jacuzzi. We were still at the Marriott, but Ace was taking us to look for a crib in the next couple of days. Car theft had paid off in a major way, and we were getting paper. Between the two of us, we had stacked close to $10,000. This was considered chump change to the big timers, but everybody had to start somewhere.

"What's on the agenda tomorrow?" Ali relaxed with her head back.

"I'm thinking we hit Auburn Hills. There's a Pistons game going on, and you know the parking lot will be hot." I thumbed through the iPad on my lap.

"Girl, they got that bitch sewn up. It's impossible to make it out of there in one piece."

"You're right. Well, maybe we can try downtown." I turned the iPad off and put it into its case. "All I know is I need to find some dope shit." We laughed.

"I feel you on that, but for real we need to be talking about what's going on between you and Ace." She stared at me, and I stared back like the cat that had swallowed the canary.

"What are you talking about?"

"You know damn well what I'm talking about. That nigga calls or comes by every single day to check on you. He drops off special gifts for you like you're his girl, and I see the looks y'all be exchanging when y'all think I ain't paying attention."

"It ain't like that." I smiled. Truthfully, I had also noticed the flirting exchanged between Ace and me. However, neither of us had acted on it, so it was nothing as far as I was concerned.

"Let me find out y'all fucking." She laughed.

"Anyway," I said, changing the subject, "let's take this conversation back to the money. I know we aren't supposed to be keeping anything from the cars, but the last two whips had purses in them. I went through them and found three credit cards." I looked around to make sure we were still the only ones in the pool area.

Alicia's eyes widened, and she laughed. "Girl, I ain't even going to lie. Two weeks ago, I snatched a whip at the gas station. The man was trying to spit game to the chick behind the counter. He left the keys and his wallet in the car. I took the car and kept his wallet. I was going to ask you what you thought we should do, but I didn't want you to get mad at me. I guess great minds think alike." We busted out laughing.

"Bobby would die if he found out, but I say we seize the opportunity and start another hustle."

"What would we do with the cards though?" Ali was all ears.

"I say we milk them for all they're worth. Let's buy shit and flip it. I'm talking all the hot shit in the stores right now." I continued to bounce my ideas off of Alicia for about thirty minutes, and she was an eager beaver. We needed to set some things in motion before we jumped out there feet first, but I knew we were on to something big.

"I'll be back. I need to go get my phone." I stood from the chair and retrieved my iPad. It was time for my weekly check-in with Gran. I didn't owe her anything, but out of respect I wanted to assure her that I was alive and well. I also needed to make sure the same could be said about her.

"Okay," Alicia replied, and I left her soaking in the warm water.

Just as I exited the pool area, two things caught my attention: the flashing lights coming from outside, and the two officers standing at the receptionist desk.

"Fuck!" I turned on my heels and headed back to the pool. Prayerfully, the cops weren't there for me and Alicia, but I wasn't one for taking chances. "Ali, let's roll!" I began grabbing her clothes off the chair and tossing them at her.

"What? What's going on?" She hopped out of the water like the shit was on fire.

"I just spotted two cops at the front desk."

"Shit!" She slipped the Aeropostle cover-up over her swimming suit. "Are they here for us?"

"I don't know." I scanned the room for an exit. Bingo! There was one in the corner. "Come on." I waved for her to follow.

"What about the money?" She stopped dead in her tracks.

"Fuck that money!" I snapped. Who gives a fuck about money when you could possibly be facing charges? "I'll send Ace by here later. If the cops ain't here for us, then the money will still be in the room when we get back."

"Naw, homie! I worked my ass off for that dough. I gotta go back." She turned and headed out of the pool room. If my hand could've reached across the room, I would've slapped the piss out of Alicia. She was too greedy for her own good, and sometimes it burned me up.

Didn't she know that going up there to retrieve some shit they had probably already seized was the dumbest idea she had this year?

I watched my girl fly out of the room, and I shook my head but kept it moving toward the exit. She had made her choice, and I had made mine. I looked at the sign on the door, and my stomach turned. The huge white sign told me that if the door was opened, it would set off an alarm. "Fuck it!" I said and pushed the door open because turning around was no longer an option.

# Chapter Nineteen

As soon as I hit the bricks, the alarm starting going crazy, but I didn't care because I was out of there. Without looking back, I ran like my life depended on it, and before I realized it, I was three blocks away and barefoot. In my haste to flee, I'd totally forgotten to grab my flip-flops from the side of the pool chair.

Onk! Onk! Onk! I heard the police sirens before seeing the squad car roll up on the side of me. "Shit!" I tried my best to appear normal, but being barefoot in a bikini was a dead giveaway that something was up.

"Where are your shoes?" a white officer asked.

"Oh, I got locked out of my apartment," I lied and kept on walking.

"Where is your apartment? Maybe we can help." They pulled the car over and parked.

"Really, Officers, I'm cool." I rolled my eyes.

"It's not a problem. Protect and serve is what we do." The black driver pointed to the words that were printed on the side of the car. I wanted to ask these men where all of that protecting and serving was when someone was in a real life-and-death situation, but I played cool.

"Honestly, I'm good. My brother is on the way with my spare keys." I politely smiled.

"Janelle, the jig is up." He unfolded a piece of paper and turned it toward me. The photo I'd taken for my school ID was blown up as big as shit. Instantly, my stomach turned, and I almost wet myself. I knew we'd been found out and I was about to go down for grand theft auto. I looked from side to side to see if I had an escape route, but the white cop peeped my game and called me on it.

"Go ahead and run." He laughed. "I was the star on my track team." He began to stretch his limbs.

"Look, I ain't gon' run. Y'all got me. But first, tell me what I'm being arrested for." I turned around to face the wall and placed my hands behind my head.

"You're not under arrest." One of them laughed. "Somebody reported you as a missing person and led us to the Marriott with reason to believe you'd been shacking up there."

"Are you for real?" I was relieved yet annoyed. The only person in the world who would report me missing was Gran. I'd checked in with her every week and had even made the mistake of calling her from the hotel phone.

"Come on, girl, let's ride." The white cop held the back door open and gestured for me to get in.

# Chapter Twenty

"Janelle, I've been so worried about you." Gran put on a show down at 1300 Beaubien. "Thank you, Officers, for finding her." She smiled.

"No problem, ma'am," they responded.

"Please remember that Janelle must show up for court on Monday," the white officer added.

"Court?" I frowned. "What do I have to go to court for if I wasn't arrested?"

"You have to appear before a judge because you've been cited for being a delinquent."

"I thought this was a warning." I folded my arms.

"This is a warning, but it has to be documented in case you pull this stunt again. The judge will let know what will occur if you have any more incidents, but if you stay clean, then your record will be expunged on your eighteenth birthday."

"Thank you, Officers. I don't think my granddaughter will have time to make any more trouble because she will be on lockdown from this point forward."

Gran pinched my ear all the way from the police station to the car, which was parked two streets over from the building.

"Why did you call the police?" I asked once we were riding down I-75.

"Because, Janelle, you needed to be taught a lesson! You ain't grown!" She turned down the gospel music that was playing in the background.

"Gran, I will be seventeen in two months. You can't lock me down forever." I rolled my eyes.

"I might not be able to lock you down forever, but I bet for damn sure you'll be locked down for the next fourteen months." That was the exact time until my eighteenth birthday. "I made the mistake of giving up on your father too soon, and look how he turned out. I will not watch you walk in his footsteps to hell."

I rolled my eyes and listened to my grandmother preach all the way back to her apartment. A few times, I contemplated opening the car door and jumping out, but I remained cool. I knew the opportunity for me to get away would present itself again. I just had to wait and be patient. Gran talked a good game and meant every word of it, but it was impossible for her to watch me twenty-four-seven.

Little did I know that from that day forward she would be on me like white on rice. I was once again cooped up in her small apartment, dodging the rats and avoiding the roaches. There was no privacy in her presence. She was like a drill sergeant. Gran told me when to wake up and when to go to sleep. I couldn't talk on the phone or even take the trash out by myself because she feared I would come up with some escape route. The woman had gone so far as to tell me I couldn't close the bathroom door when I took a shower or used the restroom. I told her she was delusional if she thought I wasn't going to close the bathroom door. After all, there was no window in her tiny bathroom, so it's not like I could've fled. She had already confiscated my cell phone, so I couldn't text anyone.

"Janie, I'm doing this for your own good. One day you're going to thank me," she said over the dinner table one night. I played with the soupy slop she'd fixed me while I watched her eat a steak, salad, and baked potato.

Her intention was to remind me that this was what my dinner would be in jail. I knew what Gran was trying to do, so I played along.

Although this was the last place I wanted to be, I was content because I had a plan. One day while Gran was in the shower, I grabbed her house phone and called Ali. She was relieved that I was okay, and I was relieved that our hotel room hadn't been raided and the operation was still going smooth.

"So what are you going to do? Bobby has been asking about you, and I found another wallet with two credit cards."

"Tell Bobby I'll be back, but I have court on Monday, so I have to sit tight until then. Tell Ace how much money we've got saved and tell him to find us a place to live, pronto. Fuck them hotels." I stopped mid-conversation to hear if Gran was still showering. Once I was satisfied that she wasn't on her way out of the bathroom, I continued. "Tell Ace to meet me down at the courthouse on Monday. My hearing is at eight thirty, so I should be out of there in at least two hours."

# Chapter Twenty-one

Monday came in no time, and I was thankful. "Janelle, let's go," Gran called from her bedroom, failing to realize that I was already dressed and waiting at the front door.

"I'm already ready," I called back as she entered the living room.

"Why are you so thrilled to be going to court?' She side-eyed me and grabbed her purse.

"I'm not thrilled, just ready to put this issue to bed," I responded nonchalantly as we headed down the hallway toward the elevator.

The Jamaican woman across the hall had her door open, and smoke was pouring into the hallway. "Hello der, Ms. Doesher." She waved to Gran. "Me apologize for da smoke. Me burnt ta curry goat me was preparing for me dinner."

I wondered why this lady was up cooking dinner this early in the damn morning, but I remained silent.

"That's okay, Margie." Gran waved goodbye to her neighbor and pushed the button for the elevator. As we waited, I watched three roaches crawl across the wall, and I rolled my eyes.

"Gran, may I ask you a question?"

"You just did." She stepped into the elevator when it arrived. Someone had littered chicken bones and a few potato wedges from KFC on the ground. I kicked a few pieces to make myself a path.

"Why don't you want to move?"

"Because this is all I can afford." She pressed the ground level button.

"All of those times my father offered to put you in a beautiful home, why did you pass?"

"Because Julius's money was no good to me." We reached the lobby, and she stepped off and tried to power walk all the way to the parking lot. I could tell she was getting real annoyed with my line of questioning, but I continued.

"Why?"

"Janelle, you're too young to understand the significance of what I'm saying. All you see is the glamorous life, but you have no idea what happens behind the scenes." She started up the car, and I fastened my seat belt.

"All you do is see the bad in people. So what my father sold drugs! He wanted to take care of you. Why can't you see the good in that?"

"Let's be clear, your father was no saint!" Gran wagged her finger. "You should try worshiping the Lord instead of Julius."

"Gran, you stay in the church twenty-four hours, seven days a week, praying to somebody who allows you to wake up every morning in a rat-infested environment." I shook my head and looked out of the window. "I thought your Savior said He would never see the righteous forsaken." I hadn't paid that much attention in church, but I did pick up on little tidbits here and there.

"True my building isn't in the best condition, and I do wake up every morning in the grit and grime of poverty. But what you fail to realize, dear granddaughter, is out of everything you said, the most important fact that remains is I wake up every morning."

The debate continued all the way until we walked inside the 36th District Court building. After waiting in line for almost a century, we finally walked through the metal detectors and proceeded toward the courtroom. The place was packed with people who were there to see the judge for various reasons. I hoped this wouldn't take all day.

One by one, each case was called, and I watched people leave either smiling, crying, or in handcuffs. The time on the clock above the judge's seat indicated we had been waiting the better part of two hours to be called. I hoped Ace wouldn't leave thinking he had already missed me. Today was the only day I had to escape.

"Janelle Renee Doesher, please rise and approach the bench," the bailiff called.

*Finally!*

"Ms. Doesher, I see here that you were issued a warning for running away from your grandmother's home. Is this true?" Judge Sylvia Waters asked while reviewing my paperwork.

"Yes, ma'am."

"I'm curious as to why you ran away, so please enlighten me." She placed the paperwork on her desk and focused her attention on me.

"Truthfully speaking, Your Honor, she's mean." I heard a few giggles coming from other defendants in the courtroom.

Judge Waters banged her gavel and demanded order in the court. "Ms. Doesher, do you know that there are approximately 1.7 million homeless teens in the United States?" Before I could respond, she continued. "And of that 1.7 million, thirty-nine percent of those teens are under the age of eighteen just like you." She paused for dramatic effect. "Seventy-five percent of that 1.7 million are addicted to drugs or alcohol their first year on the streets. Records show that five thousand young people die on those streets every year due to illness, suicide, and assault. Do you really want to become a statistic just because your grandmother is mean?" This time she waited for an answer.

"When you put it like that, no, I don't want to become a statistic." At this point, I had to say all the right things in order to not piss this lady off. I could tell she didn't play any games.

"Sweetheart, the world is a cruel place that will chew you up and spit you out. Don't be in such a rush to grow up. Soon you'll be grown, and nobody will care one way or another about your well-being." She smiled partially and collected my case files. "Again, this was only a warning, but should you run away again, you will be placed in the juvenile detention center for a mandatory six months. Do you understand?"

"Yes, ma'am." I nodded, and she banged the gavel.

# Chapter Twenty-two

"I hope you heard what she said, Janelle," Gran said as we made our way out of the courthouse.

"I heard her." I scanned the surrounding area for Ace.

"The next time, you will go to jail," she repeated.

"Gran, I heard her." I spotted on the corner the familiar face I was looking for, and I knew I was about to make a break for it.

"I'm sorry you think I'm mean. I'm just concerned," she explained.

"Gran, I love you." I wrapped my arms around her as tight as possible. "I know you do what you do out of love, but sometimes it comes across in the wrong way. But it's all good." She was shocked by my gesture, and I could tell it caught her off guard. We hadn't ever had any kind of loving gestures exchanged between us. "I'm sorry I give you a hard time, but it's in my nature."

"Well, come on now. Let's get from down here and head on over to the pastor's house." Gran dismissed my embrace and began to head toward our parking spot. My hug had her so rattled that she walked a whole ten paces in front of me. Without another word, I made my exit and headed toward my ride.

"Welcome back, baby girl." Ace winked and fled the scene in the stolen Dodge Durango. He could've picked me up in his own car, but there were too many cameras surrounding the court building. If Gran decided to once again call the police on me, those cameras would've been the first thing they checked, and they would've run Ace's license plate.

"It feels good to be back." I smiled and relaxed in the seat after strapping up my seat belt.

"I have something for you in the back." He nodded, and I turned to see what he was referring to.

"Aw, Ace, you're too sweet." I blushed and grabbed the bags from Saks and Victoria's Secret. The Saks bag contained a beautiful pink strapless dress along with matching heels from the Devereux collection. "What's the dress and shoes for?"

"I have something special planned for us." He never took his eyes from the road ahead.

My eyebrow raised in surprise. "For us?" I repeated.

"Yeah, for us." He changed lanes and passed a senior citizen in a Buick. "I realized while you were gone that I can't stand being away from you." He stopped at the red light and gave me his full attention. The hazel coloring in his eyes twinkled. "I think I love you, Janelle, and I want you to be my girl."

"What have you been smoking?" I rolled my eyes, but inwardly my stomach was doing backflips.

"I haven't been smoking shit." The light turned green, and he put the whip back into motion. "I know I sound crazy, but I'm feelin' you for real." He licked his lips and sent chills down my spine.

"You could have any girl you want, Ace. Why you want me?" I'm not going to lie. Secretively I'd fantasized about him once or twice over the years, but I shook it off because I knew I wasn't his type. He only saw me as a sister, or so I thought.

"I don't want no other girl!" he snapped. "I said I want you."

"But, Ace—"

"Let me finish," he interjected. "My love for you runs deep, girl. You're the first thing on my mind when the sun rises, and you're the last thing on my mind at night before I say my prayers. I know you're sort of like my godsister, but I've always had feelings for you. I tried to put them on the back burner, but after spending all this time with you, our chemistry is undeniable."

"So why are you just now acting on these feelings that you supposedly always had all this time?"

"Because I didn't want to cross Julius." His eyes met mine, and I wanted to kiss him right then and there. "You know your father thought no nigga would be good enough for you. I knew I could be that nigga, but I didn't want to bite the hand that was feeding me, so I chilled."

There was silence between us as we both took in the importance of where this conversation was headed. On the one hand, I was ready to fall into his arms and stay there forever. On the other hand, I knew love had no place in the streets. He was a hustler, and so was I. Eventually love and hustlin' would clash.

"Janelle, say something," he urged.

"Ace, I'm not sure what we're doing, but I'm willing to give it a try." I smiled and reached for his hand.

"I promise I'll do right by you." He squeezed my hand.

"Now what's in the Victoria's Secret bag?" I looked at him sideways. "It better not be lingerie! Don't think I'm about to sleep with you just because you asked me to be your girl." I let go of his hand with an attitude and reached into the bag. Ace didn't say anything when I pulled out a bath set. Instead, he busted out laughing, and I did the same.

# Chapter Twenty-three

We pulled up to a stunning condominium complex in Redford, Michigan, where Ace stopped at the security booth to flash some sort of badge. The older guard lifted the gate and waved us through. The place was well taken care of, and by the looks of the vehicles parked in the lot, I could tell that some financially stable individuals lived here. "Welcome home, Janelle." He parked in the driveway of one of the units.

"This place is beautiful!" I knew he and Alicia were working on our living arrangements, but I didn't think they would take the search beyond the city limits of Detroit.

"If you're in love with the outside, wait until you see the inside." He smiled, and I followed him into a home that resembled a smaller version of a New York brownstone.

Once inside of the home, I was in awe. The high cathedral ceilings, mahogany wood flooring, and stainless-steel appliances had me speechless. After the passing of my parents, I would have never in a million years thought I could live this way again. There were two bedrooms and three bathrooms, as well as a loft area that overlooked the open-concept living and dining area.

"That one is your room." He pointed to the room on the left side of the house. Without hesitation, I turned the doorknob anticipating a huge blank canvas, but what I found brought tears to my eyes.

"Ace." I sniffed. "Where did you find this?" Right before me was the very bedroom set I'd had at my parents' home. It was my custom-made black sleigh bed with leather in the headboard and footboard. The vintage dresser and nightstand were made of mirrored glass, and the hot pink chandelier glistened just the way I remembered. Ace had added a hot pink thinking chair, a pink fuzzy rug, and one hot pink accent wall to make the room pop. I loved it! "Thank you so much." I sniffed again.

"Baby, I told you I will do everything I can to make you happy." He walked up behind me and held me close. Feeling the safest I'd felt in a very long time, I closed my eyes, leaned my head back onto his chest, and sobbed like a baby. I cried long and hard for every time I couldn't cry at Gran's house. I cried until there were no more tears.

When I stopped, I noticed Ace was crying too. In that moment, we were kindred spirits sharing the loss of our parents. On that day, I vowed to love Ace with all I had. No matter what, I would be there for him as I knew he would be there for me. Nothing but death or a jail cell would keep us apart!

"Damn! Y'all caking like that?" Alicia called from the doorway of my bedroom. She was standing there with a Kool-Aid grin.

"Shut up." I wiped my tearstained face.

"All right, Janelle, I'll pick you up at nine." He kissed my cheek and dapped Ali on his way out.

"I knew y'all was fucking." She plopped down on my bed, and I lay beside her.

"We haven't had sex yet." I rolled my eyes.

"What are you waiting for?" She laughed.

"Unlike you, I'm no ho." I giggled, and she hit my arm.

"Keep on talking that shit and I'll cancel the surprise I had for you."

"What surprise?" I stopped laughing.

"Come on, you'll see." She got off the bed, and I followed suit.

"Where are we going, and how will we get there?" I asked, confused because she was heading toward the front door and neither of us had a car.

"I'm taking you to the salon to get your shit tight before the date." She hit the garage opener, and my mouth dropped.

"Whose car is this?" I walked around the 2012 Lexus RX 350. It was gun metal on the outside with a charcoal interior.

"It's mine. Do you like it?" She beamed like the proud owner she was.

"It's beautiful." I wanted to sound happier for my friend because the midsized luxury SUV was a definite step up from the bus line. However, I was worried it would draw too much attention.

"Well, then, what's the matter?" she asked, sensing my apprehension.

"Don't you think this is too flashy and expensive for a seventeen-year-old? People are gonna start talking, and God forbid you get pulled over. How will you explain this?"

"Chill, J, you worry too much!" She unlocked the whip, and we hopped in. "People are always gonna talk, and fuck the police!" she spat. Alicia was hotheaded, and I didn't want to piss her off, but she needed to be more careful.

"Ali." I sighed. "Did you cross your t's and dot your i's?"

"Yes, mother." She started the engine. "I put the car in my aunt's name when I got it from the dealership." She backed out of the garage and closed the door behind us.

"How much did it hit you for?" I asked, referring to the cost of the vehicle.

"I put ten racks down, and I'll make payments on the other twenty-eight thousand every month."

"Alicia, you need to start saving a little better." I didn't want to sound like her mother, but it had to be said. Her spending habits were reckless, and she needed to be put on notice.

"Look, I'm taking you out to get your hair done, not to be lectured to." She turned up the bass in her sound system. "Don't forget, I'm older than you." She smiled, and I did too, choosing to drop the issue for now.

# Chapter Twenty-four

We pulled up to a beauty salon called Hair Politics and parked the car. On the inside, a woman greeted us at the door with a tray carrying champagne flutes. I looked back at Alicia to see what was going on. Obviously, this lady didn't know we were underage. "Would you care for a mimosa?" She smiled with a mouth full of Lumineers that were so big her lips didn't fully close.

"No, ma'am, just water for me." I smiled politely.

"I'll take mine and hers too since she doesn't want one." Alicia reached for the glasses, and we followed the woman toward the back of the facility. I took notice of the tasteful décor, classical music with violins playing through the building, and pictures of celebrities like Christina Aguilera, Celine Dion, and Cameron Diaz hanging on the wall. The one thing that struck me as odd was the fact that not one of the stylists we had passed was African American. Don't get it twisted, I have no discrimination against Caucasian people, but only a colored woman would know what to do with my type of hair.

"We originated in Los Angeles, and now we have salons in Las Vegas, Atlanta, Michigan, and Arizona." The host gave us the rundown.

"Ali, what are we doing here?" I whispered as Alicia guzzled from her glass.

"You'll see," she said as we reached our destination.

"This is Dalia, and she will be your stylist." The host turned on her pricey heels. "Please let me know if you need anything else."

"You must be Janelle," Dalia said. She was a very beautiful Dominican woman with long tresses of jet-black hair. "Alicia has told me all about you."

"Yes. I'm Janelle." I looked from her to Alicia, still trying to figure out what I was doing here.

"Hop on in the seat and we'll get started." She patted the red leather chair.

"And what exactly are we getting started on?" I quizzed.

"Well, Alicia told me you have all of this beautiful hair that no one sees because you keep it hidden in a ponytail. So I'm going to do a Dominican press and make your hair bone straight." She began to undo my ponytail to assess what I was working with.

"Will you use a pressing comb?"

"No, I only use this brush and a blow dryer." She pointed to her supplies. Sensing my apprehension, she patted my shoulder. "Just trust me."

Eventually, I relaxed and let her do what she needed to do. I didn't complain when she washed my hair in ice-cold water, and I didn't even complain that the heat from the blow dryer was killing my scalp. In the end, the finished product was more than awesome. My hair was as straight as ever, and it hung way down my shoulders. I shook my head from side to side and admired my new 'do in the mirror. After Alicia paid Dalia, I thanked them both, and we headed back on home so I could get ready.

# Chapter Twenty-five

"Come on, damn!" Alicia called from the living room. She couldn't wait to see me in the dress, so I emerged from the doorway with a few poses.

"You look like a doll." She admired the gold dress and matching shoes. I accented the outfit with the few pieces of jewelry I'd acquired when we first started hustling. "Ace is gonna be all over you."

"Hey, can I ask you a question and you respond honestly?"

"What's up?" She looked up from polishing her toenails.

"Now that Ace and I are dating, does that bother you? I know you sort of had a crush on him, and I don't want you to feel like I stepped on your toes."

"J, ain't nobody thinking about Ace. Yeah, the nigga is cute, but I've been knowing he was feeling you. I was only flirting to be silly." She blew me off. I didn't want any drama with my girl, so I was glad to have cleared the air.

We talked a few more minutes, and at nine o'clock on the dot, there was a knock at the door. "Oh, my God, he's here." I panicked while grabbing my purse.

"Relax, you look beautiful." Alicia went to open the door. "What up, killa."

Ace stepped into the house wearing a black Calvin Klein suit with a matching shirt and tie. His shoes were black Mauri gators, and his wrist was adorned with a crazy Rolex.

"What up, Ali." He gave her a five and walked over to me. "Baby, you look breathtaking." After handing me a single red rose, he leaned in for a hug.

"You look good yourself." I tried to compose myself.

"Shall we?" He pointed to the door.

"We shall." I smiled and followed him out.

Once outside, I could not believe my eyes. There was a horse-drawn carriage waiting for us. "I can't believe you did this for me." I blushed.

"Why not? You're worth it," he whispered into my ear. His lips were so close to my flesh that it made me shudder. Ace helped me up into the carriage, and we took off out of the complex and onto the main street. People pointed and waved. Some cars even blew their horns and drivers gave us the thumbs-up.

"This is very romantic." I laid my head on his shoulder and stared at the stars.

"I'm glad you like it, baby." He wrapped his arms around mine and held me until we arrived at the restaurant. "I hope you're hungry." He held my hand and assisted me from the carriage.

"I love this place, Ace." Havier's was one of my favorite restaurants in Michigan. It was owned by an old-school hustler from the seventies who retired from the game and went into the culinary business. My father once told me the place was packed every night with everybody who was anybody in the dope game. Havier ran it for over twenty years before succumbing to cancer. One of his children took over ownership, and now it was a popular spot among the younger generation of dope dealers and fly girls.

"Your father used to have me swing by here every Friday to pick up carry-out for you and your moms." He opened the door, and we were shown a table.

"I remember that." Girls' night every Friday was a ritual that my mother and I shared. We would rent tons of movies, order Havier's, and paint each other's toenails. "Boy, this place brings back memories."

Ace must've sensed my sadness, because he reached for my hand. "I'm sorry, baby. I didn't think this would make you cry. We can leave." He stood.

"No, Ace, it's okay. Sit back down." I wiped my tears.

"Are you sure? Just say the word and we're out." He pointed toward the door.

"I'm sure." He had gone out of his way to make this night special for me, and I was not about to ruin it with my tears. Ace lifted his menu and began to study it. I left mine on the table because I knew exactly what I wanted.

"Oh, hell no!" some chick snapped while approaching our table. "I know you ain't up in this piece with another bitch." She slapped the table and glared at me. I didn't know who she was, but I returned the stare, although I didn't want to deal with another one of Ace's hoodrats. I balled up my fists and prepared for battle. I would not be caught off guard again!

"You need to check that shit and keep it pushing." Ace spoke in a low but stern voice.

"Or what, Anthony?" She rolled her neck. "First you tell me this bitch is your sister, then you quit calling me, and now I see y'all out on a muthafuckin' date."

"Things have changed." He reached for my hand.

"Yeah, things have changed." She snorted. "A month ago this bitch looked like a broke-down hoodrat, and now you got her looking ghetto fabulous."

At the mention of what I looked like a month ago, I realized this was the same chick who was in the car with Ace the day I ran away from Gran's house. "Look, you need to get the fuck away from this table." I stood.

"What you gon' do, bitch?" She squared up. I noticed three of her friends standing behind her, but I was unfazed. My mother once told me to take the one with all the mouth and make an example out of them, so that's what I did.

Crash! I hit that bitch across the face with the saucer they had on the table for bread and appetizers. Instantly, her nose split and blood gushed from her face.

"My face!" she screamed while attempting to reach for me. I ducked and punched her on the side of her face. I was sure her ear was ringing from that blow, because she grabbed it.

"That's my muthafuckin' sister," one girl yelled and tried to attack me. She was a good 250 pounds, but I wasn't scared. As soon as she stepped up, I popped her right in the face too. By then my first victim had regained her composure and tried to assist her sister with jumping me.

"Get the fuck off of her." Ace grabbed the girl by her weave and pulled her away, but that's when all hell broke loose. Outraged that Ace had chosen to put his hands on their friend, the other two women headed over toward us and prepared to give me a royal beatdown. I had bucked several times while growing up, but never had I faced off with four bitches. *Oh, well, win some, lose some. These bitches may end up getting the best of me, but I'm not about to make it easy.*

Picking up one of the chairs, I held it like a weapon. Pop! Pop! There were two shots let off into the ceiling, which blew out one of the light fixtures, causing sparks to fly and everyone to scatter. Ace tucked the gun into his waistband and grabbed my hand.

"Let's go." He ushered me toward the back door and around the building.

I remembered our transportation. "We will never make it out of here on a damn horse."

"Naw, my whip is right here." He unlocked the car, and we sped off into the night.

# Chapter Twenty-six

My hair was a mess, the dress was ruined, and I'd lost one of my shoes. Nevertheless, we laughed all the way until we pulled up to Ace's crib, which thankfully was around the corner. "That shit was crazy Joe Louis," he joked, referring to the legend with iron fists as he unlocked the door.

"I had to do what I had to do." I removed the one remaining shoe I had on and followed him into the bachelor pad. The place reeked of marijuana, and there were beer cans and alcohol bottles everywhere.

"Sorry about the mess. I would've cleaned up if I knew we would have to take a detour over here." He went into his room and grabbed a pair of sweatpants, a T-shirt, and Reebok flip-flops for me.

"Sorry I ruined the date." I slipped the dress over my head, completely exposing my nude breasts and panties. I mean it wasn't like he hadn't already seen my birthday suit.

"Don't worry about it. I'm just sorry old girl showed her ass." Ace tried to look away from me but not for long. "You look sexy as fuck!" He licked those lips I loved to death.

"Thank you." I began to do a slow striptease then stopped. "Where is your roommate?"

"He over at his baby mother's house." Ace sat back on the La-Z-Boy and reclined.

"What if I told you I wanted to sleep with you?" For some reason, I had grown a pair of balls. I was ready to take this friendship to the next level, and I was tired of waiting for him to make the first move.

"I'd be a liar if I said I haven't been feeling the same way lately." He stared at me seductively and pulled me down toward him. The heat coming from between my legs was intense, and my heart rate quickened.

"What if I told you I was a virgin?" I straddled his lap and felt him tense up.

"Then I would tell you to save yourself for someone you thought was worth it." He slid me over and grabbed the remote from the coffee table. I tried not to feel a certain type of way about his rejection, because he was right. However, I knew Ace and trusted him. If I was going to lose my virginity to anyone, I wanted it to be him.

"You are worth it." I kissed his neck, and he tried to resist the urge to return the gesture. To be honest, I wasn't sure what had made me so horny all of a sudden. It could've been the rush of what happened at Havier's, or it could've been the fact that he had kept his promise to my father and held me down. Deep down inside, I knew Ace was my prince, and whatever the case may be, I was ready to give him all I had.

"Baby, as much as I would love to go there with you, I realize what you have is precious and it only should be shared with your husband." His hazel-green eyes pierced my soul, and I felt deflated. Over the years, I'd seen him with woman after woman, and now I was wondering why he didn't want me.

"It's cool." I stood and walked into the guest bathroom to finish getting dressed. Maybe I was moving too fast, but I could've sworn he felt the same way about me. After all, the nigga just told me he loved me this afternoon. Pulling myself together, I walked back into the living room, but

Ace was gone. I started to call his phone, but then I heard music coming from his bedroom. Slowly, I approached the door and pushed it open. Ace was shirtless, standing at the stereo that was on top his dresser.

"I'm ready to go." I folded my arms.

"Janelle, sit down on the bed."

"No! Let's go."

"It wasn't a fuckin' question. Now please just sit down on the bed." Again those beautiful eyes mesmerized me, so I did as I was told. I watched as he reached into his drawer and clutched something in his fist. "I didn't mean to make you mad. I only said that you should save yourself for your husband because I want to be that nigga." He dropped to one knee and produced a ring. It wasn't as big and glamorous as you might've imagined, but it was just enough and meant the world to me.

"This was my mother's ring, Janelle, and it's the only thing I have left besides memories. I know we're young, but we were made for each other. I planned to propose when the time was right but—"

I pulled him in for the most passionate kiss I could muster. "I love you, Ace! I always have and I always will."

"I love you too, baby!" He slipped the ring onto my finger and began to nibble on my belly button.

In that moment, I gave myself to him in more ways than one. Ace had me open, and I wasn't ashamed. He had taken my virginity and stolen my heart all in one night. Together we vowed to withstand the test of time.

He was mine, and I was his from that day forward. I was Bonnie, and he was Clyde. We rode with and for each other with no questions asked. Many people despised our relationship, but everybody respected it.

# Chapter Twenty-seven

Almost a year had gone by without incident, and for the first time in a long time, everything was on point. My relationship was steady, and the credit card operation was running smooth. My pockets were getting fatter, and no one in Bobby's crew was hip to our side hustle. I wished life could always operate this smoothly, but I knew the good times wouldn't last forever.

"Sometimes you can be so hardheaded," Ace spoke into my cell phone. We had just had a slight disagreement about him wanting me to leave the hustle and play the good wife. He knew like I did that he had the game fucked up.

"Ace, I'm out here working. I ain't got time to be arguing." I scoped the scene while clutching the cellular device.

"Baby, I'm not trying to argue." His voice softened. "Can we talk about this over dinner?"

"Ace!" I was so damn frustrated, but he made it really hard to stay angry with him.

"I'll see you tonight. Love you," he said hurriedly and ended the call before I had time to object. I needed to collect my thoughts, but there was no time to do so before another voice entered my space.

"Here comes the truck, right on schedule," Alicia spoke into the walkie-talkie from her position on the corner. Like clockwork, the brown UPS came to a stop in front of the abandoned house. I watched from the park across the street as the driver went up to the door and pressed the buzzer. On cue, Donna, our hired help, walked from the side of the house and greeted the man. I couldn't hear the conversation, but she was smiling, and he was too, so everything was velvet. After a few minutes of small talk, the driver went to the back of his vehicle and retrieved several packages ranging from small to large. I expected him to leave after placing the last package at the side door, but he stopped again and made small talk. I could see Donna beginning to panic, so I prepared to head over and assist her.

Just as I stood up from the bench, the deliveryman turned around and headed back to his truck. I waited five minutes then proceeded to go over there. "What was that about?"

"That nigga insisted on helping me carry all these boxes in the house, but I told him that my man would have a fit if I let another man in the house while he wasn't there." She smiled.

"Good work." I peeled off a $50 bill and handed it to her. "Be here at the same time next week."

"Okay, Jane, I got you." She clutched the money for dear life and scurried away. I watched my mother's best friend until she disappeared in the alleyway. I knew Donna was headed to the nearest trap house for a fix. Saddened by the reality of the situation, I shook my head at what she'd become but didn't dwell on it for too long, because those were her demons, not mine. One day she would face them at the crossroads, but today she had to deal with them as best she could.

"That shit was smooth!" Alicia pulled up in front of the house and yelled from the window.

"Come help me load this up." I carried a box and tossed it onto her back seat.

"This is the easiest hustle I've ever done."

"You can say that again." I slung another box over my shoulder. Cautiously, I surveyed the area out of habit. The last thing I needed right now was a nosy neighbor calling the police and blowing the whistle on this whole thing.

After the car was finally loaded, we headed home to take a look at the goods. I was extremely pleased. Our inventory was full with two sixty-inch flat screens, one MacBook Pro, four laptops, ten Kindle Fires, five iPads, and nine iPods.

"Now how are we supposed to get rid of this shit?" Alicia glanced around our living room, which had become a makeshift electronics department store. When we first started jacking cars, we had a couple of fiends standing at the gas station offering people a fill-up for half the price. Next, we started using the stolen credit cards to buy gift cards to places like Walmart, grocery stores, and restaurants. We also sold those for half. Profits were good but could've been better. That's when I had the idea to purchase shit online and sell it for less, but I needed to call in an expert on the subject.

Ding-dong! At the sound of the doorbell, I smiled. "Help is on the other side of that door."

"Who did you call, Janelle?" Alicia looked at me with skepticism. I didn't reply. Instead, I swung the front door open.

"You're just in time. The goods just got here." I hugged my girl.

"I was at the salon in the muthafuckin' chair about to get my hair done, but when I heard you had those goods, I sped over here." Keisha stepped into the living room and removed her tan Burberry peacoat, which was wrapped around her tiny waist. It was hardly cold enough for a peacoat, but Keisha was all about labels. If it was name brand, she rocked it no matter what season it was.

"What's up, Alicia." She gave a half smile, and I watched as Alicia flipped her the bird.

"Janelle, let me holla at you for a second." She pulled me by my arm toward the kitchen. "What the fuck is she doing up in here? You know I can't stand that bougie bitch!"

"Girl, you have to put your feelings in check right now because this is about business." I patted Ali on the shoulder. Keisha was my homegirl from the Brewster Housing Projects. Her uncle hustled up under my father and we played together as kids. For some odd reason, these chicks had always had a rivalry with one another. For the life of me, I didn't know why.

"What does she have to do with our business?" She folded her arms like a spoiled kid.

"You know like I know that Keisha is the best booster in the projects. She specializes in selling stolen shit, and her clientele is off the hook. I figured we could load her up with the goods and let her work that magic." I turned to exit the kitchen, but Ali stopped me.

"Is the bitch leaving a deposit?" Alicia rolled her eyes.

"Now you know me better than that." I gave her the "for real you think I'm that stupid" face and headed back into the living room. "So what do you think, Keish? Can you handle all of this?"

"Girl, this shit is worth over seven racks on the street." Keisha looked up from her calculator.

"So how long you think it'll take you to move this?" Alicia asked grudgingly.

"Give me 'bout a week." Keisha stood from the couch and put her coat back on. "So what's the breakdown?" She popped her bubblegum.

"You keep three and give us four. I need two racks now, but you can give me the other two grand when it's sold." I ignored the side-eye Alicia was giving me.

"Cool!" Keisha went into her Alexander McQueen bucket purse and handed me several crisp green $100 bills.

"Back the fuck up." Ali shook her head. "You're giving her three thousand dollars while me and you got to split four? I'm not a math wiz, but that shit ain't adding up! Why do she get more money?"

"Keisha is the one taking all the risks." I counted through the green bills and handed Alicia her cut.

"Anyway," Keisha sighed, obviously irritated with Alicia, "I'll call you when all this is gone and bring you the rest of your dough."

"Thanks, girl!" I hugged her, and the scent of Chanel No. 5 drifted into my nostrils. I had to admit Keisha was a bad bitch from head to toe. She had the face of a model and the body of a stripper. Maybe that's why Alicia was jealous?

"You know I'm all about the money, boo. This is right up my alley. Let me have my brothers get this shit and I'll be on my way." She waved her brothers in, and they began taking out the merchandise like professionals.

"FYI, you better re-up, because this order is going to sell like hotcakes," she warned us, and sure enough, that's exactly what happened.

# Chapter Twenty-eight

As soon as Keisha was out of the house, Ali got started on me. "For real, it's like that? You just gon' ignore my input and make business deals without me?"

"Bitch, get your panties out of that knot and calm down. At the end of the day, it's all about the Benjamins. Now, if you bring me someone who can outsell Keisha, then I'll take her off the team." I went to retrieve a bag of Better Made chips from the top of the fridge and grabbed a Faygo pop. There's nothing like those Michigan classics. "What is your beef with her about anyway?"

"Nothing." Alicia headed into her room and closed the door. I rolled my eyes and headed into my room. I needed to hook her up with a dude fast because she needed to get laid.

Ding-dong! I turned back toward the door and looked through the peephole. It was Ace. I sighed before answering because I wasn't prepared for another heated discussion.

"Hey, baby." I kissed him and headed back into my room. He locked the door and followed suit.

"Come on. You ready for dinner?" He stood in the doorway.

"I really just want to chill tonight." I sipped from the can of grape pop.

"What's the matter?" He pulled the 9 mm from his pants and placed it on the dresser before lying beside me on the bed.

"Just some shit with Alicia, nothing serious."

"I just seen them niggas from the projects leaving here. What was that all about?" He took my chips and began to eat them.

"Just business! My homegirl Keisha is flipping my merchandise for me. She just came through with her brothers and picked the stuff up."

"How well do you know them niggas?"

"Ace, I've known Keisha since forever." I sighed. Sometimes his overprotectiveness was overbearing.

"You act like you mad at me for giving a fuck!" He stood from the bed and went in the bathroom. "I'm just concerned for you and Alicia, that's all. You can't do business with everybody, but if you say she cool, then that's that. Ain't nothing left to talk about."

As soon as he closed the door, his cell phone rang. It was a private call.

"Who in the hell is this?" I snapped.

"Tell that nigga he dead!" Click.

For a second, I just stared at the phone in awe. Did this nigga just receive a death threat?

"Who was that, baby?" Ace shook his hands dry and came back over to the bed.

"Ace, somebody just called and said you were a dead man." I handed him the phone.

"That shit ain't new, so don't worry about it. These clowns always blowing up my phone with these prank calls." He relaxed like nothing had happened.

"Baby, this is serious business. How long has this been going on?" I didn't like this one bit, but Ace was unfazed.

"Speaking of business," Ace said, looking at me and changing the subject, "when will you take me up on my offer to leave this city? After all, we are engaged." He played with his mother's ring on my finger. The plan was for us to wed on my eighteenth birthday. After that,

Ace wanted to move out of state and live an honest life. I didn't have cold feet, but I wasn't ready to become Suzy Homemaker. Ace wanted kids, picket fences, and a dog. All I wanted at this point in time was to get money, point blank period.

"Baby, I think we should push the wedding back at least until I graduate." I held my breath for his response. Graduation wasn't too far away, so I hoped he wouldn't be too disappointed. Before he could make a remark, his cell phone beeped. He didn't say anything. Instead, he stood from the bed and grabbed his gun.

"I'll holla at you later. Some shit just came up."

"What came up?" The jealousy inside of me was apparent. "That better not be another bitch!"

"Janelle, chill with all of that." He walked to the door. "One of my spots just got robbed. I'm going to handle it, and I'll be back."

"Let me go with you then." I grabbed my purse.

"No." He stopped me.

"Ace, I'm going with you, and that's that!" I grabbed my gun from under the kitchen sink and another one from the kitchen drawer that was concealed inside of a Ziploc box.

"What do you think you're doing?"

"It's called having your back. Now let's ride." I slid the smallest weapon inside of my purse and headed for the door.

Within a matter of twenty minutes, we were parked outside of Ace's spot on Snowden. The entire block was quiet, and I knew shit wasn't right. Inside the house, there were no lights on, and the streetlights had all been shot out. As if he could read my thoughts, Ace reached for the shotgun in the custom compartment under his back seat.

"Let me call this nigga Damien and find out what's poppin'." He loaded the shotgun while placing the call. The phone rang several times before someone picked up.

"What up, boy," Damien spoke over the speakerphone.

"I'm on the block. Where the fuck y'all niggas at?" Ace looked at me and shook his head.

"Oh, you on the block right now?" Damien sounded like he was up to no good. I could hear the sneakiness in his voice, and so did Ace, because he ended the call without another word and put the car in gear. Before we had time to pull off, a car came blazing from a side street and opened fire on us.

"Duck, Janelle." He dived on top of me and wrapped his arms around me in an attempt to shield me from the bullets that sprayed the vehicle. Every single window in the car was broken, and glass flew everywhere. It could've been just my imagination, but I felt the fire of the small metal weapons and could smell the gunpowder. Each time a shell casing hit the floor I cried because I was scared to death. Ace hadn't made a sound, so I feared the worst. With my eyes closed, I blindly reached to open the car door, and we slid out onto the pavement.

"Baby, please tell me you're okay." I wiped the snot running from my nose onto the back of my hand.

"Shh!" He placed a finger up to his mouth, and I sighed in relief. Ace was bleeding profusely. I knew this wasn't a good sign, but now was not the time to panic.

Our assailant's car had slammed on the brakes and was driving in reverse toward our car. I glanced up and down the darkened street for an escape route, but there was none. The way out of this situation was to shoot our way out.

Once the car had come to a stop, I could hear footsteps as someone walked around the car, stepping on the pieces of shattered glass.

"Yo, that nigga ain't in here."

"Find his ass then. He has got to be out here somewhere," another voice demanded. It sounded like Damien, Ace's roommate, best friend, and partner.

Ace looked at me and began to count on his fingers. I could tell he was in obvious pain, but it was do or die. By the time he reached three, we both stood and began busting our guns at Damien and his crew. Shell casings flew everywhere, and one of them even burned my arm. I took out the fool standing in the street while Ace lit the van and its passengers up like a Christmas tree. Some managed to flee the vehicle, but in the dark, we couldn't make a positive ID.

"Let's go!" Ace limped over to his destroyed car, and we fled the scene.

"Baby, are you hit?" I panicked.

"No, I'm good," he lied.

"Anthony, let's go to the hospital," I demanded.

"And tell them what?" he yelled.

We could hear sirens blaring in the distance, and my heart skipped seven beats. We didn't have time to dump the guns because we needed to park the car ASAP. It had more bullet holes than I cared to count, and the cops would've pulled us over in a heartbeat.

# Chapter Twenty-nine

Ace had taken the back roads all the way to my apartment. I breathed a sigh of relief once we were safely pulling the car into the garage. "Fuck!" He hit the steering wheel.

"Baby, calm down."

"One of them pussy niggas is still out there though." He hit the steering wheel again.

"That's okay. We'll find him."

"We don't even know who Damien had working with him on this, so how are we going to find the nigga who got away?" He clutched his stomach and laid his head back on the headrest.

"Baby, please come inside so I can check you out."

"I'm cool, Janie. This ain't shit."

"Ace, your whole shirt is soaked in blood. Please come in the house." The last time I saw this much blood, my father was dying in the hallway.

"Baby, I need to get my shit out the crib before the cops find Damien's ID and go there." Ace stepped from the car and attempted to walk straight but immediately doubled over in pain. Not only was his shirt covered in blood, but his jeans were too. Even so, he was determined not to let me see him sweat. "Let me see your car keys."

"Baby, you're bleeding profusely," I pointed out.

"I said I'm good." He stumbled a few steps and leaned up against the wall for support.

"Ace!" I was scared to death. This nigga couldn't die on me today. Didn't we have plans to get married?

I ran up the stairs and banged for Alicia to open up. After a second, she flung the door open with attitude. "What the fuck is you banging on the door for?" She had a bat in her hand.

"I think Ace got shot! Help me get him in the house," I yelled, and she flew down the steps. Together we carried him up the stairs and into the living room. He was losing a lot of blood and feeling woozy.

I lifted his shirt and searched frantically for the entry wound, but the only thing I found was a piece of glass protruding through his flesh. *Thank God!* I grabbed my cell phone and called my neighbor Tameka. She was in her last year of medical school, and I knew she would be able to help us. As the phone rang, I remembered she was finishing up her residency at the local hospital, but I prayed this was her day off. If Ace didn't receive some sort of medical attention soon, it could possibly be too late.

"Hello?" My neighbor sounded as if she was in a good sleep. I almost felt bad for waking her.

"Hey, Tameka, it's Jane. My boyfriend fell on a piece of glass and is bleeding all over the place. He doesn't want to go to the hospital. Could you please come over here and help him?" I waited while she got her bearings.

"Let me grab my bag and I'll be on the way."

"Okay, thank you, girl. I really appreciate you." I ended the call.

"Janelle, I ain't got time to be getting worked on and shit. I have to get over to my apartment." Ace tried to get up, but Alicia and I pushed him back down.

"Baby, I got it. You stay here with Ali and let Tameka help you. I'll be back." I kissed his lips.

"That shit ain't safe. Wait for me," he yelled.

"Baby, the cops could be at your spot soon. I need to get in and get out, and I can't do that if you're with me." I grabbed my purse and headed toward the door before he could object.

"Be careful."

# Chapter Thirty

Pulling up to Ace's house, I decided to park three doors down instead of in the driveway. While walking down the block, I surveyed the scene and clutched my pistol with a death grip. Everything appeared normal, but as I entered Ace's and Damien's house, I felt paranoid for some reason. I brushed the ill vibes off and began to move through the joint like a thief in the night.

Going from room to room, I removed anything I thought Ace might've wanted like pictures, jewelry, weapons, and money. Of course, I hadn't bothered with shoes and clothes because that shit was easily replaceable. Next, I went into Damien's room and looked for his valuable shit. It wasn't like he'd be using it anytime soon, so it was fair game. As I rummaged through his closest, I found a safe hidden behind a massive hole in the wall. The hole was semi-covered by a bunch of clutter on the floor. I could see that it had been left open, so without hesitation, I reached my hand inside and removed the contents, which consisted of a few green bills, a scale, and about a pound of crack cocaine.

As I tossed the items into the garbage bag, I heard the front door of the apartment open. "Oh, shit!" I cussed. Where was I supposed to go? The only ways out were the window in the kitchen and the front door. Thinking fast, I jumped into Damien's closet.

"You sure that nigga ain't here?" someone asked.

"I told you, Damien gave the word and it's done! That nigga Ace is probably in a body bag right now," the other man replied. I could hear them in the living room moving around, and my stomach hit my guts.

"That's fucked up. What he kill that nigga for anyway?"

"Nigga, I don't know. Something about wanting to be solo and cut out the middleman," the second man replied, and I listened close. "See, Ace got the connect through that nigga Chucky, and Damien wanted it for himself, but the only way Charles was gonna fuck with D is if something happened to Ace," the second man explained, and I shook my head. Niggas wasn't loyal at all. Everybody was out for self. No wonder Ace was extra paranoid.

"Well, let's hurry up, Kirk, and do what we have to do and get out of this bitch."

"Nigga, what you scared for? It ain't like Ace coming home no time soon."

I smirked 'cause these fools had no idea.

"I know, man, but I don't like being in a dead nigga's house."

"Fuck that. I'm cool. This is the easiest money I've ever made! The nigga D paid us two hundred dollars just to come over here and order a porno on the cable box and call his baby mama."

"Well, order the movie, call the bitch, and let's go," the paranoid man demanded.

"Naw, bro. We had specific instructions to call her from the house phone and let the call run for two hours."

"Why we can't just dial the bitch and hang up?"

"Because if the police look at Damien as a suspect, he can say he chilled at home, ordered a flick, and talked to his baby mama. That alibi is airtight, ya feel me?"

"Fine then! You make the call, and I'm making myself something to eat."

"Make me a sandwich too."

"Nigga, fuck you. Make your own damn sandwich."

The men bickered for the better part of their stay, and I was annoyed, to say the least. Not only was I trapped in this dirty-ass room, but my stomach was growling, and I had to pee. To make matters worse, when the men started to walk around the house, I had to conceal myself inside of the hole in Damien's closet and hide under a shitload of smelly clothes and dirty underwear.

Just when I was about to doze off, my cell phone vibrated. "Yeah," I whispered.

"Baby, where are you?" Ace sounded like he was drowsy, but I was glad to hear his voice. Up until his call, I'd silently feared the worst. There was no telling if that broken glass had pierced an artery.

"I'm in Damien's closet. Some dudes came over to set up his alibi, and I didn't have time to get out, so I'm hiding."

"What? I'm on my way," he barked.

"No, Ace. They're about to leave anyway. I'll be home in a few. Stay put." I didn't need him out here in the streets when he wasn't 100 percent in the best health.

"All right, but if you ain't home in thirty minutes, I'm coming over there." He ended the call, and I placed the cell phone back into my pocket. I knew Ace was as serious as a heart attack and would surely be on his way if I wasn't home in exactly thirty minutes. Lucky for me, the men left about three minutes after my call. I grabbed the garbage bag and made a break for it.

# Chapter Thirty-one

A few days had gone by since the shooting incident, and Ace was lying low. He'd found out through street gossip that Damien's brother was the person who escaped from the car the other night. It bothered him that he didn't know where Damien's brother was, and he intended to find him before he found Ace.

My baby was extra paranoid, and rightfully so, but it was driving me crazy. He wanted to know where I was every hour of the day, so he had me on house arrest. Thankfully, business was booming, which gave me a reason to step out every now and then. Keisha had stayed true to her word, and within a couple of days, the first order was gone. She'd put the word out to all of her clients, and within that same week, the orders began coming in faster than we could receive the deliveries.

Alicia and I had only acquired a total of nine stolen cards and had already milked them bitches for all they had. After using them up, we tossed them in the sewer and went to retrieve more. Truth be told, the credit card business was booming far more than car theft. The amount of money Bobby paid me for three cars I made in less than an hour by selling stolen merchandise. Quiet as it's kept, the only reason I was still jacking cars was that I hoped to find a credit card left behind in someone's purse or wallet. I knew Bobby would shit two bricks if he ever found out that we had broken the rules, but I was on a mission to get paid by any means necessary.

"Where you going?" Alicia looked up from her iPad. Ace had made a run to visit with Uncle Chucky, so I used the time to get out of the house.

"Donna has a package coming in today. I'm going to pick it up, and I'll be back." I slipped my Sperry boat shoes on and grabbed my keys.

"Do you need me to go?"

"No, it's cool. I got it. You can chill." I tossed her the deuces and headed outside. Just as I stepped off the porch, I noticed a black Jeep Patriot pull up, and I knew it was Ace. He was riding around in a rental car.

"Hey, you lookin' good, ma." Ace rolled down the lightly tinted window and smiled.

"Boy, stop." I giggled for no reason at all. He just had that effect on me.

"Fa real, girl! You gettin' all thick and shit. Tell me your boy ain't putting it down." He popped the collar on his Ralph Lauren shirt and emerged from the whip.

"You calling me fat?" I snapped. Honestly, I had gained about five pounds from all the good eating I'd been doing, but it was nothing a few laps around the block couldn't fix.

"Not at all." He raised both hands in surrender.

"Anyway, what you doing back over this way? Don't you have a meeting with Chucky?"

"I do have a meeting, but on the way there I decided to pick you up something special. I could've kept them with me until I came back, but I decided they might mess up my reputation in the streets if someone sees me riding with them." He opened the back door and produced two dozen beautiful red roses.

"Wow!" I exclaimed. "What are these for?"

"Just because I love you." He leaned in for a kiss. "You really had a nigga's back the other night. If you wasn't there, things might've ended up different."

"Thank you, baby!" I took the flowers and admired them. "I told you that I got you, forever and always."

"That's for sure." He kissed me again and headed back to the SUV. "Where you going?"

"I need to go check on a shipment." I unlocked the new chrome Altima I'd purchased a few days ago. Alicia begged me to get a Lexus to match hers, but I wasn't into the flashy shit. My ass wasn't trying to draw no more attention to myself than I currently had.

"You doing it big, ma, but just be careful," he warned before pulling off. Ace was overprotective and always worried about this or that when it came to me out on the streets. Call me young and naïve, but I couldn't give two fucks about some hater lurking in the distance waiting to steal my shine.

My and Ali's hustle was doing numbers. There were so many packages coming that we had to set up shop at five more vacant homes across the city. I recruited a few more crackheads to sign for the merchandise, and business was running smooth. As long as I was getting money, I would always have haters. They were part of the game. Being fearless eventually might have been my downfall, but fear would never be the reason I went bankrupt.

# Chapter Thirty-two

I pulled up at the park across from the delivery house and cut the engine. I surveyed the area, and all was well. I glanced at the time on my cell phone and noted that the UPS truck should be pulling up any minute. With time to spare, I dialed Gran.

"Praise the Lord," she answered.

"Hey, Gran. How have you been?" I reclined in my seat and clutched the phone between my ear and shoulder. Ever since my last runaway at the courthouse, Gran and I seemed to have come to some sort of understanding. She didn't want me to be locked away, but she did want to know that I was doing the right thing while out of her presence. As long as I checked in with her on a regular basis, she stayed off my ass.

"I'm just blessed, Janie. How about you?"

I rolled my eyes toward the sky, but my voice remained steady. "I'm cool, Gran. Just working, that's all."

"That's good. I was so happy when you called and told me you got a job." She sounded genuinely happy, and I knew it was because she didn't know what kind of job it was.

"Do you need anything?" I watched the truck pull up.

"No, baby, I'm fine." She sighed. "Did you decide if you were going to come back home yet?" Gran coughed.

"No, ma'am. I'm going to stay with Ali."

"Are her parents okay with that? I don't want those folks thinking of you as a burden."

"Yeah, it's cool. I'm only there a little while longer, and then I graduate." There was no need to raise her blood pressure and tell her about my condo, so I didn't. I knew after the first stunt she pulled by calling the cops, the less Gran knew, the better.

"When are you coming by here so I can see you?"

"Soon," I replied as I scoped the argument ensuing between Donna and the deliveryman.

"Janelle, you say that all—"

"Gran, I've got to go. I'll be there soon, I promise." I hated cutting her off and ending the call so rudely, but I needed to see what was going on with Donna. The deliveryman had her pinned up against the side of the house by the throat.

Stepping from the car, I raced toward the commotion. "What are you doing? Get your hands off of her!" I pulled on his arm.

"You think I don't know what's going on over here?" He let Donna go and turned his attention toward me. "I've delivered in this area for three years, and this house has always been vacant. All of a sudden a crackhead shows up and begins to receive packages every week. I'm no rocket scientist, but I know there's some illegal shit going on."

"Calm down with that illegal nonsense." I smacked my lips.

"I should call the police right now." He reached into his pocket, but I stopped him.

"Look, what will it take to make you look the other way?" I gave him an icy stare that told him I meant business.

"I don't want no part of this." He shook his head and looked around like someone was watching.

"Everybody wants a piece of the pie. Just name your price and it's yours." I folded my arms. I watched the white man turn beet red as sweat dripped from his forehead. What he didn't know was I had done my research and knew he had a gambling debt on the streets. He had taken a second loan on his house and was upside down in the financial department. "Name the price and all of your problems are solved," I provoked him.

"Ten thousand," he blurted out, and I almost laughed but kept my composure.

"Is that the best you can do? Dream bigger!"

"Fifteen thousand?" he asked like he was unsure and looked to me for reassurance.

"That sounds fair, Neal. Fifteen it is then."

"You're just gonna give me all of that money right here, right now?"

"Of course I didn't come out of the house with fifteen racks!" I yelled. "But let's meet tonight at Belle Isle, and I got you." I smiled the sweetest smile I had.

"Belle Isle?" He looked skeptical. "Why there?"

"Come on, Neal, I know you've caught a few gangster movies and you know how this works." I played it cool, and he laughed at my joke. "I can't be coming to your crib or have you come to mine. We need to meet at a mutual spot."

"Okay." He nodded and relaxed a bit. "I get off my shift at six."

"Cool, that gives me four hours to get your money." I glanced at my watch. "Meet me by the zoo entrance at seven. Oh, and I'll need your ID until we meet again."

"I'm not giving you my license. Are you crazy?"

"You will give it to me if you want that fifteen thousand." I held my hand out. After a minute of contemplation, Neal handed over his license. I swear he had to be the dumbest fucker in Detroit.

"Are you going to kill me?" He looked from me to Donna, who was as high as a kite.

"I'm not going to kill you, Neal. I'm putting you on payroll." I laughed.

"What if I don't want to be on payroll?"

"The chump change you make as a deliveryman can't afford you the lifestyle you've always wanted, right? Well, if you look out for me on my deliveries, I'll look out for you." I winked and headed to my car. Stopping halfway, I turned. "You have to keep this little secret between us, because if anyone finds out about my operation, then I will kill you."

# Chapter Thirty-three

"Are you fucking serious?" Alicia paced back and forth after I told her about my run-in with Neal.

"Chill. I got this handled." On the way home, I had already called one of my goons and told him to head over and check Neal's house out.

"You better hope you do have this handled, because this man could drop a dime on us and fuck this whole thing up."

Before I could continue the conversation with Alicia, my cell phone rang. "Hello."

"Yeah, we at the spot and it's empty. Your dude lives with his old lady and a dog, but no kids." JJ spoke in a hushed tone.

"Okay, sit tight and wait for my instruction." I ended the call and turned my attention back to Alicia. "Like I said, it's covered."

At seven o'clock on the dot, I walked up to the vacant zoo entrance and found Neal waiting patiently inside his gray Ford Five Hundred. He was still dressed in his brown uniform, which told me he came straight from work. Tap. Tap. I knocked lightly on the car window with my knuckles. After he unlocked the vehicle and let me inside, I instructed him to pull into an empty parking space.

"Let's make this quick!" he demanded.

"No problem." I reached into my duffle bag, and he jerked. "What the hell?" I asked.

"I thought that was a gun." He grabbed his chest. I was willing to bet money that the nigga had just wet himself.

"You need to calm down." I pulled out his driver's license and handed it back to him.

"I'm nervous! Wouldn't you be?"

"There is a police station on this island. If I were up to something shady, why would I meet you here?" I looked at him sideways.

"You're right. I forgot about that." He sighed and leaned back in his seat. Just then I heard a computer's voice demanding that we speak louder for further recording.

"For real, Neal? You're recording this?" I was pissed off at myself for not seeing this coming.

"I . . . I . . ." he stuttered.

"I was trying to be nice and put some money in your pocket, and this is what you do?" I lied. The truth was I had no intention of giving this man a dollar. Initially, I regretted having to kill him, but now he'd just made things much easier.

"I'm sorry," he apologized.

"Too late, game over!" I yelled and erased the recording from his phone.

"Please understand where I was coming from and forgive me," he begged with tears in his eyes.

I sighed. "Fine, I forgive you. Now let's get down to business. First things first, I need you to write something for me." I handed him a piece of paper and a pen.

"Okay, I'm ready." He put on his glasses.

"I'm sorry," I said aloud, and he wrote.

"I'm sorry about what?" He looked up at me just in time to see me pull out a .22-caliber handgun with my gloved hand. "If I don't come home in two hours my wife will call the police," he threatened.

"Call your wife." I shoved his cell phone back at him.

"No!" He shook his head. "I'll kill you dead with my bare hands before I do that."

"Suit yourself, but I'm sure you'd like to check on her and make sure she's still breathing."

"Oh, my God!" He immediately grabbed the phone and dialed home.

"Neal?" A woman's weary voice spoke through the speakerphone. She had been crying and was obviously in distress. "What have you done to us?"

"Sharon sweetheart, I'm sorry," Neal cried.

"For years, I've begged you to get help for your gambling addiction, and now it's come to this." She was tired of dealing with his nonsense, I could tell.

"Sharon, I'm sorry. I'm sorry for messing up everything. Your parents were right. You should've married that lawyer instead of the likes of me." Neal knew this was the last time he would ever speak to his wife, so I let him get everything off his chest. "I'm the reason we don't have any children. I'm the reason that the home your parents left you is going back to the bank. I'm the reason our marriage is failing, Sharon. My whole life I've been a screw-up." He smirked. "The only thing I've done right is loving you."

"I love you, Neal." Sharon sniffed back some tears.

"I love you more, Sharon. I always have." By now the floodgates opened, and Neal was inconsolable. He dropped the phone into his lap and laid his head on the steering wheel. Just then my cell phone rang. It was JJ.

"All right, boss lady, it's your call."

"You know what to do." I looked over at Neal and felt somewhat bad. "It's time to lay that bitch down." And just like that, we heard a pop.

"No!" Neal cried as I handed him the gun.

"Your turn."

He stared at the gun and then back at me like he wanted to blow my head off.

"You have nothing left to live for, so what good would it do you to shoot me?" I raised an eyebrow.

"You're right." He nodded, and I let myself out of his car. Before I had even closed the door good, I heard the shot that sent Neal to meet his Maker.

Glancing back inside the car, I saw blood and flesh everywhere. His eyes were wide open, but the back of his head was missing.

# Chapter Thirty-four

"This is WDIV, and I am Carla Hartsfield." A reporter for the eleven o'clock news appeared on the television as Ace and I lay in bed. "We have breaking news coming from the city's east side tonight, where apparently a couple far in financial debt has committed suicide. Donald Martin in on the scene with the latest."

At the mention of the familiar story, I grabbed the remote and turned the volume up on the fifty-inch television mounted to the wall.

"Well, Carla, I'm standing here in front of this two-story home on the thirteen hundred block of Charlevoix where police responded to reports of gunfire. Neighbors say at approximately eight o'clock, they heard multiple gunshots coming from this home behind me. The victim's name has been released as Sharon Duncan. When police officers responded to the call, they found an apology letter written for her husband, but here is the kicker." He paused. "Police officers also responded to gunfire on Belle Isle around the same time. Upon responding, they found a male victim slumped over the steering of his vehicle with a gunshot wound to the head. By his side were a cell phone and an apology note. Detectives called the last number the deceased man dialed, and it rang at the house you see behind me. It was later determined that the victims were husband and wife. Although this appears to be a suicide in both cases, neighbors and family members are outraged and calling for some type of action."

"Neal and Sharon had their whole lives ahead of them, so why would they commit suicide?" some woman cried as they flashed a previous interview with her. "She just told me yesterday that she was taking Neal to Florida for their anniversary. People with those types of plans don't commit suicide." The news then switched to a clip of an interview with yet another woman. I knew she had to be their neighbor because she was standing there in a bathrobe and rollers.

"Sharon didn't commit suicide." She puffed on a Virginia Slim cigarette.

"And how do you know this, ma'am?" the reporter quizzed.

"Because I heard two gunshots instead of one. How in the Sam Hill can someone shoot them self twice?"

At the mention of the neighbor's revelation, I turned the television off and tried to calm my stomach. I'd specifically told these fools how to murk the bitch and make it look like an accident, but evidently, the plan went sideways, and someone switched the game up. "Shit!" I cursed under my breath.

"What's wrong, baby?" Ace asked without opening his eyes. He was pretending not to be asleep, but the painkillers my neighbor had him taking were like dope.

"It's nothing. I just have stomach pains. Go back to sleep." I patted his arm and stood from the bed.

"Where are you going?"

"Over to Alicia's room to see if she has any medicine." I closed the door behind me and hustled across the house.

"Alicia, this is fucked up." I stormed in without knocking, but the room was empty. The bitch had the nerve to be on a booty call when I needed her most. "Damn!" I sat on her bed and collected my thoughts for just a second.

Instantly, I sprang to my feet and grabbed a pair of her gym shoes. After slipping them on, I went to retrieve my purse and cell phone then sprinted to the door. On my way out, I called JJ and told him to meet me in the parking lot of Fairbanks Elementary. It was one of many of the abandoned schools in Detroit.

# Chapter Thirty-five

I had to have been pissed to leave the house with a tank top and a pair of pajama shorts on, but it was what it was. These niggas had me so heated I couldn't wait on the inside of the car, so I waited on the hood, attempting to let the cool night air calm my nerves.

As soon as I spotted the green Cadillac pulling up, I went ham. "I told your dumb asses what needed to be done. I gave you the whole plan piece by piece, and we went over it three times. What happened?"

"Man, the bitch told her dog to attack me." JJ puffed on a Newport cigarette. "I raised my gun, prepared to off the Rottweiler, but she jumped in the way."

"Where did you shoot her at, JJ?" I massaged my temples, trying to figure why his ass didn't lock the dog up when he first got there.

"I shot her in the arm and then in the head." He tossed the cigarette butt.

"Who else knows what you did tonight?" I folded my arms.

"Nobody knows but me and you, fam, I swear," he pleaded.

"Did you cover your tracks back at her house?"

"Yup." He nodded. "I wore rubber gloves, wrapped plastic around my gym shoes, and set the scene up to look like a suicide."

"All right, fam." I gave him a dap. "There ain't nothin' we can do about it now. Just sit tight for a while. I'll be in touch." I headed toward my car, and he headed toward his. Before he opened his door, I called his name. As soon as he turned to see what I wanted, he saw my gun. Boom. Boom. Two shots dropped that nigga where he stood, and I pulled off like it was nothing.

I was back in the bed before my spot had gotten cold and Ace was none the wiser. Sleep didn't come easy that night because I tossed and turned until the crack of dawn. By the time I had dozed off, my stomach had woken me back up and I was vomiting.

"Shit!" I lay on the bathroom floor, balled up like a baby. I'd been throwing up off and on for two weeks now. I knew what the deal was, although I desperately wished it was something else.

"You need to see a doctor," Ace spoke from the doorway. He was topless with white gauze wrapped around his abdomen and gray basketball shorts on.

"I'm not sick. I'm pregnant." I sat up and placed my back against the wall.

"Janie, are you sure?"

I nodded, on the verge of tears. He stepped into the bathroom and sat down beside me. "I missed my period."

"Come here." He pulled me toward him and cradled me. "It's okay, baby. Don't cry."

"I'm too young to have a baby."

"All things happen for a reason." He rubbed my hair. "A baby is a beautiful thing. Your parents are gone and so are mine. With this baby, we can start our own family." This baby situation was right up his alley, but I was glad to have him here to comfort me. Most girls my age who give their boyfriends this type of news would end their relationship.

"You're right." I sniffed. "Do you want a boy or a girl?"

"I want a daughter." He spoke softly.

"Me too." I smiled "What will we name her?"

"Julianna," he answered as if he had already given it some thought.

"Why Julianna?" I looked up into his hazel eyes.

"We can name her after Julius, your father." He shrugged.

"Baby, that's so thoughtful." I kissed him passionately. Ace was the sweetest hardened hood nigga I'd ever known beside my daddy. I never thought I would find true love like the love my parents had, but Ace was my Clyde, and I was his Bonnie.

Before we could take our conversation any further, there was a knock on the door. "You expecting anybody?"

"No." I shook my head. "The security guard didn't call and say anyone was coming."

"Who is it?" Ace stood from the floor.

"It's Chucky."

I didn't know why but there was something about the way my uncle said his name that put knots in my stomach. I stood from the floor in time to see Ace open the door.

"What up, Chucky." Ace bumped fists with my uncle.

"Hey, Unc." I tried to pull my nausea together and smile, but I was greeted with a stone-cold stare from my uncle.

"I need to holla at you about some business." He stepped into the condo and walked over into the living room.

"What's wrong?" I could tell something was off. Uncle Chucky never showed up unannounced, so this visit couldn't have been a good thing.

"Where's Ali?"

"She's out with a friend," I replied.

"What's good?" Ace folded his arms.

"Y'all niggas up in this bitch playing house?" Chucky frowned.

"Is that why you came by, to check in on me?" It was none of his business what I was doing in my spare time.

"The reason I came by is to find out why y'all fucking up the hustle?" His jaw muscles tightened.

"What are you talking about?" I played dumb. I needed to see just how much he knew before I started fessing up about shit.

"Ace, can you leave us to it for a minute?" Chucky asked, and Ace obliged. "All you had to do was steal cars and get paid!" he yelled once Ace was in the bedroom with the door closed.

"That's what I did, so why are you mad?" I yelled back.

"Janie, I'm mad because you crossed the line by stealing those credit cards. That shit is a no-no. You know better." He sighed.

"Stealing cars wasn't paying all my bills," I defended myself since I was busted.

"You make four hundred gotdamn dollars a car!" he pointed out.

"And at the end of the day, that's not enough. I saw an opportunity, and I went for it."

"Don't you realize that's some hot shit!" He shook his head in disbelief.

"You act like stealing cars ain't some hot shit."

"That's different because you worked under someone affiliated with an organization. You get into trouble and they've got your back. When you go independent, you don't get no protection."

"I'll find my own protection then," I threatened.

"It ain't that easy, Janie." Uncle Chucky took a seat on the suede cocoa sectional.

"Look, Unc, at the end of the day, I'm making shit happen. Do you know how much money is on those stolen credit cards? I make more off of those damn cards than I do from the cars." I needed my uncle to see why I did what I did. "I'll talk to Bobby and see if I can persuade him to see things my way. Hell, all of his workers need to follow suit. There is big money in credit card fraud."

"Janie, Bobby don't want no part of that. You think you're the first genius to think of that master plan?" He stood. "The shit is too hot, and he can't take that risk. He asked me to let you and Ali know you're out."

"Fuck him then. I'll start my own organization." I laughed.

"Do what you got to do, but be careful. When the ball drops, remember it's all on you, baby girl." He kissed my forehead and left without another word.

# Chapter Thirty-six

Just like that, Alicia and I had been fired, but it was all good. I could show a nigga better than I could tell him. Ali and I were hell-bent on going independent anyway. I loved proving people wrong, and this situation was no different.

The next morning, as usual, we went out and stole some hot whips just like we would've done for Bobby. But this go-round nobody was interested. I called every crook in the business, and everyone passed on our merchandise. People were loyal to Bobby's organization, and Uncle Chucky was right. Without his connection, nobody wanted to fuck with us, but I wasn't easily deterred. I just needed a day or two to come up with a master plan.

Luckily, we had three more credit cards to rack up charges on. They would tide us over until we figured out our next move. Either way, Bobby and Chucky were about to see how me and my girl could get down.

"Fuck Bobby anyway!" Alicia spat as we pulled into the Brewster Housing Projects. For some reason, the place was packed. I had to circle the strip twice before deciding to say fuck it and double park. Keisha had called me earlier and asked me to come pick up some money since her car was in the shop.

"These niggas is everywhere." I grabbed my purse and stepped from the car.

"It looks like they having some sort of block party." Ali shielded her face from the sun. There was a moonwalk set up for the children, several barbeque grills smoking, and loud music playing out of somebody's car. Everyone was rocking white shirts and sipping from red cups.

"If I weren't around, you wouldn't be able to get up in here." Keisha unlocked her security gate and let us in.

"What's the deal?" I nodded to the crowd of folks.

"Girl, they having a celebration for this nigga named Damien." She locked the door again and showed us into her living room. Her place was plush as hell to be located in the projects, and big, too.

"What did Damien do and why are they celebrating?" Alicia peered through the vertical blinds.

"He got killed last week and today was his funeral. His brother Smoke runs these projects, so he got the whole crew plotting to catch the nigga who did it." Keisha went into her bra and removed a stack of money. After realizing that the Damien she was referring to was the same one Ace had killed, I continued with questions and listened closely.

"They know who did it?" I glanced at Alicia, who had already caught my drift.

"Yeah, girl, you know news around this piece travels fast. It's supposed to be some nigga named Ace or some-thing like that." She counted out the money and placed it into two neat stacks on the kitchen table.

"Damn, I feel sorry for Ace 'cause those niggas are deep," Ali played along.

"Yeah, Smoke and his crew don't play, either. They are probably gonna get drunk tonight and mourn his brother, then rip some shit up in the morning." Keisha laughed and brought over the money.

"Well, let me get the hell out of here before all hell breaks loose." I laughed. "I ain't trying to get caught up in no crossfire."

"I know that's right, boo, but you safe in here. Ain't nobody dumb enough to step foot inside these projects."

"See ya later!" I waved while retrieving my cell phone to relay everything I'd heard to Ace.

# Chapter Thirty-seven

On the way back home, I received a call from Mrs. Dorsey, one of Gran's neighbors. She informed me that my grandmother was ill and that I should come over and check on her. At first, I debated whether the call was a setup, but then I remembered my birthday was in a few days. Therefore, being arrested and going to the juvenile detention center was no longer an option.

"I'm on my way," I told the concerned neighbor and headed to the nearest grocery store for soup, orange juice, cough medicine, and tea. Although my grandmother and I weren't on the best of terms, I would always be there when and if she needed me.

When we pulled up to Gran's building, Alicia frowned. "No wonder you ran away. This place is horrible." She took in the sight of junkies and prostitutes standing out front. It was time for my grandmother to move, and I wasn't taking no for an answer. After asking Alicia to give me a few minutes, I stepped from the car.

"Hey, baby girl, are you looking for a good time?" A streetwalker approached me with a bikini top, fishnet tights, and pleather boots.

"No, thanks." I bypassed her and headed into the run-down apartment building. Upon entering, I noticed the security lock on the door had been broken. That meant any Tom, Dick, or Harry could come and go as they pleased. Walking toward the elevator, I gagged from the strong urine smell. This building was no place for a sixty-something single woman. After stepping off the elevator, I continued down the hallway toward Gran's door and was damn near side-swiped by some little kids playing in the hall.

"My bad," a snot-nosed boy apologized.

"It's all good, little man." At least the boy had some manners. Tap. Tap.

"Who is it?" Gran called out.

"It's me, Gran."

"Well, hello, stranger," she stated with more attitude than I thought she would have for a sick person. "And just where have you been?"

"Gran, you know the game," I replied. I was not about to get into it with her again, so I proceeded with the conversation. "Mrs. Dorsey called and told me you weren't feeling well. I stopped by the store and purchased you some things to help you feel better." I placed the bag down onto her dining room table.

"Did you purchase that mess with drug money?" She coughed and went to sit down on the couch.

"I'm not a drug dealer," I said, telling the truth.

"I ain't stupid, Janelle Renee Doesher." She knew I hated when she called me by my whole name.

"Gran, nobody called you stupid." I went into the kitchen and retrieved a spoon for the medicine and a cup for the orange juice.

"So why are you lying then? Do you think I'm blind? I see the fancy clothes on your back, not to mention the car you pulled up in. If you ain't selling dope, then you must be selling pussy."

"Gran!" I had never heard her use foul language, and frankly, I didn't like her implying I was a ho.

"Janelle, I'm old enough to call it like I see it." She coughed again.

"For your information, I'm not selling either of the two!" I slammed the glass down on the table. "Now are you going to take this medicine?"

"Leave it there. I'll get it later." She turned away from me and went back to peering out the window.

"You're welcome." I rolled my eyes and left the old woman to her misery. I had more pressing issues to deal with, like Ace and his beef with Damien's brother.

# Chapter Thirty-eight

I stepped into the house and watched Ace pace the floor like a madman. "Tell me again what that pussy-ass nigga said?"

"He didn't say anything to us, but we heard he has the entire projects ready to murk you." I placed my purse on the couch and took a seat.

"These niggas is wildin'." He flexed his muscles out of anger.

"Whatever you need, I got you, bro." Alicia sat down beside me. I had never seen Ace so heated, but I guess you get like that when there is a bounty on your head.

"Naw, fuck that. I'm rolling solo. I'm riding on these pussy-ass niggas tonight. I gotta catch these fools slippin' before they find me."

"Baby, the projects are sewn up. Ain't nobody getting through there." I tried to talk some sense into him. If Ace went on a solo mission into the jungle, he was bound to get killed.

"Janelle, there ain't no other way. Your girl said they were getting drunk tonight and the shit would hit the fan in the morning." He sat beside me. "Think about it: all them niggas will be in one place at the same time, intoxicated and off their A game."

"You're right, but you can't do this alone."

"Who else can I do it with? My best friend tried to kill me, so who knows if the other niggas in my circle are loyal?" Ace did have a point, and I felt him 100 percent, but I was totally against sending him out alone.

"Me and Ali are ridin' then."

"What?" He shook his head. "What do I look like putting two girls out there in the middle of that shit? Not to mention the fact that you're carrying my seed." He stood from the couch and Alicia looked away.

"Ace, we are all we've got, baby. If I send you out there alone and you don't come back, this baby won't even matter 'cause I'll die of a broken heart." I was dead-ass serious.

"But if I let you come with me and something happens to you or my baby, I'll die."

"Well, at least we'll all be together."

He pondered over my words for a minute and sighed, "Let's get ready because we're leaving as soon as it gets dark."

# Chapter Thirty-nine

Nightfall came, and it was show time. Ace called in a few favors with Chucky and was able to secure some heavy artillery. Of course, he didn't divulge what was about to go down or the fact that I was involved. He supplied Ace with two MAC-11s, which were machine weapons developed for the U.S. military. It held thirty-two rounds in the magazine and had some major blowback. I really wanted to shoot one, but Ace gave me specific instructions to be the getaway driver. I would've put up a fuss but decided not to press my luck, so I left well enough alone.

Slowly, we drove through the projects in a stolen Town & Country with the windows down and back door open. Alicia held her gun on her lap and Ace did the same. My nerves were a mess, and my hands were clammy. I prayed no one innocent would get caught up in the crossfire, especially not a child. "There they go right there." I pointed. "Are y'all ready?" My palms were moist from grippin' the steering wheel for dear life.

"I'm always ready," Ace replied. Alicia said nothing as she lifted her piece of steel.

"Remember to aim for that nigga Smoke," Ace reminded Alicia, who was so fixed on what was about to happen that she barely heard him.

"I got you," she finally responded right as we pulled in front of the house Smoke and his boys were gathered in front of.

"One. Two. Three," I counted, and all hell broke loose.

Bang. Bang. The shots exploding from the heavy artillery were earth-shattering. The minivan shook, and my eardrums ached in pain. People screamed and scattered like roaches. I saw a few niggas drop to the ground but was unsure if they'd been hit or if they were just taking cover.

"Stop the car," Ace demanded.

"What?" Was this fool crazy? "Ace, we can't stop now." I shook my head, prepared to put the pedal to the metal and speed the hell away from here. A few men from Smoke's camp had gotten up from the ground and started pulling out pistols of their own in retaliation. Pop! Pop! Pop! Bullets sprayed in our direction. Thankfully, none of them made a connection with our vehicle.

"Stop the fuckin' car!" Ace looked from me back to the passenger window just in time to see the gang of niggas headed straight toward us. Before I had the opportunity to question the command he had issued a second time, he opened the door and hopped out of the moving minivan.

"What the fuck is this fool doing?" Alicia stared in disbelief. "Janelle, he's gonna get us all killed." She looked at me for some sort of clarity. However, I didn't have time to respond because I sprang into action.

Immediately, I went into survival mode and grabbed both of the 9 mm handguns I'd stashed in my purse earlier just in case we needed them.

"J, what's up?" Alicia looked at me sideways. I was sure she thought I was just as crazy as Ace. Even so, I wasn't about to leave him hanging like a wet rag. See, Alicia and I were a team, but me and Ace operated as one unit. If something were to happen to him, I would no longer be able to function. Therefore, it was necessary that I keep him alive.

"I'm going to give my nigga some assistance." I guessed being a down-ass bitch was in my nature. "Take the wheel," I instructed my friend. Without hesitation, she jumped into the driver's seat. "Turn the van around and shoot out of the window like your life depends on it. The police will probably be here soon, so keep that engine running. If you see those flashing blue and red lights, take off even if we ain't back in the car."

"Fuck that, J. I ain't leaving y'all." She shook her head from side to side.

"We'll be all right, believe that!"

"You promise?" Looking into my eyes with the innocence of a child, she watched through the window as if she were being left at a daycare center, wishing and hoping like hell that we returned.

"I promise." Then I gave her a pound.

"Well, in that case, I guess I'll see you on the other side." She winked.

"See you on the other side."

I exited the van and crept around the back. I could see that Ace was still standing and holding his own. As a matter of fact, he had already dropped three men. There were only two more we had to worry about. Bang! I let off a single shot and hit one dude in the chest. Instantly he clutched at the wound, but he continued to fire in my direction. As bullets whizzed past me, I ducked and dodged. Eventually, the shooter collapsed onto the grass. I was sure it was due to the amount of blood that he had lost as well as the lack of energy.

"Janelle, what in the hell are you doing?" Ace looked upset. However, now was not the time to be arguing with me. "Get back in the van!"

"Ace, it's called having your back, and you're welcome."

"I don't need your help, girl. Go get back in the van." He pointed toward where Alicia was parked, but I wasn't having it. If he didn't know how down I was, he would surely learn tonight.

Out of the corner of my eye, I saw Smoke ducking behind a big green electrical box. His gun was pointed directly at Ace, who was so busy yelling at me that he'd forgotten we were in the midst of a shoot-out. Clear as day, I could see the scowl on Smoke's face just as he pulled the trigger.

Attempting to scream was useless because my voice was caught somewhere down in my stomach. Without hesitation, I sprinted toward Ace as fast as I could and threw all of my weight on top of him. The collision was so hard that we both fell to the ground with a loud thud. I hit my head on a rock in the grass and was bleeding pretty badly.

The fall was just the distraction Smoke needed to escape. Turning on his heels, he began to run through the low-income housing development like a bat out of hell.

Checking the magazine on his gun, Ace sprang to his feet like a jack-in-the-box. "I'm out!" he yelled in anguish. If Ace didn't kill Smoke tonight, he would surely come back for Ace. We couldn't allow that to happen. It was time to put an end to this madness so that we could move forward with our lives.

"Here, take mine." I handed him both of my guns. When he looked down and saw my bloody forehead, his mood softened.

"Are you okay, Janie?" I could tell he was torn between ensuring I was okay and catching Smoke. Inside I smiled. Even in the midst of mayhem, my man was a gentleman.

"I'll be all right. Now go get him!" I yelled, scrambling to my feet as best I could.

Ace took off like a track star behind Smoke. Within minutes, they were both out of sight. The fall had me slightly dizzy and a little shaken up. My stomach felt queasy. Therefore, I leaned over, prepared to throw up, but the only thing coming out was spit.

Just as I was beginning to get my bearings, I heard sirens and saw the police lights approaching in the distance. I scanned the parking lot for Alicia. Per my instructions, she was gone. "Damn!" I cursed. The police were extremely close. I knew it was only a matter of minutes before they would be swarming the place.

Surveying the area, I tried to plan an escape route. Unfortunately, I was unfamiliar with the projects. I didn't know whether to go left or right. Then I remembered my homegirl lived nearby. In a flash, I dashed toward Keisha's house, hoping like hell she was home.

# Chapter Forty

"Keisha, open up. It's me, Janelle!" I yelled and banged on her door for a minute straight before I realized her car wasn't parked out front. "Shit!" My heart raced. By now, I could hear the police dogs barking and a helicopter circling the area above. I couldn't call Alicia because I didn't have my cell phone on me. Furthermore, I had no idea where Ace was. Quickly, I contemplated kicking Keisha's door in but decided against it. I didn't want anyone to hear the noise then point the police in my direction.

With no other options, I casually stepped off the porch and commenced walking toward the front of the housing complex. If I could just make it out of here, get to a main street, then I was sure to be in the clear. However, the second I began walking, I was hit with the helicopter spotlight, which was looming overhead. Praying like hell that I hadn't been made, somehow I knew shit had just gotten real.

"Fuck!" I rolled my eyes at the sea of people surrounding the crime scene. The shooting had only taken place twenty minutes ago. Even so, news traveled fast in the hood. Everybody and their mama was outside trying to see what was going on. There was no turning back, nowhere else for me to go. Therefore, I continued to walk, doing my best to calm my queasy stomach and wipe my bloody face.

Apprehensively, I made my way into the center of the commotion, portrayed myself as one of the onlookers, and stopped to check out the crime scene. There was a gang of people whooping and hollering about their lost loved ones. Several others attempted to offer their version of what had gone down. As each individual provided a different account of what they had seen, I smirked within. So far, nobody's story was even believable, which meant the police had no leads.

With my head down, I bypassed a few officers who were roping off the crime scene. Out of respect, they were also covering the deceased with white sheets. "Not my baby. Lord, please tell me that's not my son lying there." A light-skinned woman was being restrained by family members who were attempting to keep her from seeing her son in his current state.

I looked over to see that the man she was referring to was the same one I had dropped with one shot. Truthfully, I felt bad for the woman. Nonetheless, that was the game. All of this could have been avoided if Damien and Smoke hadn't tried to kill Ace. If shit would've gone sideways and they had actually succeeded in executing my man, then it would've been my tears that were being shed and not hers.

After making it through the throng of bystanders, I could finally see the main street in the distance. Yet, I noticed a few more obstacles in my path. In an effort to locate potential witnesses, several police officers were interviewing neighbors. Everyone was so busy with one thing or another that no one even bothered to look my way. Prematurely, I exhaled a sigh of relief. Just as I thought I was in the clear, nearly home free, this big black woman raised her hand and pointed directly at me.

"That's one of the shooters right there, Officer!" she exclaimed. "I saw that lady right there shooting one of those guns." In her pajamas, the large woman stood in the doorway with a baby on her hip and another toddler tugging at her leg.

"That woman right there?" the male officer asked in disbelief.

"That's what I just said, didn't I?" She placed a chubby hand onto her free hip and rolled her eyes. I promise, if looks could kill, I would've murdered that bitch with my gaze right then and there. Hadn't she ever heard about the "no snitching" rule? Where was her loyalty to the G code?

"Excuse me, ma'am, may I speak to you for a second?" the officer calmly stated while speaking into his walk-ie-talkie at the same time. "This is Officer Tidesdale requesting assistance near the Mack entrance of the Brewster Housing Projects."

"What do you need to talk to me for?" I tried to play it cool, but internally I was sweating bullets.

"I would just like to ask you a few questions." He pre-tended to smile. "It's only routine, ma'am." While reach-ing to unfasten the clasp on his holster, he approached me with caution.

"If this is routine, tell me why you're walking up on me with your weapon drawn." My hands were already raised in surrender.

"This is standard protocol when apprehending a sus-pect, ma'am." A veteran officer wouldn't have provided me with so much information. Therefore, this cop had to be a rookie. My ass would've been laid out with my face in the dirt, my feet crossed at the ankles, and hands cuffed behind my back.

"I'm pregnant, Officer. Do I look like a killer?" I asked just to mess with his mind. Although I wasn't really show-ing, it gave him something to consider before shooting my ass. The moment he paused to ponder my statement, I took off like a bat out of hell and didn't look back. I needed to get the hell out of dodge before his backup arrived.

"Freeze!" he yelled as he proceeded to pursue me on foot. I was gone with the wind. I had him by a few yards. Even with a baby on board, my feet didn't fail me. For that small blessing, I was thankful. That was until a police car came out of nowhere and barely avoided hitting me. Screachhhh! Tires slid across the pavement. The squad car began to smoke.

"Lie down! Put your hands behind your back, or I will shoot!" The driver of the smoking vehicle emerged to apprehend me.

"I'm pregnant, sir! I can't lie down on the ground, but I can spread my hands across the car," I tried to reason with the man. However, someone had obviously pissed in his coffee, and he took it out on me.

"Bitch, you'll do as I say!" The officer from the vehicle damn near body-slammed me down to the ground then cuffed me.

"Please stop. You're hurting me!" I screamed out in pain. This was no exaggeration either. Now I was fearful for the safety of my unborn child due to the unnecessary use of force the officer utilized.

"Hey, bruh, that's a female. You ain't gotta treat her like that." A bystander came to my defense.

"Get the fuck out of here before I arrest your monkey ass too!" After flipping the onlooker the bird, the old cop returned his attention to me. With a comment like that, I knew I was dealing with a racist prick. Cringing inwardly, I figured this was not likely to turn out in my favor.

"Who the fuck is you calling a monkey? Cracker!" The spectator looked pissed beyond measure.

"I'm talking to you and the gorilla that had you, you black bastard!" The cop laughed as he yanked me up from the pavement then bent me over the hood of the squad car.

"Ahhh!" I screamed. "Man, this hood is hot. It's burning my face." I tried to lift my head. However, he forcefully held it down while enjoying my agony.

"I'm calling the news on you two bitches!" The bystander pointed at both officers while pulling a cell phone from his pocket. He then proceeded to record the incident. "Hold tight, li'l mama. We 'bout to get paid off this shit. I'm calling Sam Bernstein on that ass!" His mention of the popular attorney from television commercials did nothing but irritate the veteran officer.

"Get that clown and his phone out of here," the older cop instructed the rookie, who shooed the man away as best he could. While his partner was away, the vet took the opportunity to body search me. He began with my vagina. Vigorously, he palmed my private area and made a circular motion around my clit. After that, he smelled his fingers like a pervert. I could feel his manhood rising and rubbing against my ass.

"Isn't it department protocol to have a female officer frisk me?" I knew my rights. This fool was definitely not following the department's code of conduct.

"Do you have any weapons or drug paraphernalia that I should be aware of?" he asked, blatantly ignoring my question.

"You are one crooked muthafucka to be violating my rights like this." I rolled my eyes as his nasty ass began to fondle my breasts.

"You ain't got no rights, jailbird." He smirked while turning me around to face him.

"Oh, I got your jailbird." As hard as I could, I kneed his perverted ass right in the balls then watched him double over in obvious agony. Obviously, the pain didn't last too long, because he stood up and sucka punched the shit out of me. Blood sprayed from my mouth. I prayed like hell that I still had teeth.

"Brisbane, what in the hell is going on over here?" the rookie asked as he marched back over to the car.

"The bitch was resisting arrest." He assessed the damage done to his swollen knuckles while rubbing his aching nuts at the same time.

"How was she resisting arrest? When I left here, she was already in handcuffs." Looking at the damage that had been done to my face, the rookie shook his head.

"Are you questioning me?" The vet raised his voice. There was no response from the rookie. "Read her her Miranda rights and let's head back to the precinct."

"What if this gets out?" the rookie inquired. He was as nervous as a $2 ho in church on First Sunday.

"It won't get out. Her word means nothing, and you ain't gon' say shit. Now read the bitch her rights and let's roll."

# Chapter Forty-one

For the entire ride to the police precinct, I laid my head up against the squad car window cage with my eyes closed. I contemplated how in the hell I was going to get myself out of this situation. Particularly since I didn't have a lawyer. This was quite a predicament to be in. Nevertheless, I knew enough to know that if there was no evidence, there was no case. As far as their fat-ass witness went, I could easily have someone handle her before the trial even began. So that didn't really faze me.

Believe it or not, I was more concerned with the lesson I was going to teach Officer Brisbane than I was with being a free woman. I was eager to teach the racist cop a thing or two about respect. I couldn't wait to catch this fucker by himself and beat the dog shit out of him.

"Let's go, convict." The vet opened the car door and pretended to help me out of the back seat while copping one last feel of my tits. If I hadn't been afraid of him hitting me again, I would've spit right into his eye sockets.

As we made our way through the double doors, I received a few glances from concerned officers. Yet no one stopped to inquire about what happened to my face. Assumingly, the men and women in blue lived by the "don't ask, don't tell" policy.

"Have a seat. I'll be right back." The vet pointed to a folding chair against the wall and instructed the rookie to guard me.

Squatting down beside me, the rookie whispered into my ear, "I want to apologize for the way my partner handled the situation."

"No offense, homeboy, but it's way too late for apologies." I turned away from him. Honestly, I did appreciate what he was trying to do. But where was all of that kindness when his partner was assaulting me?

"I'm sorry, so very sorry." The rookie stood back up and headed over to the water fountain for a quick drink.

"Janelle?" Someone called my name. I looked up to see Officer Bryant, the cop who let me get away after shooting Gudda at the trap house. "Girl, we have to stop meeting up like this." He smiled, then immediately frowned when he noticed the burn on my face as well as the busted lip. "Holy shit! What happened to your face?"

"Why don't you go and ask that officer over there?" I nodded to the rookie who had damn near choked on the water he was gulping.

"Yo, Tidesdale. Tell me what the hell happened here." Bryant hemmed his fellow officer up against the wall. The commotion caused a small stir in the precinct. But for the most part, no one gave two shits about what was going on. Therefore, they continued to mind their own business. "Did your partner Brisbane do this?"

"What do you think?" Tidesdale replied in a low tone. The veteran officer must have had a reputation for the shit he did to me, I assumed.

"Oh, hell no! Not today! And not with her! Where is he?" Bryant's chest moved up and down as his jowl muscles tensed.

"He's down there filling out paperwork." Tidesdale pointed. Bryant was so outraged that he took off down the hall like a bat out of hell, almost knocking someone to the ground. I watched as he rounded the corner, then laid my head up against the wall to collect my thoughts.

However, before I had time to process anything, I heard my name again. This time, my heart skipped three beats.

"Janelle, what are you doing down here?" Gran stepped away from the officer who was walking beside her. With worry in her voice, she wobbled over to me.

"Gran, what are you doing here?" I answered her question with a question.

"Someone robbed me on my way into my apartment building tonight. They took my purse and the keys to my apartment." She sat down beside me. "My building manager called the police then called the maintenance man to change my locks."

"Gran, are you okay?" Now I was the worried one. "Did they hurt you?"

"No, I'm not hurt. Just shaken up, that's all." She sighed. I looked down and noticed her hands were trembling. For years, my father had offered to move Gran into a safer neighborhood. She always refused.

"Mrs. Doesher, let's go into my office to finish your report." The officer had waited patiently for us to converse. However, now he was ready to conclude his business with Gran.

"Are you in trouble, granddaughter?" Gran asked before reaching out and gently touching my face.

"No, ma'am. I fell earlier and messed myself up, that's all." I lied with a straight face. She didn't need to worry about anything else. There was already enough on her plate. "I'm just waiting for a friend to finish up reporting her stolen car." With my handcuffed wrists buried between my thighs, she had no choice but to take my word for it.

"Okay, well, I should be done soon if you need a ride." She headed off down the hallway.

After about an hour of waiting in the hallway like a sitting duck, I noticed Bryant and Brisbane approaching. I exhaled. Good, bad, or ugly, I was ready to face the music.

"Looks like you're free to go." Brisbane sorrowfully unlocked my handcuffs with a sour look on his face.

"What happened, change of heart?" I smirked.

"You've got to be one lucky little bitch," he mumbled.

"That's enough!" Bryant dismissed his coworker. "Janelle, the captain decided to release you due to lack of evidence. However, he still has you on the suspect list, so don't go out of town."

"Please believe I won't be skipping town anytime soon. I've got business to handle." I spoke loud enough for Brisbane to hear me. "See you soon, playboy." I smiled as he continued to walk back down the hallway. Knowing he had fucked up, he tried to play it cool.

"Janelle, would you like to file an incident report regarding what Brisbane did to your face?" Bryant asked.

"No snitching, remember?" I lived and would die by that rule. Too bad there weren't others who were more like me.

"Suit yourself." Bryant shrugged. "Should I call someone to pick you up or can I drop you off somewhere?"

"Can I use your phone to call my friend?" I liked Bryant. In spite of that, I didn't know him well enough to give him my address. Therefore, I opted to call Alicia.

"Who is this?" She didn't recognize the number. Naturally, she was on the defensive.

"It's me, Janelle."

I heard a huge sigh of relief on the other end of the phone. "Thank goodness you're okay. Where are you?"

"I'm at the precinct downtown." I gave her the address and instructed her on how to get here.

"Okay, sit tight. I'll be there in twenty minutes." She ended the call, and I handed the cell phone back to Bryant.

"Thank you."

"No problem, Janelle. Come on, let's wait outside." He pushed the door open for me. The night air was muggy and stale, but I wouldn't dare complain. Just an hour ago, I didn't know the next time I'd be a free woman.

"So what's up with you?" I took a seat on the top step, and he followed suit. He sat so close to me that I scooted down just a tad. I didn't want to make it obvious that he was too close. Nevertheless, I didn't want him to get the wrong impression either.

"What do you mean?" He looked at me with one eyebrow raised.

"Why do you always help me?" Sometimes you had to question people's motives. I learned from my father that if something is too good to be true, then nine times out of ten, it probably is.

"Well, I help you based on the relationship your father and I had." He sat back and removed the navy blue Detroit baseball cap from his head. Bryant worked narcotics. Therefore, he wasn't confined to a uniform. Typically, he dressed in plain clothes which often consisted of urban wear. He was a young man, probably mid-twenties, and looked too good to be a cop.

"Okay, I would be more apt to understand your rationale if my father were still alive and you were still on payroll," I whispered. "But he's dead. And I don't have any money to pay you with. So, the fact that you continue to assist me is bewildering."

"Janelle, money isn't everything." He looked away from me yet continued talking. "Growing up, your father was good to me."

"What do you mean growing up?"

"Julius used to hustle from the apartment right next to the one I shared with my mother. He was about sixteen then, and I was perhaps nine. Each day, I would see him making more money than I could ever dream of. And he saw me every day searching for loose change in the hallways. My mother was a single parent, always robbing Peter to pay Paul, so to speak. I got tired of seeing her struggle and work so hard. One day, while she was at work, I went over to his apartment and knocked lightly. Your dad came to the door rocking an Adidas tracksuit and more gold chains than Mr. T."

Bryant laughed while continuing to reminisce. "I told him I wanted a job. He asked me what kind of job. I said to him it didn't matter as long as I could make money to help my mother pay the bills and put food on the table. He stared at me for a minute then asked what I wanted to be when I grew up. I admitted I wanted to be a police officer. It was then that he acknowledged he was a bad guy, so he couldn't give me a job. For a second, I reflected on his words. Then I declared if I could get paid like him, I wanted to be a bad guy too. He laughed and patted my head, then said to me to never try to be something I'm not. I felt discouraged and began to walk away. But he called me back and stated that if I stayed in school and didn't get into trouble, he would help my mother out."

Deep in thought, he paused as if he were watching a movie of his life. "Admirably, Julius remained true to his word. He even sent me to college. When I graduated magna cum laude, he bought me my first car. Sitting in the second row, right beside my mother was Julius. He also attended my graduation from the police academy. Your father was like a big brother to me. That's why I look out for you the way I do."

"Wow, that's deep." I was happy to hear the story about my father.

"Man, I was devastated when he was murdered." Bryant shook his head.

"Speaking of that, do you have access to his case files? Have they discovered who killed my parents?" A while ago, I decided to place my parents' deaths in the back of my mind. However, every now and then, the thoughts and images gnawed at me.

"I reviewed the file front to back. It indicated there was a search warrant for the property. And when the police arrived, your father began shooting."

"They ambushed the house with smoke bombs. However, no one knocked on the front door to present the warrant. As a matter of fact, the men on the surveillance cameras wore ski masks. My father began shooting because he thought it was a home invasion."

"The report made no mention of that. Are you sure that's what happened?" Bryant sat up straight.

"That's a day I will never forget." I looked at him like, duh! "Don't you guys have the surveillance tapes?"

"The report mentioned nothing about tapes. I'm going to have another look at the case file. I'll keep you posted."

"Okay, we'll talk soon." Noticing Alicia's Lexus pull up to the curb, I stood to leave. For obvious reasons, she had ditched the stolen Town & Country we'd used in the drive-by. I was relieved. "I have to go. My ride is here."

"Call me if you need anything," he shouted as I hustled over to Alicia's whip.

"Girl, I was worried sick about you." Ali exhaled after I was securely situated inside of the vehicle. After observing Ace sitting in the front seat, it was my turn to exhale.

"Baby, what happened? Did you get him?" I knew Alicia was worried about me. Even so, I was more concerned about Smoke.

"That nigga should be on his way to the morgue right about now. I left him stanking in the gutter," Ace replied calmly. All the while, he was watching me with a puzzled look through the pull-down mirror. "What the fuck happened to your face?"

"Some cop put his hands on me, but it's nothing."
Brushing off my true emotions was the only way to keep
Ace calm. If I had expressed how upset I was, he surely
would've reacted in a brash manner and ruined my plan
for revenge.

"Fuck you mean it's nothing?" Ace turned around in his
seat to face me.

"It's nothing. Just chill." I sighed.

"Bryant?" Alicia asked while merging onto I-75.

"No. Some asshole named Brisbane." The pounding in
my head was treacherous. Therefore, I closed my eyes
and rested my head against the headrest.

"Some man put his hands on my pregnant fiancée, and
you want me to chill?" Ace's question was rhetorical.
Therefore, I didn't respond.

"First thing in the morning, we goin' to see that nigga,"
Ali declared.

"You damn right we goin' to see that nigga." Ace turned
on the radio and leaned back in the passenger seat. I had
my own plans when it came to Brisbane. For that reason,
I didn't say a word and just let 'em talk.

"Do you think you need a doctor?" Although Alicia was
concerned, all I wanted were pain pills, my bed, and a
pillow.

"No, I'm good. Just get me home as fast as you can."
The freeway was practically empty this time of night.
Effortlessly, she navigated the lanes as a local radio station,
WJLB, played in the background. They were bumping
some great music, which allowed me the opportunity to
relax, if only for a little while. Realizing this was the calm
before the storm, I took it all in before my showdown with
Brisbane.


After the run-in at the projects, Ace decided it was best
for me to lie low for at least a week. I did as instructed

and stayed out of the streets, with the exception of going to school or to my doctor appointments, which was where I was coming from today. Because both Ace and Alicia were busy, I had gone by myself. I didn't mind the alone time. It allowed me to think without distractions. These last few days, my mind had been on overload. I was mentally fatigued.

The minute I pulled up to the crib, it was my intention to jump into the bed and hibernate. Unfortunately, as I rounded the corner, I noticed Keisha's Ford Fusion parked in the driveway. Not only had we already handled our business for the month, but I had informed her that the credit card operation was over as well. Hence, I felt the visit was out of place. Keisha was extremely disappointed that her pockets would take a hit. Nonetheless, she took the news in stride, and we promised to keep in touch. *So why is she here?* I wondered silently while walking up the steps. *Is she trying to settle the score with Ali?* With a scowl on my face, I placed the key into the lock. I honestly didn't know where the beef between them stemmed from. Right or wrong, I was always on Alicia's side. Keisha was my girl. However, Ali was my sister, and I would battle any bitch for her.

Upon entering the foyer, I stopped and listened for a possible cat fight between the women but heard nothing. Next, I walked though the condo and spotted Keisha's Hermès bag on the couch along with a pair of Jimmy Choo heels sprawled across the floor. *What in the hell?* I twisted my face up and headed straight for Alicia's bedroom. Providing only a slight knock, I turned the knob and entered. To tell the truth, I didn't know what I expected to see on the other side of the door. However, nothing could've prepared me for what I did find.

"Oh, shit, baby, make me cum," Alicia moaned. My eyes widened. Her eyes were closed as she lay back on top of her bed, with one hand behind her head and the other palming Keisha's head like a basketball.

"Damn, baby, I missed this good shit." Keisha's tongue slid up and down between Ali's parted legs. I almost pissed myself. I'd known both of these girls forever and had no inkling that either of them was playing for the other team. To make shit crazier, Alicia was my best friend. We shared almost everything, so why hadn't she told me about her sexual preference?

Just as I was about to make my silent departure from the bedroom, Alicia's eyes popped open. I was cold busted. "Janelle," she called out.

"Janelle?" Keisha lifted her head, obviously offended. "What you mean, Janelle?"

Without a word, Alicia pointed in my direction.

"Oh, my God, Janelle!" Keisha tried as best she could to cover herself.

"I'm sorry. I didn't mean to barge in. I thought you two were in here fighting, and I was coming to break it up. I didn't know y'all were in here fucking." I closed the door, but Alicia was hot on my trail.

"Look, can we talk?" She stepped into the living room in just her bra and panties. Wrapped in a sheet from the bed, Keisha came out of the bedroom behind her boo. "I can explain."

"You don't have to explain anything to me." I shook my head. "It's none of my business what you do in your boudoir." I was telling the absolute truth. Nevertheless, Alicia insisted on explaining.

"Me and Keisha used to mess around back in the day. But we broke up, and that's why we were beefing."

"Tell the whole truth," Keisha chimed in.

"At the time, I wasn't sure if I wanted to be a full-fledged lesbian or if I was bisexual." She paused long enough for Keisha to add her two cents again.

"She cheated on me with a dude. That's why we broke up, Janelle!"

"Okay, that's all fine and good. Like I said, it's none of my business. But why did you keep this from me?" I cared nothing about her and Keisha's relationship. On the other hand, the fact that she'd been fronting . . . What actually had me puzzled was her pretending to be someone she wasn't. We were as thick as thieves. or so I thought.

"I didn't want you to view me as being weird, peculiar, or strange." She took a seat beside me.

"Alicia, you know me better than that. I would never judge you for something like that. Come on now." A lot of people frowned upon the homosexual lifestyle. Not me. I left the judgment up to God. Nobody's perfect, and no single sin is greater than the next.

"I'm sorry, Janie. I was going to tell you. I just didn't know when or even how." Alicia wrapped her arms around me. "You forgive me?" she asked in baby dialect.

"It's all good. Just don't let that shit happen again!" I pinched her arm. How could I get mad at her for keeping secrets when I had a few of my own? Granted, my secret was in regard to murder, which by the way was a much bigger deal than being a lesbian. Yet again, it was all good. "Are you guys an item again?"

"Yeah, I'm ready to go all the way this time." She winked at Keisha, who was blushing like a schoolgirl.

"In any case, I'll support you girls without a doubt." Alicia was my best friend in the whole world, and Keisha was a close friend. If they wanted to be together, who was I to stand in their way?

# Chapter Forty-two

At seven o'clock the next morning, I was startled awake by someone lying heavily on the doorbell. I looked over at Ace, who was comatose as usual, and I rolled my eyes. Today was Sunday, and I was trying to rest. Until I got rid of the intruder, sleep wouldn't come again. Grabbing the switchblade from my nightstand, I approached the door with a vengeance. "Who the fuck is it?"

"It's Chucky!" My uncle sounded like the Big Bad Wolf ready to blow my house down.

"What's up?" I yanked the door open with much attitude. "What you keep ringing the doorbell for?" After wiping sleep from my eyes, I placed the switchblade into my pajama shorts.

"Tell me what the fuck went down in the projects the other night?" He barged into the living room like a madman and awaited my response.

"If you left your bed to come over here this early in the morning, then I'm sure you already know what happened." I yawned.

"Janelle, I'm here because I want you to tell me that your stupid ass didn't do what I think you did." He mean-mugged me, and I returned the stare down. I didn't know who Chucky thought he was to be bossing up on me, but I didn't like it one bit. Tired of his temper tantrums, I squared up to him. Chucky was pissed but so was I. He had no right to come into my home and think it would be okay to speak to me any ol' kind of way.

"No disrespect, but who the hell are you talking to, Unc?"

"I'm talking to a young-ass girl who's gon' fuck around and get killed or end up in jail 'cause she thinks she's made of Teflon." He sat down on the sofa. "Had I known you were going to be involved in that shit, I never would've given Ace those guns. Now it's just a clusterfuck of bullshit, and you're caught up right in the middle."

"I've been cleared." I shook my head. "It's all good."

"True, you've been cleared by the police, but what about the niggas in the projects? Once they find out you were in on that shooting, they gon' come for you."

"Unc, we deaded all those niggas. Ain't nobody coming for me."

"Let's hope not, Janelle. That's a battle you're not ready for." He sighed.

"I'm not a little girl anymore, Chucky. Trust me, I can handle this." I sat beside him and patted his knee.

"I know you're grown. It's just hard for me to accept it. In my eyes, you'll always be that little baby with a snotty nose and pissy diaper." He chuckled and started coughing at the same time. Due to years of smoking, his lungs were dreadful.

Ace must've heard the bickering. Wearing nothing more than a pair of boxer briefs, he entered the living room. "What's up, Chucky." He nodded. "You good, J?"

"Yeah, she's good, nigga," Chucky answered on my behalf in a malicious tone of voice.

"I was talking to my girl." Folding his arms, Ace stared Chucky down with those hazel-green eyes I loved to hate. At times, his pupils were warm and inviting, but sometimes they were cold and piercing.

"Oh, now you wanna be overprotective. Where was that overprotective shit the other night when you took her to do a damn drive-by?" I could tell things were about to get ugly when Chucky stood.

"I don't have to explain nothing to you, dog." Ace stood his ground. "What me and Janelle got going on is between me and Janelle."

"Modern-day Bonnie and Clyde, huh?" Chucky smirked.

"Yeah, something like that," Ace replied.

"Newsflash, dummy: they both die in the end. Do you want to be responsible for the death of your pregnant girlfriend?"

"Ain't nobody gon' get her killed. So you can chill out with all of that shit."

"Y'all young'uns think you know everything." Chucky shook his head and headed to the door. However, he stopped short then turned around to face Ace, who was still standing in the same position up against the wall. "As a matter of fact, since you got this, go out and start your own operation."

"What are you saying?" Ace shifted his body.

"I'm saying you're cut from my team."

"Fuck you and your team!" Ace was up off the wall and now in Chucky's face. "You think you big and bad, but you're really a bitch-made nigga!"

"Li'l nigga, you better remember who taught you the game and show some respect!"

"The only nigga who ever taught me shit was Julius. You were just a bitch-ass sidekick." By now, both of them were so close in each other's face that it was merely a matter of time before all hell broke loose.

"A sidekick?" Chucky was offended. "Homie, you better check my resume, because I do this shit."

"You don't do shit but hide behind your money. You just a pussy playing the part of a real nigga." Ace was all the way turned up. "If Julius hadn't been killed before he made the announcement, then the whole organization would've been mine."

The last expression to come from Ace's mouth had my mouth wide open. Did Uncle Chucky take my daddy out in order to keep the trap to himself? While I sat there pondering what the hell was really going on, Chucky had charged at Ace. They were on the ground scuffling like wild animals.

"What is this?" Alicia had finally emerged from her room, where she had been holed up all night with Keisha.

Crash! The men knocked over a ceramic lamp from the coffee table. "Stop it!" she yelled. However, it was useless. I knew better than to throw myself between two men.

"I'm gonna call the police." She grabbed the phone from the receiver but no one budged. They kept at one another until Ace was on top of Chucky, beating him like he had stolen something. I thought Chucky was going to die, which was the only reason I intervened.

"Please don't kill him," I begged. "Ace, please, please, please don't kill him."

Ace was apparently angry that I had discontinued the WWE match. Nonetheless, he obliged and got off of my uncle.

"Get that nigga outta here." He was out of breath, yet still in good shape. If I had to pick a winner of this round, it definitely wouldn't be Chucky.


Although the fight was still on everyone's mind, no one had time to dwell on it when there were bigger fish to fry. The time had come for me to pay Brisbane a visit. I was eagerly anticipating the reunion. Bryant had called a few hours ago with the information I needed to make Brisbane pay for what he had done.

"Where is this nigga at? He was supposed to be home an hour ago." Ali huffed and puffed in the passenger seat of the rented Chevy Impala, which was parked down the street from Brisbane's address.

"You don't think your boy played us, do you?" Ace sat in the back seat with his eyes fixed on Brisbane's crib.

"No, Bryant is legit and his information is good. Everybody just needs to chill." I leaned my head against the headrest. If anybody was gonna be antsy, it should've been me. Nevertheless, I was as cool as a cucumber. I knew it was only a matter of time before Brisbane came home.

"So what you gon' do now that you're not rolling with Chucky?" Alicia made small talk while we waited.

"I got some shit lined up," was all Ace said. Although I didn't know what he meant by that, I was confident that my man wouldn't be down and out for long.

"There he go right there." I smiled as the headlights on his Buick passed us and turned up into his driveway. We all sat silently while watching him exit the car, retrieve his workbag from the trunk, and then head up the porch steps into the single-family home.

Exactly sixty seconds after he entered the house, we stepped from the car and proceeded down the street. It was slightly past midnight. Everything was quiet in this little suburb.

Boom! Boom! I banged on the door. Alicia concealed herself in the shadows to my left. Ace was to my right. We could hear Brisbane fumbling with the chain locks on the other side of the door before he opened it. "Who are you, and what are you doing here this time of night?"

"You don't recognize me?" I asked with a sneer as he skimmed over my body with his eyes.

"You're that girl from the projects."

"I told you I would see you soon."

"Look, girl, you've got three seconds to get off my property before I bust a cap in your black ass." He brandished his department-issued weapon in my face.

I laughed. "I dare you, old man."

"One. Two." In an effort to warn me, he started counting. By the time he got to three, I forced my gun into the pit of his stomach. Alicia and Ace emerged from the shadows, standing right beside me with their guns aimed to the left and right side of his head.

"What is all of this?" He raised his palms in surrender.

Removing the gun from his hand, I forced him into the house. "Don't get scared now, old man." I laughed at the wet spot between his legs.

"Is it money you want?" Pulling money from his pants pocket, Brisbane bitched up like a female. I was amused.

"I didn't come for the dough but I'll take it!" I snatched the currency from his clutches and began to count aloud. Dude only had $63. Now I was insulted. "After what you did to me the other night, you better have more than this for my troubles." I smacked him across the face with the bills. If he was going to bribe me with money, he could've at least made it worthwhile.

"I can get more. Give me a date and a time."

"Shut up and sit down." Ace pointed to a wooden dining room chair. Brisbane was hesitant but the look on Ace's face meant business. If he had things his way, Brisbane would've taken a bullet right between the eyes the moment he answered the door. I wanted to have some fun first.

"Tie this nigga up and do what you came to do so we can get the fuck out of here," Ace instructed me while Alicia made her way around the house searching cabinets and drawers. Dropping to my knees, I placed the book bag I was wearing on the ground. It contained bungee rope and duct tape. While I was working on Brisbane's ankles, Ace worked on his brain.

"So you like to hit women?" he asked with a straight face.

"Man, that was a mistake." Brisbane shifted uncomfortably in the chair.

"You fucking right it was a mistake, a big mistake, player. Any man who lays hands on a female is a bitch! What's worse is any man who lays hands on my chick is a dead man." Ace reached back and knocked the dog shit out of Brisbane. Spit flew from the corner of his mouth, and blood oozed from his nose. Ace repeated the punishment several times until both of Brisbane's eyes were swollen shut, and his face was lumped up like a sack of potatoes.

"Enough." I prevented Ace from swinging again. He looked deranged, like a rabid animal with rabies. Sweat dripped from his face. His breathing was erratic.

"Is that all you got, pussy?" Brisbane asked with swollen lips.

"Just let me kill this man," Ace pleaded with me as Alicia reentered the living room.

"All this old man has is two hundred dollars in the nightstand and a wall safe with guns and knives." She smacked her lips, noticeably disappointed.

"Does the safe have a key lock or a combination code?" Instantly, I saw dollar signs. Those guns would sell like hotcakes on the black market.

"Key lock," she replied.

"Grab his key ring from that coffee table and get the guns. Leave the knives," I instructed. When I directed my attention back toward Brisbane, he was laughing. "What's so funny?"

"You three stooges are hilarious. First, you break into my home at gunpoint. Then you assault and rob me like you didn't know I was cop. The second I get out of this chair, I'll have all of your asses awaiting trial in county lockup."

"Who told you were getting out of this chair?" Ace aimed the gun for Brisbane's head. I closed my eyes tightly. Even though I wasn't new to death, seeing brain matter soar all over the place was nothing I would ever get used to.

Ding-dong.

I'd expected to hear the sound of the gun going off. Instead, the damn doorbell chimed.

"Be quiet," Ace warned Brisbane.

Alicia flew into the living room like she'd seen a ghost. "What the fuck?" she whispered, and I shrugged.

As I crept up to the front door, I almost shit on myself when I saw the female officer standing on the porch with a patrol car waiting out front. Easing away from the door, I informed them it was the police. Panic consumed the room.

"Leave out the back door now," Ace instructed.

However, Ali shook her head. "The back door has been bolted closed. The only way out is through the guest bedroom. All of the other windows are barred shut."

Ding-dong. The doorbell rang again. This time it was accompanied by knocking. "Dad, if you don't open up in one minute, I'm coming in."

"My daughter has ten years of experience on the force. You might as well surrender now." Brisbane laughed.

"Shut the fuck up!" Ace popped Brisbane one last time with the butt of the gun. That put him right to sleep. I grabbed the duct tape, which kept getting stuck to my latex gloves, and I covered his mouth.

"Dammit, you should've just let me kill him in the first place," he said while turning back to me. The doorbell rang again.

"Let's go." Alicia ran down the hallway. Ace and I followed suit. Ace endeavored to force the window open. It was dry-rotted and wouldn't budge. We all attempted to open the window again but it was no use.

"Fuck!" I was beginning to panic. According to Brisbane's daughter, our minute was up. From the bedroom, I could hear the front door open. My heart sank.

"Dad!" the woman screamed. "Oh, my Lord, what happened to you?"

All of us froze in place, holding our breath until Ace spoke up.

"To hell with this shit! We're not going out like this." Taking the butt of his gun and smashing the window, he instructed me and Alicia to run like Forrest Gump. Thank God the bedroom was on the main floor. My days of jumping from two-story homes were over.

"Eastpointe Police Department. Come out with your hands up," Brisbane's daughter yelled from the other side of the closed door. She was merely feet away from us, but it didn't matter. One by one, we all hopped through the window like it was on fire and disappeared into the cover of night. I could hear the officer calling for help on her walkie-talkie. Looking back, I could see her watching us flee. Fearful of leaving her father alone, she wasn't going to chase us, I was fairly certain. It was just the opportunity we needed to get away. By the time her backup arrived, we would be long gone.


Back at our house, Ace was furious with me. "Do you see what transpires when we do shit your way? We could've gone to jail tonight!" He paced the bedroom floor.

"I know. I just wanted that bastard to feel some pain before putting him out of his misery." I lay on the bed, applying Vaseline to my feet.

"Well, he's in pain all right. But he sure ain't dead. That means we've got to get at this man again before he gets at us. Shit, he knows it was you. It won't be long before he identifies me and Alicia too." He dropped his head into the palm of his hand.

"Ace, the old man will probably just leave well enough alone and call it square because of what he did to me." I sounded more confident than I actually felt. Truth be told, I had fucked up and I knew it.

"Look, get some rest. You have school in the morning. We can talk about this shit tomorrow after you take your finals." He leaned down and kissed my head before turning off the lamp and leaving me alone in the room.

Terrified the police might bum-rush the condo and arrest all of us for attempted murder, I could barely sleep that night. I needed to put an end to Brisbane for good. Right now, all I could do was wait. Currently, he was probably laid up in some hospital bed under heavy police protection. With his injuries and old age, I assumed he would be down for at least a month. That would buy me some time.

But I don't have to tell you what happens when you assume.

# Chapter Forty-three

"You look so pretty!" Keisha applied the final touches to my makeup. Tonight, we were headed off to prom with Alicia. I couldn't have been more excited. She attended Oak Park High School, the same school I went to before moving in with Gran. All of my old friends went there. Since I left, I'd been counting down the days to see them.

Ace had surprised me with the tickets two weeks ago. He wanted to take my mind off the Brisbane issue. I decided to let my hair down this evening. My gown was canary yellow, trimmed in rhinestones, with a split up both of my thighs. My hair was styled like Kim K.: long bombshell curls. My shoes were none other than Christian Louboutins. I told Ace not to spend so much money on a pair of shoes, especially with the baby on the way. Looking down at them now, I was glad he didn't listen to me.

"Come on, we better get this party started before they start fussing." Keisha grabbed the red clutch that matched her red dress, and then we headed out my bedroom door.

Upon entering the living room, my mouth fell open in amazement. I didn't know who was more stunned, me or him. Ace looked like a million dollars standing there in his white suit, canary yellow button-down shirt, and yellow and white Mauri gators. The canary yellow diamonds around his neck and on his wrist gave the outfit just what it needed. The cherry on top was the white Bossalini hat with a yellow feather.

"Damn, girl, I'm about ready to remove that dress and say forget the prom." He licked his lips in anticipation and smiled.

"There will be plenty enough time for that later." I winked and turned my head to check out Alicia. "Wow!" was all I could say. I had never seen my best friend rocking men's clothing. Don't get me wrong, my homegirl was fierce. Nevertheless, I was caught off guard by her skinny black pants, red button-down shirt, red and black tie, and red Converse sneakers. Her hair was pulled back into a simple ponytail. However, the smile on her face was priceless. She and Keisha loved one another as much as Ace and I did. It was exhilarating that she felt comfortable enough to be herself these days.

"Come on, y'all, let's go." Ace ushered everyone toward the door, and we were on our way.

Before going to the prom, we stopped to have dinner at Havier's. Although the place was packed, we spoke with the hostess and were immediately shown to a table. My parents' longtime connection with the eatery and with Havier himself ensured we were shown favor.

"This is really nice." Before reviewing the menu, Keisha took in the beautiful surroundings and calm atmosphere.

"You'll love the food." As always, I didn't bother reaching for a menu. I was going to order the meatloaf, candied yams, greens, and cornbread. Most girls going to prom would probably be trying to eat light. I was four months pregnant and wasn't concerned about that.

A few moments after taking our seats, the waitress placed water on the table and took our orders. Ace ordered smothered pork chops, Alicia ordered baby back ribs, and Keisha ordered a salad.

"I'll be right back. I need to use the restroom." I excused myself from the table. On the way to the bathroom, I was greeted by several people. Some of them I knew, and some I couldn't remember. They all offered condolences about my parents. It touched me. They had been dead for nearly two years. People still had love for them.

Just as I reached the ladies' room, someone grabbed me from the back. "It's been a long time, little girl." Gudda stood before me with a smirk on his face. The last time I saw this fool he was bleeding to death in his trap house.

"Damn, I guess you didn't die." I laughed although I was only partially joking. "Ace told me whenever you shoot someone, make sure you kill them. Now I see why. When you let niggas live, they become thorns in your ass. What do you want, Gudda?" While attempting to make eye contact with Ace, I rolled my eyes. Our table was clear across the room and his back was facing me.

"Oh, I'll tell you what I want. Come take a walk with me." He removed a 9 mm from the small of his back then pulled me close enough to push it into my side without anyone noticing.

"I'm not leaving this building." I tried to pull away, but he tightened his grip and proceeded toward the back exit.

"Janelle, baby, is that you?"

I turned slightly to see Michelle. She was one of my mother's friends from back in the day.

"Hey, Auntie." I smiled inwardly but kept a straight face. Auntie Michelle was a real street bitch. She knew what was up.

Gudda was familiar with her pedigree. Therefore, he tucked the gun into the front of his pants before turning us around.

"Where you taking my niece, nigga?" She raised an eyebrow with her hand deep inside of her Chanel bag.

"We're going to talk and catch up on old times." Gudda was still holding me closely.

Auntie Michelle wasn't having it. "You ain't got shit to talk to a seventeen-year-old about, boss."

"Michelle, I see you're still meddling in other folks' business." Gudda smacked his lips. "Get the fuck out of here if you know what's good."

"Listen here, you got 'til the count of three to let my niece go. Ya feel me?" She pulled her small revolver from her bag and aimed straight for Gudda's balls. He was instantly immobilized. That was about the same place I had shot him.

"You got it, ma. Just chill." He raised his hands and allowed me to leave. As I hurried toward Michelle, Gudda dashed straight out the back door.

"I never did like that nigga." She laughed while placing her gun back into her purse.

"Thanks, Auntie." I hugged her and thanked God for favors.

"Is that a baby bump?" She rubbed my stomach and smiled. "Boy or girl?"

"I don't know yet. Hopefully, it's a girl."

"Who's your baby daddy, and what's the nigga's resume?" she questioned me just as Ace approached us in the hallway.

"Girl, I thought you had gotten stuck in the toilet or something," he joked. "Hey, what's up, Michelle."

"Oh, shit! Don't tell me you're the baby daddy." She hugged Ace then me. "I told your mama y'all was fucking." She laughed. "I wish that heffa was still here so I could see her face. Damn, I miss your mama." She sighed.

"Me too," I replied.

"Call me if you need me. Auntie loves you, Janie." She rubbed my stomach one last time. "You better do right by her, Anthony, or I'm coming to see you."

"Yes, ma'am." He nodded. We watched her walk away. "Come on, baby, the food should be out by now."

I didn't want to tell him that Gudda had spoiled my appetite. That would've ruined our night. Deciding to keep this run-in to myself, I went back to the table as if nothing had ever happened.

# Chapter Forty-four

As we pulled into the parking lot of the Roostertail banquet facility where the dance was being held, there were three police cars parked near the front entrance with flashing lights on and sirens off. I didn't know why, but my stomach began to feel queasy, and my palms began to sweat. There was a line of cars trying to get past the police. Two officers were stopping each car and asking questions. I noticed a squad car sitting at the rear of the parking lot.

"They must be checking for open alcohol containers or something," Ace rationalized.

"Yeah, people are known for drinking and driving on prom night," Ali responded.

Although the scenario was ideal, I knew better. "Ace, I think we should turn around and do something else."

"Girl, we're all dressed up and shit, so we're going to the dance," he said, blowing me off.

"I don't have a good feeling about this," I admitted.

"Baby, chill. We're legit tonight, so no worries. We don't have any drugs, liquor, weapons, or warrants out for our arrest," he joked. Everyone laughed except me.

Fifteen minutes later, it was our turn to face the cops. My stomach felt as if it were on the spin cycle. I was very lightheaded. "Good evening, Officers." Ace put on his best behavior. I looked straight ahead out of the front window.

"This won't take long, young man. I promise." The first officer spoke nice and calmly. "Would you and your passengers please present your state identification card, driver's license, or school identification?"

Ace, Alicia, and Keisha quickly produced their cards. However, I took my time retrieving mine and handed it over reluctantly. The officer flashed a flashlight over all of the ID cards. As he stared intensely at one of the IDs, I could tell that somebody in this car was going down.

"Sir, do you mind pulling your car over?"

"No, I don't mind, but what's up?" Ace asked.

"I'll explain it all after you pull over and turn off your engine." The officer pointed over to where he wanted us to park. We followed instructions and did as we were told.

"What the fuck is up?" Ace asked everyone.

"I told you we should've left." Shaking my head, I nervously waited for the officers to approach us.

Tap. Tap. There was a knock on my door. "Janelle Doesher, please step from the vehicle with your hands up."

"What?" I knew someone in the car had done something wrong. But I honestly didn't think it was me.

"What did you do, Janie?" Alicia asked as I opened the car door. Because I had no answer, I didn't respond.

"Janelle Doesher, you're under arrest for trespassing." He read me my rights while beckoning for a female officer to frisk me.

"Trespassing?" I was completely baffled until I recognized Brisbane standing beside his car, lighting a cigarette. A million thoughts invaded my mental space, such as how in the world did this fool know I was going to be at the prom tonight?

"I got you now, you dirty son of a bitch!" Brisbane let out a heavy laugh, and I snapped.

On instinct I ran over to where he stood and tried to attack him. I didn't care about nothing at this point. His ass needed to get got. Brisbane dodged my offense and ran around the car like a bitch, trying to stall until his fellow officers had detained me.

"Janie, I got you, boo. Don't worry!" Alicia called out from the window. She would've been out of the car too if it weren't for an officer blocking the door.

"I'm good, just make sure Ace is all right." I didn't resist arrest as the female officer slapped cuffs on me and walked me toward her vehicle. There was no need to make the situation any worse, so I remained calm.

For hours, I waited inside of a holding cell before I was granted a phone call. "Let's go, prom queen." The lady cop gestured for me to follow her over to a desk. My four-inch Louboutins had been removed for fear that I would use them as a weapon. Consequently, I sauntered barefoot across the cold, sticky jail floor. I had requested footies but they just laughed at me. "Dial nine and then one to make your call."

"Thanks." I picked up the desk phone and dialed the first person who came to mind.

"Hello." Officer Bryant sounded as if he were asleep.

"It's Janelle. I'm in trouble. Can you help me?" I paused.

"Story of my life." He laughed lightly while still trying to wake up fully. "What's the info?" He sighed. I ran down all the necessary information to him.

Just like clockwork, Bryant was there to get me within the hour. "Thank you, Jesus!" I could see him through the cell bars as he approached me.

"Don't thank me just yet. I had to call your grandmother." He stood beside the officer as she unlocked the cell to allow me to leave.

"What? Why?" I was confused.

"This isn't my precinct, Janelle. I have to abide by their rules. You're a minor. For that reason, the only way you could be released is to call your parent or guardian." He sighed. "She didn't want to come in, so she's waiting for you in the lobby."

"Shit!" I was not looking forward to hearing Gran's mouth.

"Furthermore, I hate to be the bearer of more bad news, but you'll have to go to court on this trespassing case if Brisbane doesn't drop the issue." He waved to an officer after recognizing him. The officer returned his gesture.

"What's wrong with that fool? He violates me and I'm the one going to jail." I knew Brisbane had to be handled sooner rather than later. For now, I was grateful he didn't hit me with attempted murder.

"I know it's not right but—" He stopped short as we approached the main entrance and saw Gran standing there with Ace, Alicia, and Keisha. "I'll get with you later, all right?" He didn't give me time to respond before he walked away. After bumping fists with Ace and waving at the ladies, he was gone like the wind, leaving me to face the wrath that was sure to come.

"Janelle, what's going on with you?" Gran asked in a weary voice. "You've resorted to breaking into other folks' property now?"

"No, ma'am, it's not like that," I tried to explain, but she cut me off.

"It never is like that, is it, Janelle? When are you going to grow up and take ownership of the mess you always seem to find yourself in?"

"But—"

"I played this game with your father. You see how his story ended, right? Do you want us to have to bury you too? At the rate you're going, you'll be dead or in prison by next year."

There was something in her speech that resonated with me. Right then and there, I vowed to myself to never be caught up in some bullshit like this ever again. I had to be more careful out here on these streets. My unborn child needed me to survive. There was no more time for playing around. "Gran you're absolutely right. I apologize for putting you through all of this. Thank you for coming to get me out; I swear this is the last time you'll ever have to do this."

"You'll be eighteen soon. Then you'll be considered an adult. Next time they won't be so lenient."

"I know, and again I'm sorry for dragging you out of your bed this time of night." I wanted to hug her. However, the fear of rejection prevented me from doing so. As an alternative, I went over to stand beside Ace.

"You were released into my custody. Therefore, you better come with me."

"Gran, I'll be okay." Before she could object, I hustled toward the door.

"Granddaughter, I'll be praying for you and the company you keep," I heard her utter through the sliding glass door as I walked away from the precinct.

# Chapter Forty-five

All the way home, we plotted against Brisbane. I had to lay that nigga down before my court date. No questions about it. "We need to make that shit look like an accident." I was turned around in my seat speaking to Alicia. "Maybe we can pull a drive-by while he's out running errands or something," I strategized.

"I'm down with that. Because going back to that man's house is no longer an option," Ali agreed. "He probably has all types of alarm systems and recording devices by now."

"Y'all can fall back this time." Ace's tone was low. "Let me make a few calls. I'll have it handled." He turned the music up, but I reduced the volume.

"I want to do this myself."

"Janelle, you're already knee-deep in trouble. I can't have you doing anything like that ever again."

Since he was pissed, I dropped the subject for now, but it wasn't over. All this meant was Ali and I would have to talk in private about what was going to transpire. That's exactly what we did.

A few days later, we sat in the pouring rain outside of the police precinct and waited for Brisbane to come out. I was parked down the street in a rented Dodge Avenger. Alicia was parked on the other side of the block in a rented Ford Explorer. Earlier, we paid a crackhead $50 to rent one car from Avis and the other from Enterprise. I felt bad for keeping secrets from Ace. However, it was the only way to execute my plan without him intervening and potentially preventing my mode of attack.

Just as the time on the dashboard hit eleven fifteen, Brisbane strolled out of the precinct like he wasn't about to die. This silly man had no idea that we were waiting and watching his every move. He tossed his bag into the trunk and slammed it closed, then made his way around the front to get inside the car.

As he cranked his engine, Alicia did the same and pulled off right in front of him. Approximately twenty seconds later, I started my car and followed suit. For about three blocks, I followed him. Suddenly, I heard a crash behind me, and my car began to fishtail out of control. My neck whipped from side to side, and I had to swerve to avoid running up on the sidewalk.

"Shit!" Someone had just rear-ended my automobile. As my car came to a screeching halt, I looked through the rearview mirror and saw an elderly man approaching me. Brisbane's brake lights came on as well. Promptly, I pulled down the Detroit baseball cap just above my eyes, and then made sure the black bandana covering my mouth was tied tightly. Gripping the .45-caliber handgun that was by my side, I decided it was now or never.

"Are you okay, young lady?" The older man who'd hit me tapped on my door. He was soaking wet. Slumped over the steering wheel, I paid him no mind and watched my target like a hawk.

"I'm a police officer. Is that person okay?" Holding an umbrella, Brisbane spoke to the bad driver as he approached the scene of the accident.

"Oh, thank God you're the police. I don't know what happened, sir. My vision started blurring because of the rain I guess, and I got a little dizzy. The next thing I saw was the back of this woman's vehicle."

"Step aside, sir," Brisbane instructed while opening my door.

Going into theatrics, I moaned like death was around the corner.

"Ma'am, please respond if you can hear me." Reaching inside of the car, he pretended to check my pulse, but the bastard copped a feel of my breast instead. This little gesture was all I needed to fulfill my mission.

While he played with my left areola, I gripped the concealed gun and started blasting. Pop! Pop! Pop! Pop! Four shots sent his body backward and stumbling to the ground. He had been hit in the neck, leg, arm, and stomach.

"Jesus, Mary, and Joseph," the old man shrieked while attempting to run back to his mode of transportation.

Pop! Pop! Two shots to the back dropped him to his knees. I knew he wasn't dead by the way his body continued to move. Therefore, I walked closer and stood over his bloody body.

"Please have mercy on me," he begged after he was able to turn around. He was a truly innocent bystander, and I knew he didn't deserve to die today, but as hard as I fought with myself to spare his life, I knew it had to be done. There was no way I could let this man live. Pop! The final shot right between his eyes was the one that sent him on to glory.

Taking one last look at the crime scene, I ran to Alicia's car. We were only three blocks from the police station, which meant we had to get out of dodge.

# Chapter Forty-six

Two weeks had passed since the shooting. There was no word on the streets about who the killer was. The media ran the story for about three days. Then it became old news and it was back to business as usual. Ace suspected that Ali and I had something to do with the murder. In spite of his suspicion, I rationalized that a crooked cop like Brisbane had more enemies than just little ol' me. Since dead men didn't tell tales, he didn't harp on the subject for too long. Naturally, my case was dismissed for lack of evidence. All they had was Brisbane's word. Once again, my butt was spared. I knew I had to do better.

For the first time in my life, I had actually considered leaving the streets for a nine-to-five type of job. I went out and applied for this and that. Ace's preference was for me to enroll in college after the baby was a year old. I debated with him about going to college versus getting a paycheck. Nevertheless, he wasn't hearing it. He informed me that he had me covered. Originally, I had my doubts. With Ace no longer making moves with Uncle Chucky, money was tight. Even so, you couldn't keep a real nigga down for long. Eventually, he linked up with Nicholas Carmichael, an Italian made man. They called him Nicky for short. He was part of the Pauletti crime family, a big organization that originated in New Jersey.

Ace had known Nicky for years while shadowing my father in the dope game. Regrettably, the Italian organization didn't do business with black people. Therefore, there was never a reason to become friendly with one another. However, that all changed the day Carmichael realized it was the black dope dealers, neighborhoods, and fiends who had the game on lock. Sure, the Italians moved huge units of product. However, it was the nickel and dime packages that were selling out every hour on the hour that kept everyone's pockets swollen. Carmichael reasoned with his boss, Daniel Pauletti. He explained that the family could offer the "blackies" cocaine and heroin on the down-low then sit back and watch their money grow. None of the other Italian crime families associated with black people, which would give them an edge over the competition. Pauletti yielded and agreed to sit down with Ace. The rest was history. When it came to the "niggers," he was now their go-to man. Although he was low-level on their squad in terms of rank, his connection and low prices made him the man among our people.

Within weeks, the streets were buzzing. People were saying Chucky was in disbelief that Ace was selected over him. Rarely one to believe shit I heard if it didn't come from the source's mouth, this hood gossip I was sure was true. We hadn't seen or heard from Chucky since our last encounter. I was convinced we would run into him sooner or later.

"Baby, are you okay?" Ace tapped on the bathroom door before entering.

"Yeah, I'll be fine." I sighed. Seemingly, graduation day had rolled around quickly. I was elated to be done with classes, yet heartbroken that my parents weren't here to enjoy the moment.

*"The word is yours, baby girl."* I thought of the words my father always told me on a consistent basis. *"You can be anything you want, baby girl. Just finish high*

*school, graduate from college, and apply yourself,"* my mother would always add. Thinking of them now put a smile on my face. I often wondered what they would think of me and the choices I'd made for myself in their absence, but today it was like my thoughts about them were on steroids. Everything I saw and heard reminded me of them. I wished we'd had more time together. I felt robbed, I felt angry, I felt jealous of the other graduates with their parents, and worst of all I felt alone.

"We made it, bitch!" Alicia brushed past Ace and hit me on the butt. Although she and I attended two different schools, our graduations were coincidently being held on the same day. "It's been a long time coming." Alicia was cheesing from ear to ear. I didn't want to spoil her moment. Therefore, I put my personal feelings on the back burner.

"I know, right? I'm so excited." I hugged my friend tightly, trying not to wrinkle her graduation gown. She was all decked out and eager to attend her ceremony. However, I wasn't prepared for mine because I had decided not to go. As long as I had my diploma, I'd be all right. Besides, the commencement ceremony was really for the parents of the graduate. There would be dozens of people there smiling for the cameras and waving at video recorders. That would only remind me of the fact that I had no reason to smile and no one to gesticulate to. Of course I could've invited Gran, but the feeling for me wouldn't have been the same as having my parents there clapping for my accomplishment.

"I really wish you were going, Janie. It's not too late!" She looked hopeful, but I shook my head.

"Nah, I'm good, but you better hurry up before you're late." I fixed a stray strand of hair from her baby-doll curls.

"I wonder if my mom will show up. I left a ticket in her mailbox last week." She wished daily that they could one day mend their fences.

"She'll be there." I winked.

"I won't hold my breath." She grabbed her purse and headed for the door. I followed her, wearing a sneaky smirk. Alicia had no idea that I'd rented a stretch 300C for her special day as well as made reservations at Erica's popular soul food joint in the city. I even sent Ace to pick up Keisha and Alicia's mother an hour ago. They were both outside waiting.

When Alicia opened the front door and spotted her mom standing beside the limo, she burst into tears. Her mom was waving a huge piece of poster board with the words I'M SO PROUD OF YOU written on it. It made me tear up.

"I didn't think you were coming." Ali sniffed.

"I wouldn't have missed this for the world." She embraced her weeping daughter into a much-needed hug. On cue, Ace walked over and wrapped his arms around me.

"Should you change your mind about going to your graduation, I'll be there for you," he whispered.

"No, I'm good, but thank you." I laid my head back onto his chest and exhaled.

Alicia turned toward me. "You did this, didn't you?"

I looked like the cat that had swallowed the canary. "Enjoy your day, sis, and tell me all about it later. I love you."

"I love you more, fam." She embraced me snugly. "This means more than you'll ever know."

"Girl, you better get moving," I urged. She hustled down the sidewalk.

"See you later, J." Ali stepped up into the limo as I waved goodbye.

"So, what do you wanna do now?" Ace stared at me seductively. I knew what was on his mind, but I had other plans. The reunion between Ali and her mother caused me to think about Gran. It was time for a visit.

I pulled up to the low-income apartment building and cringed. There were a bunch of deadbeat crackheads loitering around the property and prostitutes walking the beat. Little children played in the street without adult supervision, while a group of dope boys sipped forties from paper bags in the parking lot. Upon further inspection, I noted the grass was in need of mowing and some asshole had tagged the front of the building with spray paint.

"What's up, li'l mama?" One of the men walked alongside me, blowing a blunt and trying to spit game. This fool looked as if he were allergic to soap and water. He was dingy and dirty as hell.

"Ain't nothing up, playboy." I kept walking.

"Shit, then slide me your digits and we can make something happen." He stroked the braided chin hair on his face.

"Sorry, boo, I'm taken." As I placed my hand on the lobby door, he put his nasty paws on top of mine.

"Fuck that nigga," he spat instantly like he was offended.

I had tried to be pleasant, but that shit gets you nowhere. It was time to change my approach. "Fuck you, nigga!" While speaking, I slid my hand down into my bag and gripped the handle of my pink nickel-plated 9 mm handgun.

"Fuck you then, bitch." He jumped at me like he was about do something.

Without flinching, I pulled my gun and put it right upside his dome. "Do that shit again and it'll be the last thing you'll ever do, believe that!"

"Oh, shit!" Just like I knew he would, he stepped back with his hands up. "It's like that, shorty?"

"The minute your ass got disrespectful, you made it like that. Now get the fuck out of the way before I shoot you just for pissing me off." I was dead-ass serious, too. Men these days thought they could talk to women any ol' kind of way. But I wasn't having it. By look on his face, he had never met a bitch like me. He attempted to save face for his boys, who were watching and laughing. Even so, I could tell he was intimidated.

"Yeah, all right then. I guess I'll see you next time and we'll see how tough you are then." Having just tossed me an empty threat, he walked away like he was a boss.

"Nigga, I ain't ever scared." I proceeded to enter the building without looking back. All the same, I kept my piece out just in case another person wanted to jump stupid today.

Knock. Knock. I tapped lightly on Gran's door and placed my gun back into my purse.

"Who is it?"

"It's Janelle," I replied and waited for the door to open.

"Well, hello, stranger." She looked me over from head to toe before she decided to move aside so that I could enter her apartment.

"How are you, Gran?" I took one look at the old corduroy sofa and made the prompt decision to stand. Not only was it on its last leg, but it probably had a roach or two crawling beneath the cushions.

"I'm blessed and highly favored." She sounded like a gospel robot.

I simply shook my head. Now don't get me wrong. There was nothing wrong with religion. However, Gran took it to a whole other level with her sermons, side-eyes, and finger-pointing. In the past, I'd heard that saints were once the biggest sinners. Yet, Gran acted as if she were holier than the Lord Himself. Just because she hadn't sold dope or killed anyone didn't mean that her having a baby out of wedlock was viewed any differently in the book of judgment.

"Anyway, I just came over to check on you and see if you needed anything."

"Janelle, the Lord will supply my needs." She nodded then sat down at the dining room table. "I was just about to eat some lunch. Would you like some?" She pointed to an open can of tuna fish.

My eyes bucked. "Gran, why are you eating tuna from the can? Where is the relish, the mayo, the egg for God's sake?"

"I like it like this." She was lying, and I knew it.

Without delay, I went into her kitchen. Swinging open the refrigerator, cabinets, and pantry, it was just as I thought. With the exception of two more cans of tuna, a can of Vienna sausages, and a half-eaten pack of saltine crackers, they were all bare.

"Gran, why didn't you tell me you didn't have any food?" I was devastated. While I was at home eating steak and lobster, my grandmother was starving. We may have had our differences, but I would never see her go hungry.

"It's not your concern, Janie." She kept on eating that tuna like it was her last supper.

"You're my grandmother!" I yelled. "Please let me help you," I begged on the verge of tears. Gran was merely too damn stubborn for her own good.

"No, thank you. I don't want anything to do with that street money."

"So you'd rather starve?" I couldn't believe this shit.

"I won't starve. My food stamps come in on the fifteenth." She completed her canned meal and set the empty container down on the table.

"Gran, today is the seventh. There's no way you'll survive for eight days with what you have in that kitchen."

"Like I said before, it's not your concern." She looked at me with a straight face. "I can see that you've been eating good though." She pointed.

I looked down at my belly then back at her. "Gran, I'm pregnant." It took a few minutes for my words to resonate with her. I imagined she was going to go hard on me.

On the contrary, she actually smiled for the first time in a long time. "Babies are blessings, Janelle. Congratulations, granddaughter."

"Thank you, Gran. I'm due in four months. We're excited."

"Who's the father?" She looked as if she almost didn't want to know.

"Anthony."

"That boy your father adopted?" She appeared puzzled. "Well, isn't that your so-called godbrother?"

"We decided to date a while ago, and the rest is history."

"I guess." She sighed. "You do know you have to make sure you take care of yourself and eat right."

"Look who's talking." We both laughed, which diffused the tension somewhat.

For the rest of my visit, we talked about motherhood. She even reminisced about when my father was born. It felt good to hold a genuine conversation with my grandmother, one that wasn't phony or forced. When it was time for me to leave, I was even able to talk her into letting me give her some grocery money. We were making progress. I prayed things remained this way.

# Chapter Forty-seven

Surprisingly, my visit with Gran lasted three hours rather than the anticipated three minutes. I was headed home to catch a nap when my cell phone rang. It was Ace. "Hey, I'm headed home now," I said.

"Meet me downtown at the Detroit Princess boat. I have a surprise for you." He spoke with the wind whistling in the background.

"What kind of surprise?" I smiled.

"If I told you, then it wouldn't be a surprise, would it?" He laughed. This man was always going out of his way to spoil me, and I loved every second of it.

"Okay, let me go home and change. I'm way too under-dressed for the boat ride." The denim shorts and pink tank top with a pair of Old Navy flip-flops weren't exactly my "going out" attire.

"Chill, girl, I got you. Just bring your sexy ass on down here. I'll be waiting out front." He ended the call, and I amped up the volume on my radio.

Within half an hour, I was parking downtown and calling Ace. He had already spotted me and was striding over to me with a garment bag and a box of shoes. "What's up, cutie? Where's your man?"

"Ha-ha, very funny." I leaned in for a kiss as he rubbed my belly.

"I got you a li'l something. Come on, you can change in one of the bathrooms on the boat." He grabbed my hand.

"You are so good to me, Ace. What did I ever do to deserve you?" I knew that shit sounded corny, but it was exactly how I was feeling.

"Baby girl, I'm the lucky one. There are so many bitches out here claiming to be a down-ass chick. I know I got a real one. That's why I gotta take care of you." He winked.

"I love you!" Never in a million years did I think Ace and I would be together, but I was sure glad we were. He was the yin to my yang. In some ways, I felt the love my parents had for one another had been miraculously transferred to us.

After stepping onto the large party boat, I entered the first bathroom I saw in order to change. Ace had purchased a beautiful coral BCBG spring dress with beaded straps and a pair of gold Gucci sandals. I pulled my hair up into a ponytail and made a bun. The look was cute yet comfortable. I knew he would like it. "Okay, I'm ready." I stepped through the doorway with my old clothes stuffed inside of the huge Michael Kors purse I was carrying.

Wearing a huge smile, Ace was leaning against the wall with his arms folded. "Damn, girl, we might have to go in that bathroom and handle some business." He licked his lips and readjusted his manhood.

"Stop playing and let's go. I'm hungry."

"Girl, you're always hungry." He rubbed my belly again and led me toward the dinner cruise dining room.

"I can't help it." We laughed as he pulled the door open. At first glance, the place was dark. I thought we were in the wrong room. Out of the blue, the lights came on and everyone yelled, "Surprise!"

"Oh, my God!" I jumped, partially scared to death and partially surprised. The room was full of my friends, most of them wearing their caps from graduation. There was a banner in the center of the ceiling congratulating all graduates. "You did all of this for me?" I turned around to face Ace, who was holding out my cap and tassel.

"Put it on, baby, and go celebrate with your friends."

"Thank you!" I mouthed after being pulled away by a few of my girls from school.

"Girl, Ace know he's fine!" Tyra put emphasis on her statement by rolling her neck around in a circular motion.

"Hell yeah!" Tamia laughed. These twins had been my girls ever since ninth grade. I often referred to them as Chocolate and Vanilla. Their mother was white and their father black. One might assume they would both be light skinned. However, Tamia was dark brown and Tyra was high yellow. "Does he have a brother? Because a bitch is trying to get hooked up."

"No, he doesn't." I laughed.

"When is the baby due?" they both asked at the same time.

"In four months." I waved back at a few familiar faces then took a seat at one of the tables covered in white linen. "Anyway, how is your mom?"

"Girl, she should be getting out in a few months." Tyra sat beside me while Tamia continued to stand. Their mom, Harriet, was busted ten years ago after bringing a shipment of heroin in from Mexico for their father, Robert. The feds knew the dope wasn't hers. They offered her an opportunity to rat on her man for a reduced sentence. Consequently, Harriet insisted she was in business for herself. Since they weren't able to prove otherwise, Harriet was sent to prison and Robert was left with his girls. He tried to do right by them and leave the game, but after a while the streets started calling. About three years ago, he was murdered while waiting in the drive-thru line at a fast food restaurant.

"So what's next for you two, college or the workforce?" I asked.

"Girl, I'm trying to find a baller to take care of me." Tyra was dead serious. "I mean, look at all of this."

"Girl, bye!" Tamia rolled her eyes.

"Well, not everybody's a genius like you. Besides, I've been to juvenile too many times to get a real job." While growing up, she had gotten into some of everything, from beating up girls with bats to stealing from the corner store. One time, she was sentenced to do real time in the county.

"I'm going to school for accounting," Tamia interjected. She always was the brains of the operation, receiving straight A's in school and scholarships to various colleges.

"Are you attending an out-of-state school?"

"No, I'm going to University of Detroit Mercy. I need to keep an eye on this one here." She pointed to her sister, who was applying lip gloss. "What about you?"

"After I have the baby, I'll probably get a job." I shrugged.

"Janelle, do you remember the day we started ninth grade?" Tyra asked. "We were in Mrs. Claskin's class. She went around the room asking everyone what they wanted to be when they got older. I said I wanted to be a model, and Tamia wanted to be a banker. Do you remember what you said?" She busted out laughing, and so did Tamia and I. Everyone's mouth dropped open when I told my teacher I wanted to be a gangster.

I'd never forget that day! She was at a loss for words, but not for long. She called my parents then told me how idiotic I sounded. Most of the kids laughed until I asked Mrs. Claskin how much she made a year. If I recall correctly, it was somewhere between $35,000 and $45,000. Then, I proceeded to inform her that one brick of cocaine was worth approximately $1,000. And even if I only sold one brick a week, I would still make more than her in less than a year. The class roared with laughter. Although I was suspended for a week, it was still funny.

"Those were the days." I continued laughing with my friends until the disc jockey commenced to playing the current hit songs. That's when we hit the dance floor to break a sweat.

# Chapter Forty-eight

The party was a huge success. I was elated to see all of my people again. A few of them had even asked me to come and hang out a little while longer, but I declined. Being pregnant sure could take a toll on your body. My back was aching and my feet were sore. So here I was stretched out across the sofa.

"Where you going?" I looked up from the *Boss Bitch* magazine I was reading just in time to see Ace heading for the door. He was in such a hurry that he hadn't bothered to tell me he was leaving.

"I just got a call from my man, Nicky. He said today's shipment should be arriving in an hour. He wants me to be at the spot when it gets there so that I can grab my order and hit the streets."

"Should I go with you?" Don't ask me why, but I was beginning to become more protective of Ace than he was of me.

"No, I'm good. It shouldn't take that long." He leaned down to kiss my lips then my belly.

"What time will you be back?"

"I'm not sure, Janie, but it shouldn't take more than two hours."

"Okay, be careful. See you later." I watched him leave the house then turned my focus back to the magazine.

"Girl, you've been in that same spot since I came home over two hours ago." Alicia emerged from her bedroom with Keisha on her trail.

"Why are you clocking my moves?" I teased Ali. "You need to be worrying about your life and stop worrying about mine. Now can you bring me some water?"

"Oh, no, heffa, I ain't bringing you shit. Get your lazy ass up off that couch and get it yourself." She laughed.

"You see how selfish she is, Keish?" I shook my head.

"She's not that bad, Janelle." Keisha defended her boo at all costs. I tossed a pillow at her, and she caught it then tossed it right back.

"Here, lazy." Ali set a cold glass of water down on the table. "Is there anything else I can bring Your Royal Highness before I go?" She bowed playfully.

"Yeah, bring me a million dollars."

"Small bills or large?" she asked with a straight face. Then we burst into laughter.

"Where are you going anyway?" I reached for the water and took a sip. "Don't y'all wanna stay in and order some food and a movie?"

"We got a room downtown for the night." Alicia grabbed her keys from the table.

"Well, don't mess around and get pregnant!" I cracked up laughing so hard that I almost peed on myself. Ali flipped me the bird. Keisha gave me a hug before leaving.

After a few hours of quiet time, I ended up dozing off in the living room. I awakened with a strong urge to use the restroom. Slowly, I stood from the couch and stretched. My joints popped as the pressure to pee intensified. I glanced at the time on the cable box and noticed it was almost midnight. Silently, I wondered where Ace was at. Therefore, I grabbed my cell phone from the coffee table to check for missed calls. However, there were none.

Quickly, I dialed his number while heading into the bathroom. After several rings, his voicemail came on. I ignored the feeling in the pit of my belly that was telling me that all was not well. Repeatedly, I dialed him, only to hear his voicemail.

Instinctively, I grabbed some clothes from my dresser and slid them on. I didn't care one bit if they were wrinkled and didn't match. After calling Ace one last time, I called Alicia.

"Hey, J. What's up?"

"Ace hasn't been home since earlier. I know something's up."

"Calm down, girl. When was the last time you spoke to him?" she asked as my other line beeped.

"Hold on." Without awaiting her response, I clicked over to the other line. "Hello."

"Janelle, sorry to call you this late. It's Kenny."

"Who?" I frowned.

"Officer Bryant."

"Oh, I'm sorry. I never knew your first name. What's up?"

"Have you been watching the news?" he asked cautiously.

My stomach tightened. "No. What channel?"

"Turn it on channel four. They're doing a story on a drug bust this afternoon. The Feds confiscated over one hundred kilograms of cocaine and arrested seventeen people. Ace was one of them."

"What?" I grabbed the remote control and turned on the news. Sure as shit, they were covering the drug bust. Ace's name was all over the television. "Oh, my God!"

"I just wanted to let you know. From what they're saying, he's facing some serious time. So you better get him an attorney quick."

"Thanks for the heads-up. Talk to you later." Completely winded, I ended the call and fell onto the bed. What was I going to do with Ace behind bars for God knew how long? All the money that we'd saved for when the baby came would have to be used to retain an attorney.

My cell phone rang, interrupting my thoughts. I answered without looking at the caller ID. "Yeah."

"Damn, you could've at least clicked over and told me you would call me back," Alicia complained.

"Girl, my bad. That was Bryant on the other end telling me that Ace was arrested a few hours ago by the Feds." Unable to believe what I was actually saying, I sighed. It's crazy because everyone in the game knew that death and prison were always lurking around the corner. Nonetheless, when that shit actually happened, you felt blindsided.

"Are you serious, Janie?" She was just as stunned as I was.

"I wish I were joking, Ali." I allowed a tear to fall down my cheek. I didn't bother to wipe it. I knew there were more to come.

"It's all good, J. We'll get him out." She tried to sell me a dream, but this was definitely a nightmare.

"Alicia, he's with the Feds. This shit is for real." I sniffed.

"Look, don't be getting yourself all upset. Ace will be home in no time. We just have to figure this shit out and keep on pushing."

Even though Ali was right, it was difficult to see the light at the end of the tunnel.

# Chapter Forty-nine

All night long, I tossed and turned. I was simultaneously nervous and angry. We didn't have a lawyer on standby. Therefore, the mission at hand today was to find and retain one. At exactly six fifty-nine, I hit the floor and began preparation for my busy day.

Knowing enough about lawyers to know they charged a hefty fee, I dropped to my knees and pulled several shoeboxes toward me. Popping the lids on all of them, I began to count the wads of rubber-banded money they housed. The sum was $34,000. I reserved $10,000 for myself, then slid the other boxes back under the bed. That money was all we had to our name. Be that as it may, you better believe I would've spent every single dollar to have Ace back home with me.

Subsequent to tossing the money onto the unmade bed, I retreated into my closet to grab a pair of black skinny jeans, a coral blouse, a white blazer, and a pair of black-and-white pinstriped wedges. I unwrapped my hair then contemplated applying makeup, which typically I didn't wear. But because I'd spent most of the night crying, my eyes were incredibly swollen.

Buzz. Buzz. My cell phone vibrated. I made a mad dash to answer it. "Hello."

"You have a collect call from a Michigan State inmate," the operator informed me. I knew it was Ace. "Press one to accept."

After pressing one, I blinked back a few tears. "Ace, are you okay?"

"I'm good, Janie. Are you okay?" His voice sounded low yet firm.

"I'm a mess, but that's neither here nor there. I heard about what happened. I want you to know that everything will be okay. Today I'm going out to hire you an attorney."

"I'm sorry I let this happen to us, Janie."

"Ace, it's not your fault. Don't worry, I got you." I wanted to wrap my arms around my man so badly, to let him know that we would get through this no matter how long it took.

"One minute remaining," the operator chimed in.

"Baby, keep your head up and your eyes open." Because prison was such a treacherous place, I needed him to be focused and stay on his toes. "This will be over soon. You'll have an attorney by tonight. I love you."

"I love you too," he said, and then there was silence. Our time was up.

My emotions were high. For the entire day, I could've sat there and wallowed in sadness. However, there was no time for that. It was time for me to play my position.

My first stop was to an attorney's office that I'd heard about through other niggas in the hood. Allegedly, he was the go-to guy for street criminals. I certainly hoped he could assist us.

"Welcome to the office of Tom Hanson." A white clerk smiled from behind the receptionist desk. "Do you have an appointment?"

"No, I don't have an appointment, I'm sorry. My boyfriend got into some trouble last night, and we need a lawyer," I explained.

"Sorry, but we don't handle domestic violence cases." She smiled politely.

"What?" I was puzzled. "I'm not here for domestic violence." I frowned.

"Oh, my goodness! I'm terribly sorry. Please forgive me." She was beet red, flushed with embarrassment. "I simply looked at your face and saw the swollen eye, so I just assumed . . ." Before going any further, she cut her statement off midstream. I wanted to remind her of what happens when people assume. However, I couldn't be angry. This woman had no idea I'd been crying my eyes out. More than likely, I would have come to the same conclusion. "Currently, Mr. Hanson is on a call, but if you have a seat, he'll be with you shortly. What's your name?" Prepared to type in my information, she turned to the computer.

"Jane Doesher." I went to have a seat on the plush red lobby furniture but quickly turned around. "Do you have a bathroom?" I was nervous as hell and needed to urinate.

"Sure, it's down the hall to the left." She pointed.

On my way down the narrow hallway, there were three offices and one conference room. The place was much larger than it appeared from the waiting area. I was quite impressed with the swank decor. There was a wall covered with pictures of Mr. Hanson and several clients, all of whom were black. Some faces were unfamiliar. For the most part, I did recognize a few athletes and one or two politicians. There were even a few Detroit rappers among the photos. Therefore, I knew this guy was legit. Feeling a bit more assured, I entered the restroom to handle my business.

On the way out, I could hear two men holding a conversation from the office across the hall. They were speaking rather vociferously, so I naturally stopped to listen.

"Tom, why do you continue to utilize your prestigious degree and avail yourself to the scum of Detroit who are thrust your way?"

"Those scum you're referring to happen to be some of my best clients," Tom replied.

"Please elaborate and help me understand why these hoodlums have such a powerful grip on you."

"Andy, you'll never comprehend this but once you go black, you never go back." Tom chuckled. However, Andy didn't seem to find the humor in his declaration. "Listen, it's simple. On average, black men in Detroit begin committing crimes around the age of fourteen. They are in and out of jail several times before they hit thirty. You know how much I love repeat offenders. Some of these niggers make more money in a week than I will make all year. Hell yes, I'll represent them all, no matter whose house they shot up, how much dope they found in the car, or whose sister they raped. Most of these niggers come to this office with cases that put me in newspaper headlines. The 'scum,' as you referred to them, are the reason my wife lives in her dream home and my mistress drives a Bugatti."

Tom continued to brag, but I had heard enough. So outraged at what I had just overheard, I left the office without saying one word to the receptionist. I would never be the reason a bastard like Tom continued to live in the lap of luxury.

As I started the car, my cell phone vibrated. It was Bryant. "What's up?" I asked as I reversed out of my parking spot.

"Hey, Janelle, I was calling to check on you and see if you're all right."

"I'll be better when Ace is out, but I'm good. Thanks for checking on me." I pulled onto the main street then pondered where to go next. At the moment, I didn't have any other references for attorneys. Nevertheless, I was determined to find a good one.

"I hear that. Federal cases are out of my league, but let me know if there's anything I can do for you."

"Thanks for the call as well as your concern, Bryant." I ended the connection and detected a huge building up ahead and to my left. Seeing the big bold words RICHARD LENNIGAN, ATTORNEY AT LAW, I figured my prayers had been answered.

Speeding hastily down the street, I pulled up to the building, jumped out of the car, and waddled into the front door. This pregnancy thing was for the birds, and I was no near my biggest stage yet.

"Hi, may I help you?" a male secretary asked with a chipper demeanor. Anyone could tell he was gay by the way he applied lip gloss to his puckered lips.

"I need to see an attorney regarding my boyfriend."

"No problem, girl. Lucky for you Richard has a free calendar this morning. Come on back, boo." He stood from his seat and I almost died. Dude was rocking spandex pants and red bottom heels. "Girl, can I get you some tea, water, coffee, or pop?" He smacked his lips.

"No, thank you, I'm good." I smiled politely.

Tap. Tap. He knocked on a large brown door then opened it. "Richard, we have a client here in need of a consultation." After he escorted me into the office, I took a seat.

"Thank you, Bradley." The Italian attorney swiveled around in his desk chair to face me. "Sorry about that. He's my son, God love him." The attorney laughed.

"No problem. He's very nice." Prepared to get right to business, I sat up straight in my seat.

"Well, let's get started. Tell me what brings you my way," he said, looking attentive.

"My boyfriend, Anthony, was arrested last night following an FBI drug raid. Currently, he's being held in federal custody. One hundred kilos of cocaine was recovered."

Mr. Lennigan jotted down several notes before looking back up at me. "Do you know when his hearing is set?"

"No, I don't." I shook my head.

"No problem. If you choose to retain me, I'll get that information." He placed his pen down on top of the table.

"Speaking of a retainer, how much do you charge?" I braced myself for the astronomical fee I was confident I would hear. This guy was as fancy as they came in his three-piece custom suit. Therefore, I was convinced he would be expensive.

"My retainer is ten thousand dollars to get started. This allows me to file all of the necessary paperwork on the defendant's behalf. Additionally, I'd attend the bail hearing, at which point I would request that the defendant be released on bond."

"So what happens after that?" I was new to this thing and needed to be educated.

"Well, if they agree to let him out on bond, then he'll come home the same day. On the other hand, should they deny our request, Anthony will remain in prison until the preliminary hearing."

"What's a preliminary hearing?" Like a student thirsty for knowledge, I was absorbing as much information as I could.

"It's simple. A hearing is where the prosecutor must present probable cause to the judge in order to detain the defendant after bail has been denied. If the judge determines there is enough evidence to prove Anthony committed the crime, then he will be 'held to answer' or 'bound over.'" He made air quotes with his fingers. "In other words, the prosecutor will offer a plea deal. If Anthony accepts it, he will be bound over to the State to begin sentencing. If Anthony rejects the deal, then he will be given a trial and we will proceed from there."

"Wow! That's a lot to take in, but I'm happy you took the time to explain it to me." I stood and shook his hand.

"It's no problem at all. I'm here for you and Anthony, day or night. I'll continuously keep you up to date." His smile caused me to feel at ease with my decision to hire him.

"Please see Bradley on the way out, and I'll handle Anthony's case right away."

# Chapter Fifty

It had been more than seventy-two hours since I'd been sitting on pins and needles waiting to hear something from Ace's attorney. I was too nervous to attend the bail hearing in person because I couldn't take another letdown. There was no way I'd be able to lay eyes on my baby and face the reality of him not being able to come home with me.

"Fuck this waiting shit. I say we just call the damn lawyer." Alicia slammed the refrigerator door. "The hearing was at ten o'clock, and it's almost two."

"It's not that simple." I sighed. "Sometimes you can be stuck in court all day." I knew this firsthand from a previous incident with my grandmother. Speaking of Gran, I decided to pick up the phone and give her a call. Our last visit was so good that it kind of had me missing the old bird.

"Praise the Lord," she answered in her over-sanctified tone.

"Hi, Gran, it's Janie." I grabbed the acetone and two cotton balls from the coffee table and began to remove the pink polish from my toes. The polish wasn't in bad shape. I just needed to kill time and calm my nerves.

"Well, how have you been, missy?" I could tell she was happy to hear from me. As usual, she played hardball. "My congregation has been praying for you and your ways during Sunday morning services."

"Is that so?" I rolled my eyes.

"The scripture says, 'For where two or three are gathered together in my name, there am I in the midst of them.' Once God gets involved, the devil has no other choice but to turn you loose and flee," she preached.

"Gran, I was just calling to say hello and let you know I was thinking about you." I politely cut her sermon short.

"When can I expect another visit from you?"

"I'll be there soon, Gran." I finished removing the polish from my last toe and closed the lid on the acetone.

"Have you been going to your doctor's appointments?" She was actually concerned, and it shocked me.

"Yes, ma'am. Everything is just as it should be."

"Good. Good. I can't wait to meet my great-grandbaby." I could tell she was smiling, which made me smile. Who knew my pregnancy could bring us closer?

"Me too, Gran. Before I let you go, is there anything you need from the grocery store or pharmacy?"

"No, thank you, Janie," she declined politely. "I'll see you soon."

"See you soon, Gran." I ended the call then placed my cell phone on the coffee table.

"How is your grandmother?" Alicia flopped down on the sofa beside me.

"She's good. Still preaching as usual but she's coming around." I laughed. "How is your mom?"

"I don't know." She shrugged.

"Haven't you spoken to her since the graduation?"

"She promised we would work on our relationship, but when I went by there the other day to see her, Tyrone was there so she wouldn't let me in." She looked disappointed. Her mom was one of those women who had to have a man no matter how good, bad, or ugly he treated her. I felt bad for my friend, so I tried to cheer her up.

"I say we blow this popsicle stand and head to the mall, my treat." I was tired of waiting around the house for the phone to ring.

"Actually, I'd rather stay in and call it a movie night. Let's order pizza, rent some movies, and go to the store to load up on junk food." She stretched.

"Okay, I'm good with that." I stood from the couch. "Let me grab my shoes, and then we can get the party started early."

As I headed into my room, my phone rang. Alicia grabbed it for me. "Hello? Yes, she's right here." She brought it over to me as I held my breath.

"Richard, what happened?" In order for Alicia to hear the conversation, I put the phone call on speaker.

"Well," he sighed. Right then and there, I knew this wasn't what I wanted to hear. "They denied bond but offered Anthony a plea deal of five years."

"Whew!" I blew out an audible breath. Five years was a drop in the bucket. *Hell, he may even get out earlier for good behavior.*

"Janelle, I regret to inform you that Anthony rejected the deal and wants to take his chance at trial."

"What?"

"He wants to go to trial." Richard sighed again, which told me he didn't feel Ace had chosen correctly.

"When does his trial start?"

"The State's caseload is backed up right now. It could be years before this case goes to trial, but I'll do my best to expedite the process."

"Okay, but if he's found guilty, what's the worst-case scenario?" I leaned against the wall for support.

"The charge he's facing carries a maximum sentence of forty years and a minimum of twenty."

There was silence on the other end of the phone as he awaited my response. It felt as if someone had just snatched the air from my lungs. I attempted to gather my thoughts and form a sentence. However, the only audible sounds coming from my body were sobs. Alicia took the phone and explained to Richard that I would call him back. He apologized and expressed his understanding.

"What am I going to do without him?"

"Janelle, we'll get through this."

"My man is never coming back?" I slid down the wall. Alicia sat on the floor beside me. "What about our wedding? What about the baby? Who am I supposed to be with now? No one loved me like Ace! Nobody loves him like me!"

"I don't know what to say right now to make you feel better, sis." Alicia was now wiping her own tears.

"I need to go lie down." I stood from the floor and retreated into my room, where I stayed for almost a month.

# Chapter Fifty-one

I heard somewhere that real niggas shed tears. Even so, I had been crying for too long. Enough was enough! The pity party I was having was pathetic. It was taking a toll on my body. Although I was six months pregnant, my body weight was less than it was before I conceived. I rarely ate, and when I did, it came back up. My hair was thin from worrying and there were bags underneath my eyes from lack of sleep. Day after day I worried myself sick about Ace. Night after night I cried myself to sleep because I hadn't heard from him. I'd been writing him letters since his first week behind bars. However, I never received any correspondence back from him. I had even gone downtown to visit him, only to discover I wasn't on his visitation list. I wasn't sure what the deal was, but there had to be a great explanation.

For now, I determined it was time to pull myself up by my bootstraps and get back to grinding. My money stash was decreasing. That meant I had to get back in the streets and come up with some sort of get-rich-quick scheme in order to keep Richard Lennigan as our defense attorney. He would be Ace's best chance at a fair trial. By any means necessary, I had to keep him on payroll. Of course, my heart was aching. I could've stayed in bed forever. No matter what, he was my nigga and I was his bitch. Determined not to let him down, I put my own feelings on the back burner and pressed forward.

Without hesitation, I swallowed my pride and made a call to Uncle Chucky. He told me to come right over.

"What's up, Janelle?" As I stepped into the foyer of his home, he greeted me with a Newport cigarette dangling between his lips. There were still hard feelings between us. Neither one of us really wanted to address the matter just yet. Therefore, we let the issue rest for now.

"Those cancer sticks will be the death of you one day, old man," I joked.

"Better cancer than one of these fuckin' niggas." He inhaled then exhaled a puff of white smoke.

"I hear that." We both chuckled. "Thanks for taking the meeting with me, Unc."

I followed him to the den, which was at the back of the house. The home reminded me of something straight from the pages of an Ikea catalogue. Everything was black, white, and red. The place was clean-cut and modern. Yet, the decor felt cold and uninviting. It also lacked a woman's touch. Chucky's wife, Vivian, left him exactly one month after their wedding. I was just a kid back then but I distinctly remember my mother telling one of her friends that Vivian left because he was abusive.

"No problem, niece." He took a seat on the red leather sofa and rested his feet on the black metal coffee table. "Now speak on what brings you here."

"Well, I know I fucked things up with Bobby a while back. I'm really sorry about that, but I think I deserve another chance."

"No fucking way!" He laughed. "Just because your last name carries weight doesn't mean I can just go around forcing people to rehire you." Chucky grabbed the green Heineken beer bottle that was resting on the end table and took a swig.

"Unc, I'm not asking to be put back on with Bobby. I'm asking to be put on with you. I'm done with stolen cars and credit cards. I want in on the trap." I sighed.

"Janie, I thought we had this discussion a while back." He took another swig. "And I distinctly remember telling you no."

"Chucky, a lot of shit has changed since then. I'm ready now." Having no other reply, I went with the first thing that popped into my head.

"Besides that baby bump, tell me, what has changed?" he challenged me.

"Last year, I was just a little girl trying to make a way for myself. This year, I'm a woman who's hungry."

"Do you know how many niggas out there are hungry?" His question was rhetorical. "It's a recession. Everybody in Detroit is hungry."

"Let me rephrase that then. I'm fucking starving!"

"You sure this doesn't have anything to do with the fact that your boy Ace is locked up?" He smirked.

"Does it matter? I'm here ready to put in work for you. That's all you need to be concerned about," I snapped and then toned it down. "Look, I'm not trying to come at you wrong. Please understand that neither Ace nor my relationship is up for discussion!"

"All right, that's reasonable." Chucky raised his hands in surrender. "But tell me how crazy I would look to put your pregnant ass up in a damn trap house."

"No disrespect, but let me worry about that."

"I always said you should've been a boy. You act too much like your father." He chuckled lightly.

"So can I get in with you or what?" I raised an eyebrow as he considered his decision. I guessed there was something in my voice or perhaps the look in my eyes, but after a few additional minutes of heavy persuasion, Uncle Chucky agreed to give me and Ali a new trap on the east side.

"The cut is sixty-forty," he explained.

"Fifty-fifty, nigga. We're the ones taking all the risks."

"This shit ain't up for negotiation. Take it or leave it. It's as simple as that." He sipped from the neck of the green beer bottle.

"Fine then. Can I at least put together my own crew?"

"It's your trap. Run it however you wanna run it. As long as my money come back right, we won't have any problems."

"Cool then." I smiled. "So when can we set up shop?"

"As soon as you give me the five grand it's gonna take for you to get your first shipment." He stood from the sofa.

"Just tell me when and where to meet you. I'll have it then." I headed back toward the door.

"Call my man Fox. He'll give you the information." He wrote Fox's number on a piece of paper and handed it to me.

"Thanks, Unc." I reached in for a hug but he stopped me.

"Janelle, we can't be family when we're handling business. From this point forward, you address me as Chucky and I'll address you as Janelle."

"Since it's like that, just call me Jane." I tossed him the deuces and headed out the door.

This was the moment I'd been waiting for. Finally, a chance to show the dope game how much a bitch like me was capable of. For years, I watched my father and studied his movements. I learned from the bad as well as the good. I couldn't wait to come up with a few of my own. Today was just the beginning. However, one day the world would remember Jane Doe.


Without delay, I arranged a meeting with my potential crew, which consisted of Alicia, Keisha, Tyra, Tamia, and my aunt Michelle. The next day over lunch at Chili's,

I laid out my proposal. It covered everything from who would handle what responsibility to how much they would each be compensated.

Because all of these women were skilled at certain aspects of the game, I felt confident with my team. Keisha, for instance, was a hustler by nature. She could sell fire in hell and water to a whale. Tyra was always messing with dope boys growing up. Therefore, she had several plugs and connections into the game. Tamia was a good girl, but for as long as I could remember she'd been great with numbers. Her intelligence would be used on the business side of things. After the money started flowing in, Tamia would be the one to legitimize our hustle and turn our dirty money into justifiable capital. Last but not least was Auntie Michelle. Previously, I said she was from the old school, but the way she whipped up crack was impeccable. There was something about the way she cut it, mixed it with filler, blended it, and then pressed it with a hydraulic jack that had the hot boys, including my father, banging down her door.

Naturally, everyone was on board with the new venture except for Tamia, who would be starting college pretty soon. She didn't want to jeopardize her education. I fully understood her position. Conversely, she did agree to assist us if we really needed her.

After dropping off my startup money to Fox the next day, Alicia and I rode over to the spot on Charlevoix with Tyra and Michelle following us. The neighborhood had definitely seen better days. Yet the location was perfect for what we were trying to do. Upon pulling up to the vacant home, I counted five men out front.

"You think they're with Chucky?" Alicia frowned.

"Let's find out." I grabbed my pistol, tucked it into the small of my back, then headed up toward the house. The men ranged in age between fifteen and possibly twenty-something. They had on the typical dope boy attire: baggy jeans and long T-shirts. They were probably local dealers who had claimed the spot for their own, or so they thought.

"Who's in charge?" Alicia asked.

"Who wants to know?" One of the boys looked from side to side.

"I don't have time for games." I blocked my face from the sun.

"We don't serve pregnant bitches," the youngest one spoke from the porch.

"Good, 'cause I ain't trying to get served." With Alicia on my ass, I continued walking toward the house. Vanilla was posted up against her Durango with her arms crossed at the chest. Michelle was peering through the passenger window while blowing on a swisher.

"Fuck you want then?" one of the other men asked while looking me up and down.

"I came to claim my spot. That means you niggas can get to bouncing!" Stopping just in front of the crew, my gaze remained relentless.

"Your spot?" the little one asked. "Bitch, we own this whole block in case you didn't know."

"Call me one more bitch and I'm going to beat your ass like your mammy should have."

"Fuck you say about my mama?" He stood from the step but was held back by one of the bigger men.

"Let that li'l nigga go so I can tap that ass." I patted my belt.

"Enough with all of that other shit. Who sent you over here?" The oldest man came off the porch to meet me.

"I got orders from Chucky to take this spot."

At the mention of Chucky, the man's face softened. "You J?" He looked confused.

"Yeah, that's me." I nodded and looked back at my girls. "Shit, when Chucky called and said to hold the spot down for J, I thought you was a nigga." He laughed.

"It's short for Jane. Is that a problem?"

"No beef this way, ma." He extended his hand. "I'm Dog, that's Tay, he's G, he's Polo, and the little nigga is PJ." The men nodded their greeting. I nodded back. "Chucky said you might need some assistance. That's what we're here for."

"No disrespect, but I have my own crew." I pointed back at my girls.

Dog didn't seem impressed with my roster. "You got an all-female squad? No offense, but you asking for trouble."

"Is that so?" I raised an eyebrow.

"Once the jack boys find out y'all bitches—I mean, females—they're going to hit y'all spot. You better get some security."

"Don't worry, I'm well protected." We had already ordered a heavy arsenal of weapons. Additionally, I had two pit bulls set to be delivered tonight. Their names were Thelma and Louise.

"Well, don't say I didn't warn you." He shrugged.

"I hope they try us, cuz. I've been fiending to bust another cap in someone's ass." I pulled the gun from behind my back and put it into my purse just to let them know we were packing heat.

"That's cute but you better stock up. The trap gets scary at night." He laughed and the other men followed suit. "The jack boys come under the cover of darkness and take all you've got."

"Ain't no punks over here. We ain't afraid of the dark or no gotdamn jack boys!" This fool had irritated me with his so-called scary story.

"I respect that, Jane. Do you and I'll catch you later." He extended his hand again. "Oh, yeah, we got the spot around the way on Hazel. So holla if you need me." He beckoned for his friends. They all left quietly.

His crew was the first of many to doubt our capabilities, but they couldn't knock the hustle. The grind me and my girls put in was unheard off. We immediately set up shop in the run-down dwelling. To make it look like something on the inside, I purchased a living room set, flat-screen television, and a refrigerator. Next, I called a locksmith to upgrade the locks. The minute it got dark outside, we unloaded the product.

# Chapter Fifty-two

Within thirty days of the new trap house being opened, our business was booming. I couldn't tell you if it was perfect timing, a great location, or the way Auntie Michelle cooked up the crack. Whatever it was had the dopefiends loving us. Tyra had also gotten a plug on pills, so we were able to extend our business to pushing ecstasy, Vicodin, Percocet, and Oxy.

Although he hadn't said anything, Chucky had to have been impressed with the amount of money we made in such a short time. My team was legit, which was why I was always thinking of ways to elevate our hustle. From day one, it was never my intention to remain a low-level dealer. I wanted to be a queen pin, bottom line. All we had to do was sit tight, play our positions, and wait until the time was right.

"All right, Jane, I'm done. Are you sure it's okay for me to leave?" Auntie Michelle called up the stairs. She had just finished whipping up a fresh batch and bagging it up.

"Yeah, go ahead, Auntie. I'll see you tomorrow." Sunday night was always slow at the trap for whatever reason. Only about two or three dopefiends came by for a fix every couple of hours. For that reason, I always sent my team home early. There was no need to keep them around when I didn't have to, which meant more money in my and Ali's pockets.

Speaking of Alicia, I pulled my cell phone from my pocket and proceeded to dial her number. After one ring,

I ended the call, remembering she was out on a date with Keisha. Over the past couple of months, they had become inseparable. I couldn't have been happier for my friend. Oftentimes, their relationship made me long for Ace. Never in a million years could I have pictured my life without him. I had no choice now. I still hadn't heard from him. I was angry, but there was nothing I could do about it right now.

Pushing thoughts of Ace to the back of my mind and getting back into G mode, I wiped my ass and flushed the toilet. In the trap, you always had to have a clear mind and a hardened heart in order to survive. Today was no different. I stood in front of the sink to wash my hands, and I gave myself the once-over. The baby face I once possessed had become more mature. The smile I once shared so freely was now a hardcore grimace. Life had been unkind to me. The pain behind my eyes was evident. At such a young age, I'd seen and done some things that most people could only imagine. However, I was a survivor.

From the upstairs bathroom I heard my dogs barking in the basement, which meant someone was approaching the house. Tap. Tap. I headed down the stairs just in time to hear the light knock, and I knew it was one of my customers. Without hesitation, I reached into my jeans pocket for the small bags of crack the fiend desperately desired.

"What you need?" I opened the wooden door slightly and spoke through the gated security door on the side of the house.

"Let me get two smalls." The female spoke softly. I recognized the loyal customer standing there in a black tank top and biker shorts. Relaxed, I continued with the transaction without hesitation.

"That's twenty dollars." I watched her lift the mail flap and slide two $10 bills inside. I opened the door about an inch or two wider and retrieved the money. Holding the money up to the light, I inspected that shit for authenticity. These crackheads were known for passing around fake money. After noting the money was authentic, I opened the mail flap and dropped two Baggies into her palms.

"Thanks, J." She smiled, grateful for the fix. I wasn't sure what her name was. What I did know was she lived a few houses down with a husband and three kids. The lady drove a nice Honda Civic, and she had a good-paying job at an accounting firm. She was what we called a functioning addict. She worked to feed her habit and did her best to hide it from family and peers. Sometimes I would see her leaving for work in the morning dressed to the nines in crisp suits, with a briefcase and a cup of coffee. By day, she was a superwoman. Unfortunately, she came undone in the evening.

Her husband knew about her addiction. He had even come over once before to beg me not to service her. I felt bad for the man. Therefore, I agreed not to exchange commodities with her anymore, but I warned him to watch her. If she didn't buy drugs from me, she would damn sure begin buying them elsewhere. Within two weeks, she made a purchase from another trap and damn near died of an overdose. The crack was mixed with rat poison. The poor woman was off the scene for a while. I figured she must've checked into rehab as a result of her near-death experience. However, that wasn't the case. The monkey on her back still had her fiending. Once again, she was a returning regular, trading coins for merchandise.

As I made my way into the kitchen to check out what was in the fridge, I heard another knock at the door. This time it was more of a banging sound. It caused me to jump slightly.

"Who is it?" I called out from the hallway, but no one answered. I waited another second or two before heading into the living room for my piece. Before I could get there, I heard a window shatter. "What the fuck?" I turned in the direction of the noise, which was coming from the kitchen, and I saw a brick lying on the kitchen floor. *One of these days, I'm gonna take my belt off and whip one of these damn kids!* The children in this neighborhood were always working my nerves with stunts like this. One time, those little fuckers torched one of the neighbor's cars.

I walked over to the kitchen window to see how bad the damage was and smacked my lips. It wasn't awful. Then again, even having to get the window fixed was not only a major inconvenience, it was also money out of my pocket. I grabbed the dustpan and broom and began to clean up the mess when there was another loud noise, coming from the front door this time. Boom! Boom! It sounded as if someone was attempting to kick the door in. Before I had time to react, that's exactly what happened.

"Oh, shit!" I dropped the broom and tried to make a mad dash for the living room where my pistol was stashed in between the sofa cushions. However, I stopped dead in my tracks when I realized who the intruder was.

"What's up, Janelle?" Gudda stood there mean mugging me. I thought after our run-in at the restaurant things were over.

"What's up with you, nigga?" Although I was a little shaken up by his presence, I had to show this fool I wasn't intimidated.

"Oh, I'll show you what's up." He took the butt of his gun and smashed it into my forehead. The blow sent me dazed and disoriented to the floor. Next, he removed his belt and proceeded to whip my ass like I was a runaway slave. I screamed out in agony, which riled up my pit bulls even more. They desperately wanted to protect me. However, the basement door was preventing that from happening.

"Where is all that tough shit now? You ain't so bad without a gun or your auntie, huh?" His deep voice echoed in my ears.

Blinking rapidly, I struggled to focus, but the room was spinning, making it a difficult task. "Get up, bitch!" He kicked me in the arm as I protected my abdomen with all of my strength. I'd die before I let something happen to my unborn child.

"I said get the fuck up!" This time, his size-twelve Timberland boot went right upside my head. At this point, all I wanted to do was cry in agony, but I wouldn't dare. Except for my vagina, there was nothing pussy about me. Therefore, I maintained a straight face and endured several body shots from his massive fists. When he had finally completed his assault on me, he picked me up from the floor by my ponytail.

"You better kill me, nigga!" I spat the blood from my mouth into his face.

"Don't worry, shorty, wishes do come true." He wiped away the blood and saliva with the collar of his shirt then punched me right in the face. I heard something inside my mouth crack. Then I felt small objects fall onto my tongue. Those were my fucking teeth. I presumed my life would end here, tonight, at the trap house. Alicia would most likely find my body in the morning.

"Take your bitch ass into the basement," he demanded, which was music to my ears. Once this fool opened the door, it would be lights out for him at the bottom of the stairs.

Each step was taken with Gudda on my ass. I silently anticipated what was about to occur. "Open the fucking door." He pushed me. I didn't hesitate.

In retaliation and without hesitation, Thelma and Louise attacked Gudda with vengeance. They bit his ass up. I watched him try to fight both of the 130-pound dogs. During the attack, he dropped his gun, which gave me the perfect opportunity to slaughter that nigga. I guarantee you I didn't hesitate.

Pop. Pop. Pop. Three shots sent the nigga stumbling to the ground. I staggered over to his body then placed the pistol right into his mouth. Pop. That was all she wrote for Gudda. His time was up.

Staggering up the stairs, I managed to retrieve my phone.

"Hey, girl, what's up?" Ali answered.

"I need you to get here quick." Due to the loss of my front top teeth, I sounded like Daffy Duck.

"What's wrong?" she asked with concern.

"This nigga just tried to kill me!"

# Chapter Fifty-three

After the incident, my girls urged me to take a few days away from the trap in order to recover. I used the time off to contact Richard to see if he could schedule a visit with Ace. I also went to see an oral surgeon about my mouth. There was no way I'd be seen with missing teeth. Dental implants were my only option. Because I didn't have insurance, the outpatient surgery hit me up for $10,000 out of pocket.

My grill was back just in time for Richard's call informing me that he was able to arrange a visit with Ace. Hence, I didn't complain, but I did wear the mask they wear at the nail shop while doing nails. They wear the mask to keep them from breathing in fumes all day. My lie for wearing the mask was that I was sick with flu-like symptoms. In all honesty, I just didn't want Ace to see my new teeth and lose his mind about what happened with me and Gudda. Thankfully, our attorney had major pull behind the prison walls. I needed to find out what in the hell was going on with Ace and our relationship.

"Please have a seat, ma'am. He'll be out shortly," the chubby corrections officer informed me before he closed the room door behind him. I sat on the cold metal seat. While waiting for Ace to show up, out of habit I nervously bit down on my bottom lip. After a few minutes passed, I stood up and began pacing the floor in my new red bottoms. On my fourth lap around the small room, I heard Ace speak.

"You look good, Janie." He walked through the door and my heart melted. He was a tad more toned than I remembered. Seemingly an inch taller as well. His shoulders were broader and his arms chiseled. It was apparent that he'd been spending most of his days working out. Subsequently, my focal point became his eyes. Those hazel-green eyes were as piercing as ever. Ultimately, I discontinued the loving stare between us and took in the mini Afro he was sporting. His hair was so curly that one would think he rolled it up at night. Yet I knew better. It grew like that when he went too long without a haircut. Furthermore, the facial hair around his mouth and chin needed to be trimmed. He sported a beard now. Although I was pissed off and wanted to hate him, my love outweighed all of my anger. Just as I had months ago, I still felt the same about him. In fact, I wanted to run into his arms and breathe in his essence.

Then I remembered why I was even there in the first place. "What the hell is going on with you?" I crossed my arms across the sheer leopard top I was wearing that pushed my breasts up.

"You came all the way down here to question me?" He tried to give me attitude, but I wasn't having it.

"You're damn right I came down here to question you!" I rolled my eyes. "First, you don't add me to your visitors list. Second, you don't call. You aren't even communicating with me via mail. Is there another bitch?" My heart raced in expectancy of his answer. I had watched too many movies where the main chick discovers her man has side bitches after he goes to prison.

"What?" He shook his head. "Why would you think something like that, Janelle? I love you with everything I got. Can't no other bitch take your spot, baby." He stepped closer to me but I wasn't done.

"Why are you treating me like shit then?" I questioned.

He sighed. "Baby, I'm facing forty fucking years in this place. I don't want nor expect you to do this bid with me." He pulled me closer. "If I go down, I want you to take my seed and forget about me. Pretend I got killed or something." He rested his chin on top of my head and held me so tightly that I could barely breathe.

"Ace, why are you talking like this? Forty years isn't that long."

"Janie, there is no use in pretending this shit is hunky-dory. Forty years is forty years, no matter how you look at it. By the time I'm released, you'll be fifty-eight and my seed will be forty with grandkids." He released the embrace.

"They offered you a plea of five years. Why didn't you take it?" The question had been burning a hole in my head ever since Richard told me he declined the offer.

"The prosecuting attorney wanted me to snitch on Nicky and the Pauletti crime family. You and I both know better than that." He shook his head. He was right, I did know better, so I didn't push the issue. Where we came from, "no snitching" was the code of the streets. Real niggas and bitches lived and died by it. "The truth of the matter is I might go down for this, Janelle, and do the whole bid. It's not fair but it's reality. I've come to accept it, and you have to do the same."

"Baby, you will get out of this. I promise." I needed him to know that I believed he would beat this thing.

"Never make promises you can't keep." He took a seat on one of the metal chairs.

"Ace, I'm making moves and setting shit up for us. I believe wholeheartedly that you will come home." I took the seat across from him.

"What moves are you talking about?" He frowned.

"Me and Alicia got a spot under Chucky." The look on his face told me he was disappointed. "Baby, don't look at me like that. It's just for the meantime."

"The trap ain't no place for you." He hit the table. "And it damn sure ain't no place for my seed."

"Calm down." I placed my hand on top of his. The corrections officer was peeking into the room. I wasn't ready for him to end our visit. "It's only temporary," I whispered.

"Do you know how many niggas are in the cemetery who have said the same thing?"

"Ace, I'm doing this for us."

"Bullshit!" he yelled. "You've been begging to be in the trap ever since your father died, so don't say you're doing this for us!"

"I am doing this for us! I need the money to pay your lawyer," I hollered back. "Listen, it was either selling pussy or selling powder!" I stood from the chair and grabbed my purse. It wasn't my intention to say all of that in the vicinity of the officer. I was beyond furious, so it was what it was. "I'm leaving."

"Janie, I'm sorry. Don't go." Ace stood with me.

"Fuck you, Ace!" I spat and banged on the door for the officer to let me out.

"I'm so sorry. Please don't go." He blocked the door.

"Why would you say some shit like that then?" I was hurt by his words and I wanted him to know it.

"Ma'am, are you okay?" the officer asked.

"She's good," Ace answered for me.

"Ma'am, are you good?" the officer asked in an aggressive tone.

"Yes, I'm good, thank you." I nodded.

"Come here, Janie." Ace pulled me away from the door and over toward the table, where he took a seat.

"Ace, I'm leaving. If that's the way you feel about me, then I'm done with you." I resisted when he attempted to pull me down onto his lap.

"Come here," he said again with more bass in his voice. "I'm sorry for snapping on you like that, but a nigga is stressed. Not a day goes by that I don't think about you or my child." Ace sighed. "I often wonder what type of life you guys will have without me, and then I get sick to my stomach. I love you, Janie. More than anything in this world. It's killing me not to be able to be there for you." He showed a vulnerable side that I had never known him to have. The tear in the corner of his eye softened my demeanor.

"What am I gon' do without you, Ace?" I blinked rapidly. He stood from his seat, walked over to mine, then dropped to his knees.

"It's going to be all right, baby." Ace lifted my shirt and pulled my waist toward him. With both lips puckered up, he began to plant soft kisses all over my belly.

"What are you doing?" Now was not the time to get freaky.

Ace stopped kissing my stomach and smiled. "I probably won't be there when you have the baby. Most likely I won't be there at the first birthday party or when my baby starts walking. Hell, I might not even be there for the first day of school. But I can at least say I gave my baby the first kiss."

"Ace baby, please don't do this to me." I tried to dab at the tears beginning to freely fall down my face.

"I'm sorry I did this, Janie. Somehow, someway I will figure this out, believe me."

"I believe you." Through my tears I nodded and wrapped my arms around him in silence until the corrections officer told me that it was time to go.

# Chapter Fifty-four

The visit with Ace had my emotions all over the place. But after receiving a text from Chucky requesting my presence at a meeting, I put my game face on. This was my first sit-down with all of the players in his organization. I was nervous to say the least. I didn't know how the fellas would take to seeing a female at the table. However, I was quite anxious to find out.

Upon entrance into Snookers, the billiard spot off of the I-96 freeway, I scanned the place for any familiar faces and saw Dog heading past regular patrons through a back door. Therefore, I followed him into a medium-sized room. The place was set up with several cocktail tables and one pool table. From the outside looking in, you would've never guessed all of this extra space was back here. "Yo, Dog, wait up," I called out, and he stopped.

"What's good, J?" He nodded. "I hear you and your girls have been doing the damn thing over there. That's what's up."

"I told you we would." I nudged him playfully. Don't get it twisted, he and I weren't BFFs. Alternatively, he wasn't that bad, and right now he was the only person in this place I knew to some extent.

"What's this meeting shit about?"

"I don't know, fam." He sipped from a shot glass then took a seat at one of the tables. "Fox stated that Chucky wanted to sit down with the heads of each trap, but that's it." He shrugged.

I grabbed the empty seat beside him and sat down. Quickly, the place began to fill up with hardened criminals. I caught a few niggas staring in my direction and gossiping like females. Yet no one had the balls to approach me until one nigga actually did walk up.

"You must be Jane Doe." The gap-toothed brother rested his beer bottle on my table. "I heard you was getting it poppin' over on the east side."

"Something like that." I smiled politely.

"That's unheard of, but I guess there's a first for everything. Right, homie?" He extended his fist to bump knuckles with Dog, who didn't return the gesture.

"What do you mean by that?" This nigga was only talking reckless because he saw me as a weak female, but he was gon' learn today.

"I mean, back in the day the trap didn't have no place for a bitch, but I see things done changed."

"Ain't no bitches at this table." I smirked.

"Yeah, okay. There's a bunch I can say about that. But for now, I'ma let it ride." He grabbed his drink and moved on to the next table.

"Don't let that nigga get you stressed." Dog patted my back.

"I'm not stressed." I brushed his hand away. The last thing I needed was to look like I was being consoled.

"Chill, J, I was only trying to let you know it was all right." He shook his head, and I felt bad for snapping but I still stood my ground.

"I appreciate your concern. But if I were another man, would you be rubbing on my back?"

"Hell no!" he snapped.

"That's my point. Just because I'm a female, don't treat me like a pussy." I smiled.

"Point taken, Jane. I feel you." He nodded just as Chucky came through the back door with a group of men on his trail.

"Who is that?" I whispered. The only person I recognized with Chucky was Fox.

"The light-skinned dude is Perry. Should something happen to Chucky, he's second in command, and the young nigga is Vito, Chucky's son."

"Son?" My mouth dropped wide open because I'd never known him to have children.

"Yeah, supposedly the little nigga has been living with his mother in Las Vegas. Until recently, Chucky didn't even know about him. Now that he's here, his spoiled ass gets everything he wants. He doesn't have to work for anything."

"How old is he?"

"'Bout twenty or so," Dog whispered as Chucky took the floor.

"I called y'all here today for the monthly meeting, so let's get to it." He paced back and forth in a Ralph Lauren Polo and a pair of khaki shorts. "First and foremost, we have a new member added to the team. Her name is Jane, and she has the spot on Charlevoix. After the meeting, stop by and introduce yourselves."

"I ain't introducing myself to no broad," someone joked, and everyone laughed except me and Dog.

"Jane might a girl but she hustles like a man. This month, her spot has outsold all of y'all. From what I heard, your spot is in jeopardy, so you better take notes from her, Nate." Now everyone was laughing except Nate. "Anyway, I brought y'all here to let you know we gon' switch things up a bit."

"What does that mean exactly?" a voice from the crowd spoke up.

"In an effort to break up the normal routine, I'll be rotating everyone. For instance, Jane and her crew will be moving to Rosemont. Vito and his crew will take over her spot."

Before he could continue, I was up on my feet in protest. "Hold on! We've worked our ass off at that house. I'm not about to let anyone take our customers."

"Janelle, you and your crew have done an awesome job, but I'm relocating you and that's the bottom line."

"So basically you're giving your son everything I've worked hard for? Why not let him build up his own trap like a real hustler?" I was pissed. A few men began to whisper and some snickered.

"Are you questioning me?" Chucky asked.

"Are you stealing from me?" I retorted.

"Enough, Jane!" he snapped. "Keep on talking and you'll be fined."

"Fuck you and the five thousand dollar fine." I removed a few green bills from my purse and made it rain all over the meeting room.

# Chapter Fifty-five

Chucky was a dummy if he thought I would bow down and kiss his ass like every other nigga on his team. My father didn't raise no fool. He should've known better than to take my spot and give it to someone else, son or not!

When I came home, I didn't bother relaying the message to the girls right away. Since we weren't going anywhere, nothing was changing. Instead, I took a nap to ease my pounding head. Regrettably, I was awakened later by the pounding of Alicia's headboard up against the wall and Keisha's high-pitched screaming. Promptly, I grabbed two pillows and covered my ears. It was useless.

Snatching the pillows from my head, I flung them across the room. Alicia and Keisha were getting it in like jackrabbits and it was getting on my nerves. I hadn't had sex in several months. The batteries in my sex toys had been swapped out more times than I cared to count.

After glancing at the clock on my nightstand, I noted it was three o'clock: primetime hour at the trap. Standing from the bed, I stretched my arms toward the ceiling as best I could without straining my belly. By now I was seven months pregnant, and my stomach was big, round, and tight. My due date was still two months away. Even so, I wished I had more time. The thought of going into labor and delivery without Ace by my side was sickening.

Sauntering over to the dresser, I removed a pair of sweatpants and socks then put them on. Next, I went to the closet, slipped on a pair of Reebok flip-flops, and grabbed my purse. As I stepped into the hallway, Alicia's bedroom door opened.

"Where are you going this time of night?" Alicia asked on the way into the kitchen.

"I'm headed to the trap. I can't sleep." I was sure I sounded grumpy. I was irritated, no doubt.

"Oh, I'm sorry, Janelle." She looked back into her bedroom. "Did we wake you?"

"It's all good. Don't worry about it. I'll catch you later." I grabbed my keys and left her standing there. It wasn't my intention to be rude, but today wasn't one of my better days.

Coasting down I-75 in silence provided the perfect opportunity to mull over the day's events. I didn't like my position with Chucky, so it was time look elsewhere for employment. Furthermore, Alicia and Keisha were beginning to work my nerves. Maybe it was time we looked into separate living spaces.

As I exited the freeway, my stomach began to hurt. Sharp pains hit me all of a sudden and I felt weak in the knees. The feeling was so intense that I contemplated driving straight to the hospital. However, I ignored my intuition and continued to the trap instead. Michelle's car was parked outside when I pulled up so I blew the horn once.

She opened the side door. "Jane, what are you doing out this late?"

"Auntie, I couldn't sleep." I swung my legs out of the car and struggled to stand up.

"What's wrong?" She came down the driveway toward the car.

"That damn Ali and Keisha been sexing like rabbits and I can't sleep." I laughed.

"So why didn't you get a hotel room instead of coming here?" She helped me from the car and up the driveway.

"This may sound funny, but I actually find peace here."

"Your daddy used to say that." She shook her head.

As we reached the side door, I saw movement in my peripheral vision. Before I could completely turn around, I heard the gunshots. Bang. Bang. "Ahh!" I screamed as hot fire hit my knee, forcing me to the ground.

"Oh, my God, Jane." Michelle struggled with attending to my needs or running for shelter. Most people would've let me be in order to save their own ass. Nevertheless, she stayed behind and attempted to pull me to safety. My purse housed my gun, but it had fallen a few inches away from where I was lying and was out of reach.

"What's up now, bitch?" The man pointed the gun and shot again, this time hitting my arm. His aim wasn't worth shit. If he were a real killer, I would've been dead at this close range. But I wasn't complaining. "Pick her up and get her in the house," he instructed Michelle, who was covered in my blood.

"What's the matter with you? She's pregnant!" she screamed.

"Shut up and do what I said." The masked man pointed the gun at her. She shrieked. "Now hurry up!"

Michelle struggled to lift my body with her 135-pound frame. She did as best she could until we were in the house.

"Where's the dope?" he asked.

"We ain't got no dope," she yelled. "Just leave us alone."

"Bitch, stop lying." Once again he pointed the gun toward her.

"I'm not lying. We ran dry over an hour ago," she insisted.

"So where's the money at?"

"It's been delivered to the stash house," Michelle replied.

See me, I would've come up off the bread and lived to fight another day. Michelle, on the other hand, was from the old school. She would die before she gave a nigga anything. Once word got out that you did, they'd think you're soft. It then became an open invitation for every Tom, Dick, and Harry to get at you.

"So you wanna be tough. Suit yourself. Both of y'all get into that closet," he barked.

Up until this point, I hadn't said anything. I was concentrating on the sound of his voice and the pattern of his movements and memorizing the shoes he had on. "Son of a bitch!" I spoke low yet loud enough to be heard. "For real, dude, is that you?" He was one of the local residents I'd had an encounter with a few days ago.

Ali and I had stopped at the corner store for snacks. When we came outside, he and his homies were leaning on Alicia's Lexus like they owned it. We asked them politely to move but they decided to get ignorant. Dude actually tried to flex on me until I revealed my gun and shot at his ass. I wasn't really trying to hit him. But now I wished I would have. This man had the audacity to run up in my spot trying to rob me while wearing the same neon green Air Max's he had on the other day.

"Get in the closet!" He snatched the mask off and threw it to the floor, no longer attempting to conceal his identity.

"You better kill me, I swear on my mother, because if you don't, you'll wish you had." With my adrenaline racing, I no longer felt the pain. He walked over to me, grabbed the collar of my shirt, and dragged me into the closet. Auntie Michelle tried crawling away, but he shot her right in the ass. Screaming in agony, she dropped to her stomach and lay flat. Old boy went over and pulled her by the legs into the closet.

Once he closed the door, she wrapped her arms around me. "Janie, if only one of us makes it out of here alive, I'm gonna make sure it's you."

"We're both going to make it," I assured her as we heard his movement throughout the house. He had to be looking for drugs, money, or anything else to make his robbery worthwhile. A short time later, the footsteps stopped. Soon, he increased the volume on the television to the max. I didn't know what the hell was going on until I saw the bullets tear into the closet door. The first two shots barely missed us. I was petrified yet pissed off because I wasn't able to do anything about it.

Michelle flung her body on top of mine as the remaining bullets ripped into the wooden door. I wanted to scream as her body rocked from the penetration of bullets, but I knew better. If he was going to think we were both dead, then I had to stay still and remain silent.

# Chapter Fifty-six

Too scared to move an inch or make a sound, I lay in the closet for hours, balled up like a baby. It wasn't until I heard, "Yo, is anyone in here? I'm trying to get serviced," that I relaxed. The voice belonged to Leroy, one of the crackheads I served. He was a middle-aged war veteran who had returned home with a habit. After years of intravenous drug use, his skin was damaged, his teeth were decaying, and he was half out of his mind. Nonetheless, Leroy was my savior at the moment.

"I'm in here." I was too weak to open the closet door myself so I stayed put.

"Y'all really need to clean up. Look like a murder scene up in here." He rambled on at the mouth while walking through the house.

"I'm in the closet, Leroy. Open the door."

"What in the hell is you doing in the closest? And they say I'm crazy." Slowly, he turned the knob and damn near leaped from his skin when he observed the scene before him. "Jane, are you all right?"

"No, Leroy, I need help. Please call Ali for me." He was a regular at our spot and real familiar with Alicia and me. From time to time, he would wash our cars or cut the grass for some free crack.

"I ain't got no phone, boss." He shook his head.

"My purse is on the ground outside in the driveway. Go get it and grab my cell phone." It probably wasn't the best idea to send a crackhead to retrieve my purse. However, my options were limited at the moment.

Leroy was back in a flash, handing me my phone. I put in the finger code and dialed Alicia.

"I've been calling you all night, Janelle! Where in the hell have you been?" She was pissed, but now wasn't the time for that.

"Alicia, get over on the east side now. That nigga we had issues with at the corner store came over here and robbed us."

"What?" she screamed. "Are you okay?"

"He shot me twice and he killed Michelle." I looked down at my aunt's lifeless body. A wave of emotion came over me. However, I couldn't allow my tears to fall in the trap house.

"I'm on my way."

"Get here fast. I think my water just broke." The liquid flowing from between my legs was a telltale sign that my baby was coming.

In no time, Alicia and Keisha were at the spot. They picked me up and carried me to the car. Then Ali went back and locked the house down. With a baby on the way, no one could worry about Michelle. Just as I did with Gudda, I would send someone to clean up the spot and move Michelle's body to another location. The only difference was I made sure they burned his ass to a crisp afterward. The coroner was probably still trying to make heads or tails of his ashes.

"So you know for sure it was old boy?"

"Yes, Ali, he took his mask off." My stomach was doing its own thing. I prayed like hell my child wouldn't be born in this car.

"I got that nigga on the real." She beat the steering wheel. Surely, he would get what was coming to him, but right now I couldn't concentrate on anything except having this baby.

"Janie, you know once they see those bullet wounds, they're going to call the police." Keisha rubbed my shoulders from the back seat. Until now, I hadn't thought about my injuries.

"I'll just tell them I was robbed on my way to the corner store or something." I shrieked from the pain in my vagina and held on to the seat belt for dear life.

"They're gonna want to know which store," Keisha continued.

"It doesn't matter. Pick one. Hell, you could be robbed at any one of the corner stores in this city." She was beginning to work my nervous system. Alicia recognized the apprehension so she turned on the radio. We rode the remainder of the way to the hospital in silence.

When we got there, emergency staff determined that I was indeed in labor, which trumped my bullet wounds. Therefore, they bandaged me up then dispatched me to the maternity floor. On the way up, I thought of Gran. "Can someone call my grandmother?" I had already been pushing for over twenty minutes. The baby was just about here.

"I already did. She's on the way." Alicia squeezed my hand.

"Push, Janelle, you're almost there," the nurse coached me.

"Push, Janelle. Push, baby." Gran stepped into the room on cue and came over to be by my side. It meant so much to me that she was here. She was the only family I had left, besides my child.

"Come on, J, you can do it." Alicia jumped up and down.

"I can see the baby's hair." Keisha smiled from behind her cell phone. She was using the camera feature to record the birth for Ace. I was exhausted and drenched in perspiration. My lips were dry and I felt cold. I'd been pushing for too long in my opinion and was ready for my baby to make her entrance into this world.

"Janelle, just give me three good pushes. I promise this will be over and your baby will be in your arms." Dr. Nolan stood between my legs in light blue scrubs. The nurses stood in the rear of the room, ready and waiting for my baby to arrive.

"J, you got this!" Alicia rubbed my shoulder.

"One," Dr. Nolan counted and I pushed. "Two," she continued. I gritted my teeth, pushing until I was blue in the face.

"This is it, baby." Gran patted my arm.

"Three." I pushed like my life depended on it and felt something ooze out of me like a ball of slime. I watched as Dr. Nolan cut the umbilical cord and remove mucus from my daughter's mouth and nose.

"Eight o'clock on the dot." One of the nurses called out her time of birth then placed her onto a machine to measure her height and capture her weight. "She's twenty-one inches and eight pounds eleven ounces."

"Here's your big girl, Mommy." Another nurse placed my baby girl into my arms. I showered her with my tears and covered her with kisses.

"Happy birthday, Juliana Antonia Valquez. I love you." As she blinked slowly, I peered into her tiny face and acknowledged that her eyes reflected a hint of hazel and green, just like her dad. Truthfully, she looked like the mirror image of Ace. In that instant, I realized it would be exceedingly complicated to look at her every day and not be distressed.

"She is absolutely adorable." Gran dabbed at a tear.

"J, you did so good." Alicia was crying as well.

"Congratulations on your miracle." Keisha rubbed Juliana's tiny hand. The moment was bittersweet. Therefore, I didn't say anything. Closing my eyes, I pretended that Ace was standing beside me, that they were his words I was hearing rather than theirs.

# Chapter Fifty-seven

Being a new single mom was definitely something to get used to. With the help of Gran and Alicia, I was making it happen. They were my support system when I needed assistance. Primarily, I kept Juliana with me. She was the apple of my eye. I loved her more than anything. Every day she was growing and changing right before my eyes, which only saddened me because her daddy was missing out.

Speaking of Ace, today I was taking Ju to visit him for the first time. To me, it was important for him to lay eyes on his daughter as a reminder of what he had waiting for him at home. The prison officials tried to give me a hard time about it. However, Richard pulled a few strings and arranged the meeting.

Beep! The sound of the corrections officer swiping his badge to enter the room captured my attention, startling me slightly. Just like the first time I was here to see Ace, my stomach was in knots and I was a nervous wreck. Sitting up straight, I put on the best smile I could muster. Juliana's car seat rested atop the metal table as she napped quietly. "You all have fifteen minutes." The officer turned then exited the square room, leaving us alone.

"Damn, Janie, you look nice." Ace stood in the doorway and looked me over from head to toe. His eyes roamed every inch of my body like a lion ready to devour his prey.

"Thank you, baby." I stood and performed a slow spin for him to see what I was working with. Then I went over to hug him. He grabbed me with so much force that I was lifted off the ground. His shoulders were tight and his back tense.

"Girl, I've missed you." Ace sounded sad, which in turn made me sad. I was aware of the fact that prison was definitely taking a toll on him. He even had a few gray hairs on top of his head. "What happened to your teeth?" He frowned.

"They're called Lumineers. Do you like them?" I couldn't keep wearing the surgical mask. The jig was up.

"It looks okay I guess, but why did you get them?" Ace never missed a beat when it came to me. Sometimes it was gift and a curse.

"I had a run-in with Gudda, but it's been handled." I hated to even say the bastard's name.

"What happened?"

"Baby, let's talk about this some other time, okay?" I kissed his lips. "I wanted to cheer you up, so I brought someone to see you."

He put me back down on the ground. "Who is it?"

"Her name is Juliana Antonia Valquez. She's three months old." I pulled him in the direction of the table in the middle of the floor and tapped on the door. Richard opened the door and handed me the car seat with our daughter waiting bright-eyed, ready to meet her father.

"Oh, shit, she's actually here." Instantly he was overcome with joy as I set the car seat on top of the table. "I didn't think I would see her in person anytime soon." Ace sat down in front of the car seat and smiled. "Oh, my gosh, Janie, she's beautiful!" He rubbed her tiny leg. Ju smiled in her sleep, which made his day.

"I went into premature labor and had her early." I specifically skipped the horrific details about what caused Ju to come early. Ace didn't need to know anything about it. "I would've brought her sooner but I had to make sure she had all of her shots first." I stood behind him and massaged his shoulders.

"I'm so glad you brought her. Thanks, baby, I really needed this today." He kissed her hand and rubbed her hair.

"Don't you wanna hold her?" I asked.

"No, I have too many germs on me. This place is filthy." He shook his head and continued watching Ju sleep.

"Baby, I brought a bunch of blankets to cover you in. If you would like to hold her, trust me, it's okay." Juliana awoke just as I went to unlock the belt on the car seat. "See, she has your eyes." I pointed and he smiled.

"She looks like the girl version of me." As I handed him the blankets and then Ju, he was awestruck. Although he was nervous at first, within a minute or two he was comfortable cradling her small body. I took out my camera phone and snapped a few shots of this moment for Juliana's photo book.

"Damn, J, she has stolen my heart already." He kissed her forehead while rocking her gently. I watched Ace with our daughter and wanted to cry. But I kept it together.

The rest of the visit went smoothly. While Ace held his daughter, I showed him the recording of the delivery so he could feel as if he were there. For a small moment in time, things felt normal again, up until the officer came to inform us the visit was over. Ace requested fifteen more minutes, and the officer obliged.

"I need to holler at you about some business." He placed Ju back into her car seat. "You know when they took me down, they took the whole Pauletti family down, right?"

"Yeah." I didn't have anything else to say so I let him finish.

"Well, I literally just got word that the wives of the men arrested have stepped up to take over the business in order to make sure the family stays afloat until this shit is worked out."

"That's what's up."

"Well, Nicky Carmichael sent a kite to me this morning asking if I had someone willing to take my spot. I sent a kite back and told him about you. If you're game, you're on."

"So you want me to go into business with the mob?" I was shocked. Ace never wanted me anywhere near the trap. However, now he was handing me a connection on a silver platter.

"You said you set up shop with Chucky in order to make money for us, right? Well, I figured if you were gonna take such a risk, then you might as well make it meaningful. The money they bring in is unheard of. If you do this shit like I know you can, then you'll be a millionaire in less than five years. Your new position with the mob makes you the number one supplier on the streets in all of the black community."

"Straight up, it's like that?" My mouth was wide open as I intensely considered what he had just said. On one hand, I wanted to be a better role model for Ju. Conversely, this connection could also be just what I needed to live the way I'd always dreamed I would.

"If you want the position, it's yours, J. Just say the word." He licked those perfect lips I loved to hate. "You know how I feel about you hustling, especially now that you've got my seed. But I know you're a grown-ass woman and you gon' do your own thing regardless of how I feel. The coins you make with Chucky is chump change compared to mafia money. So if you gon' do it, at least do it right." He made a very valid point. I was hooked.

"Thank you, baby! Count me in." I kissed him.

"Before you get all excited, you need to know these fuckers don't play. If you mess up, they come for you hard."

"I promise I won't mess this up." I was excited about the new opportunity. It was time to take my crew to the next level. I couldn't wait to get started.

"I love you, Janelle. Please be careful." When he pressed his lips up against mine, I felt a shiver from the tips of my toes all the way to the pulsation that was happening in my vaginal area. "Do you still love me?"

"Of course I do." I looked at him crazy.

"Say that shit then. 'Cause a nigga need to hear it right about now," he demanded with a smirk, all the while rubbing my thighs.

"I love you, Anthony." I slid my hand down toward the bulge in his pants and fondled him.

"Damn, I miss this shit," he groaned softly.

"You'll be home soon, don't worry." My nipples were hardened and my body was aroused. Shit would've gotten real had the officer not come back to stop the party. The rooms Richard always arranged for us were the ones inmates used to meet with their counsel. Therefore, nothing could be monitored or recorded. Before Ace left, he gave me an address and a phone number for some woman named Karla.

# Chapter Fifty-eight

I couldn't wait to tell Alicia the good news. When I did, she was just as excited as I was. We decided not to share the information with anyone else until after the meeting.

Gran came over the next day to watch Ju. Then we headed out to the boondocks to meet with Karla. The home was out in Romulus, Michigan, a good forty-five minutes away from Detroit. Pulling my whip up to the gates of the most magnificent home I'd ever seen, I marveled in amazement and endeavored to keep my bottom lip from dropping too low.

"Do you see this shit?" Ali tapped me as I went to press the intercom buzzer.

"Hello." Someone fumbled with the button. "Carmichael residence."

"Hi, my name is Jane. I'm here to see Karla." I tried not to sound nervous. However, the mansion that stood before me was quite intimidating. "This is some boss shit for real," I whispered to Ali as the ten-foot wrought-iron gate opened and I pulled inside. The dark green lawn with sculpted shrubbery was immaculate. The red rose beds were impeccable. There was even an arch-shaped driveway made of cobblestone with a white Rolls-Royce parked out front.

"Damn, I feel underdressed." Alicia straightened out her yellow one-piece capri jumper.

"Who you telling?" I had on an orange maxi dress with sandals. But the place was so fancy I felt like I should've had on a big hat or something.

"Hello, I'm Karla Carmichael. Nice to meet you." A tan woman with toned arms extended her hand. Her grip was soft yet firm, and her smile was sincere. In her eyes, I recognized the pain of missing a loved one. However, in her voice I heard the fortitude it took to bring that loved one back home.

"I'm Janelle, but you can call me Jane." I shook her hand and returned the smile. "And this is Ali."

"Nice to meet you." Alicia smiled.

"Come on in, ladies. Let's get down to business." She gestured for us to enter the grand home then closed and locked the door. The interior of Karla's home resembled something straight from the home decor pages in *Italian Vogue*. There was the allure of cream, burgundy, and gold colors throughout the residence.

"This place is absolutely gorgeous!" Alicia marveled at an oil painting in the hallway.

"Thank you, sweetheart! My husband, Nicky, and I decorated this entire place without a designer. We wanted it to be chic yet personal." She led us into a cream and copper-inspired kitchen. The sink, dishwasher, oven range, and refrigerator all resembled copper. It was the first I'd seen of its kind, and I was sort of feeling it.

"Well, kudos to you and Nicky." I smiled. "When Ace is released, and after we save up enough money to buy a house, maybe you could help us decorate."

"Oh, I would love to decorate for you. My husband speaks highly of your boyfriend, Anthony. He says he's like family and is a real stand-up guy." She pulled three teacups from the cupboard, handing one each to Alicia and me and keeping one for herself. Then she went into the kitchen drawer and pulled out a small metal flask filled with a brown liquid. She poured a shot into her teacup. "Girls, would you like a sip?" She waved the flask. Alicia readily extended her cup.

"None for me. I'm nursing," I declined.

"Well, since you can't have one, I guess I'll help myself to another." She winked and walked over to the kitchen table. "Jane, here is some hot tea if you'd like some." Karla pointed at the tea kettle resting on the table. I wanted to decline that beverage as well. However, I didn't want to offend her. Therefore, I poured just a little.

"Thank you, Karla." Alicia and I spoke at the same time.

"No problem." She took a seat at the table beside us. "So let's get down to business, shall we?"

"Anthony didn't go into much detail about this meeting. He simply provided me with your address and told me when to show up." Ace had given me plenty of information. Nevertheless, I wanted her detailed version of the story.

"Well, in case you didn't know, Nicky is a big part of the Pauletti crime family. Recently, they took a huge hit during the bust. As a result, the entire male organization is presently behind bars awaiting trial, including Anthony." She sipped from her teacup. "Never in history has every male in our organization been pinched at the same time. And with them away, we're losing money as well as our respected position with the other families. Approximately a month ago, Constance Pauletti, the boss's wife, approached the rest of the wives with an idea to not only save the business on behalf of our men but to keep the family up and running. That's where you come in. We would like you to take over Anthony's spot with our organization until he comes home." She sipped from her teacup again while looking directly at me.

"In other words, you want me to be your black salesgirl?" I also sipped from my teacup with my eyes focused on hers. I knew how most Italians felt about black people, and she was probably no different.

"Jane," she said, smirking, "not many people know this but my grandmother was a black woman. So contrary to what you believe, when I look at you, I don't see color. All I see before me is a woman ready and willing to play her position until her man returns home, just like me."

"Is this a secret between you and me, or will I be introduced to the other ladies?" I wasn't a backdoor bitch. If Karla wanted to do business with me, then she had better bring me to the table the correct way.

"Funny that you should mention it, because the other women should be here any minute now. We get together every Saturday to eat, vent, and talk shop." She tasted from her teacup, having to refill it twice. She made small talk until there was a buzz from the intercom. Karla excused herself from the table while Ali got straight to it.

"J, do you know what this means for us?" She smiled.

"It means a whole lot of trouble if we aren't careful." I shook my head. True, the Italian connection was just what we needed to dominate the dope game. Accordingly, more power virtually always came with more problems.

"They're here." Karla retuned to the kitchen with four women in tow.

"Hello, ladies, how are you?" A heavyset woman entered the kitchen with a Tupperware container and set it down on the counter. She was tall with black hair, big boobs, and very full lips. In my opinion, she needed to have some of the Botox removed from her lips and go down three sizes on the implants.

"I love what you've done with the place, Karla." Another woman entered carrying a basket of bread, never acknowledging us. She was very tan and petite with black hair.

"It's hotter than an elephant's ass out there." The oldest woman placed four bottles of champagne down on the table. "Hello, girls." At present, she wasn't much of a looker. However, I could tell that back in her heyday in all probability she was a beauty queen.

"Constance, you better watch your mouth." The final woman to enter the kitchen was carrying a box of pastries. She didn't look Italian to me. In fact, if anything, she appeared to be Caucasian due to the blond hair and blue eyes.

"I'm sixty-nine. So I'll say whatever the hell I wanna say," Constance snapped and opened the refrigerator to retrieve a bottle of Fiji water.

"Ladies, we have guests, so cut it out." With a giggle, Karla cleared her throat. "Jane and Ali, this is Amelia, Ramona, Gia, and Constance."

"Hello," I spoke, while Ali simply waved. With the exception of Amelia, everyone seemed friendly. But I wasn't too concerned with her.

"For the meeting, we brought some penne pasta with sausage and tomato sauce, pinot grigio, and a loaf of freshly baked bread. Have some?" Ramona asked while pulling plates from the cabinet.

"They don't have a choice," Constance joked. "If they're going to be a part of this family, then they have to eat like an Italian."

We all gathered our plates and moved into Karla's formal dining room. The spacious room housed a ten-seat cherry wood table, a four-tier chandelier, and a large china buffet with various family heirlooms atop. The ladies participated in small talk for a little over an hour before getting down to business.

"Did Karla fill you girls in?" asked Constance. Her husband had been the head of the family for over three decades.

"Yes, she filled us in." I nodded. "But we hadn't discussed percentages and payouts yet." It was time to get to the meat of why we were here in the first place.

"Our family has a coke supplier straight from Mexico. Every Friday morning, we send a money truck across the border. In return, each Friday afternoon, they send a shipment of pure cocaine at its finest." Constance wiped her mouth with a napkin from the table.

"Why is everything done on Friday?" Alicia asked.

"Because Friday is the border patrol's biggest day. They see over a million vehicles from sunup to sundown. It's an arduous process to be thorough when they're attempting to move line upon line of waiting vehicles."

"I guess that does make sense." Ali shrugged. "So how long does it take the truck to get from the border to us?"

"Roughly around four days." Constance took a gulp from her goblet.

"Basically we can expect the shipment to arrive every Wednesday?" Alicia continued with her line of questioning. Nonetheless, I cut in.

"Forgive me if I sound crazy. But for clarity's sake, this isn't the same transportation operation that got everyone arrested, is it?" I was sure these ladies were smart enough not to use the same routine as the one that initially got their husbands locked up. Nonetheless, I had to ask.

"No, Jane, this is a totally different setup." Ramona laughed.

"Okay, cool. In that case, let's continue. How much coke am I expected to buy and how much will it cost me?"

"I only sell kilograms. And because I like you"—she smiled—"the cost for each kilogram is ten thousand dollars." Although Constance was the one stuffing her mouth, I almost choked. Her prices were splendidly low. Most kilograms priced between $20,000 and $25,000. Hell, after we cut the coke and added filler, we could easily make a calculated profit of at least $60,000.

"Constance, when can we get started?" I was eagerly anticipating the bankroll that was sure to come. However, I reserved my serious face so that she wouldn't retract her price and charge additional.

"Jane, I'm ready to do business now. Do you have the money?" She bit down on a piece of bread. On cue, Alicia excused herself from the table and went to the car to retrieve the money we brought with us. We were actually anticipating a higher price. Therefore, we put our money together and came up with $30,000.

After finishing our business with the Pauletti ladies and loading three kilos into the trunk of my car, we were once again on our way. "So what now?" Alicia put her seat belt on.

"As soon as we get back to the city, I'ma holla at Chucky and give him first dibs on this shit." I put the car in gear and headed away from the house.

"Fuck Chucky!" Alicia spat. "That nigga tried to do us dirty by giving away our spot."

"I know, but you get more bees with honey. That nigga has Detroit on lock. If he's down, then all of our shit will be in each of his traps, which will make his competition seek us out. Then we'll have even more business."

"Dude is shady. I still don't think it's a good idea." Ali shook her head. "Think about it. Your father was the king of Detroit. Chucky was his sidekick. He probably wanted what your father had, so he set him up. Next, Ace starts working for the Italians and becomes the man. Then all of a sudden, he's behind bars. If we go in there telling him about our connection, something bad is gon' happen."

# Chapter Fifty-nine

Contrary to what Alicia thought, I knew I had to visit Chucky. Her words had given me second thoughts. Consequently, if we were to start supplying everyone with dope and not inform Chucky, the repercussions could be deadly. Ultimately, a move like that would be equivalent to taking food from his mouth. Most people would be unsympathetic about stepping on the next person's toes. In contrast, I believed unconditionally in doing good business, which was why I would alert him to not only a new opportunity but a potential partnership as well.

In an effort to locate Chucky, I stepped into the bar and went directly to the back. As usual, he was playing dice. "Hey, let me holler at you real quick."

"I'll be done in a few. Grab a seat." He never looked up.

"Look, it's about business and I don't have much time." I was ready to make moves, not sit here and wait for him.

"Speak then," he snapped.

"I got a connect on some uncut coke for the low-low. I wanted to plug you in." I watched him pause for a second.

"How low are you talking about?"

"I'm talking eighteen thousand a kilogram." I folded my arms and waited for his reaction. Even with the eight grand I tacked on, the price was lower than what he was accustomed to paying.

"Where you get this connection from?" Realizing the information I had was more important than the dice game, he stood.

"Come on, blood, you should me better than that." I laughed because he knew damn well I wasn't gon' give my connection up to him.

"I like to meet the people I do business with," he replied.

"You're doing business with me. That's all you need to know."

"How good is the grade?" He motioned for me to follow him over to a booth.

"I could hype this up all day, but I brought a sample for you to see for yourself." I tossed him a small Baggie. After carefully reviewing it, he then called one of the dice players to test it. The man poured a small line of white powder onto his hand then took a sniff.

"Woo!" He blinked rapidly. "That shit is fire right there." His nose started to run. I handed him a napkin from the table. Chucky thought quietly for a second then excused the man from the table.

"Can you drop the price for family?" he asked with a straight face.

"I don't have to remind you that there is no such thing as family when we're doing business! Remember?" Those were his exact words to me when I started hustling.

"Well, let me think on it and I'll get back with you." He stood from the table with an attitude like he was dismissing me.

"Out of respect, I came to you first. But if you're not with my deal, then I'm on to the next one! There is no waiting in this game. You should know that." I stood and grabbed my purse.

"Do what you feel you have to do. Just remember your dope won't get far without my approval. I run this city. Ain't nobody fucking with you unless I say so." He laughed then waved goodbye as I headed out the door.

I didn't know why Chucky thought he had so much loyalty in these streets. Niggas in the dope game were only loyal to one thing, and that was the almighty dollar. It was time for plan B.

After leaving the bar, I called Tyra and told her to close down the operation after she sold the last of what we had. Next, I sent Keisha to pass out one free sample to every dopefiend she laid eyes on. I was sure it was unheard of for dope dealers to pass out free dope. Yet, I viewed the complimentary samples as business cards. After they tasted my product and got hooked, they wouldn't ever wanna fuck with my competition again. Ultimately, this tactic inevitably meant more money in my pockets. Finally, Alicia and I hit the streets hard to persuade some of the other dealers to join us.

The first stop we made was to see Dog. His spot was full of niggas on the porch as usual. "What brings you this way, fam?" With his feet inside a kiddie pool, he was sitting on the porch, sipping on a bottle of water. Even though it was hell hot today, this Negro looked crazy as hell.

"I came to talk shop with you one-on-one." I took the vacant seat nearest him and placed the duffle bag on my lap. Once he asked his crew to leave, I got right down to business. "Recently, I came upon a connection for cocaine. It's top grade, one hundred percent pure from Mexico. Since I'm trying to do things on a grand scale, I'm only selling kilos."

"Damn, I usually don't fuck with that much weight. Normally it's only ounces."

"It's time to step your game up, fam." I patted the duffle bag.

"If the price is right, then I might be down." He removed the cap from his water and took a gulp.

"I'm selling them for eighteen racks." I watched Dog's eyes widen as he sat up in his seat.

"Damn! I pay Chucky more than that for the processed shit."

"Come over to my side and you'll not only have more money in your pocket but a better product." I watched as he pondered the pros and cons of doing business with me.

"You speak to Chucky on this?"

"Out of respect, I took it to him first, but he passed. So now I'm here. If you pass, I'll be on to the next one."

"Let's say I do this. What's the take?" He removed his feet from the small pool and planted them on the porch.

"There is no breakdown. Once you buy your package from me, you can sell it for however much you want."

"Square biz?" He was all ears now. "Sounds good to me, but are you sure you're ready to go toe-to-toe with Chucky? Once he finds out we crossed him, there's gonna be smoke in the city."

"I told you once before that I ain't ever scared. What about you? Are you riding with me or what?"

"Yeah, count me in, J." He nodded, and then we proceeded to conduct business.

Several meetings with additional dealers had pretty much gone the same way. Most of them were down with my prices. However, others were afraid of cutting ties with Chucky. Some joined my roster, and some stayed down with Chucky. A few of them flat-out declined my offer, stating they would never do business with a bitch. I respected the game but it was a decision they would soon regret.

# Chapter Sixty

News of my connection ripped through the streets of Detroit like a virus. Before I knew it, I was "the man," so to speak. Dealers from all over the Midwest and Canada had begun hitting me up for the goods. Within a year, we expanded the operation to Atlanta, Miami, and Los Angeles. The crew was bigger and stronger than ever, which amazed the Pauletti women on many levels. We were moving so much weight they had to expand their delivery schedules in order to keep up with the demand.

Overnight, my crew became celebrities. Everywhere we went, people took notice. For fear of attracting the Feds, I didn't like all of the attention. Yet Ali didn't mind it one bit. In her opinion, as long as we weren't caught with our hand in the cookie jar, there would be no harm and no foul. I knew better, but there was nothing I could do about it.

My crew had made over $3.2 million in a year's time. Everyone upgraded their whip as well as their address. I purchased a home in West Bloomfield. Alicia purchased a condo with Keisha. Tyra had even managed to convince Tamia to join the squad as our accountant on a full-time basis. The first thing she showed us was how to invest our money the legit way. For doing so, we paid her well.

I invested in a chain of clothing stores in each city. The retail stores were called Capa Donna and were set up in malls. In the Italian families, the word "capo" is used to describe the head of a crime family. The word "don" depicts a high-society man with money and power. Since I'm not a man, I rolled with the female version of each word. If for any reason I were ever audited, my bank accounts were all linked to that business. Furthermore, if I were to be questioned with regard to my frequent flights to each city, I would have an excuse. Alicia chose to invest in a record company that would only produce some of the dopest female entertainers in the game. The company was called Grade A Entertainment. She already had ten clients.

Money was pouring in at such an impressive magnitude that we needed buckets. In my mind, things could only get better from here. Boy, was I wrong.

"Oh, shit, we've got the AFM in the building!" the disc jockey announced as we walked into Club Haze in Southfield. People began to stare at us. A few of them even raised their drinks in a toast.

"Who in the hell is the AFM?" I asked Alicia, who was in front of me. Tonight, she had invited everyone out to celebrate the success of one of her artists who had a single playing on the radio. Typically, the club scene wasn't for me. However, Gran offered to watch Ju. Because I hadn't been out for a while, I agreed.

"It means All Female Mafia," she yelled over the music. I didn't know where he had gotten the name from, but it was kind of catchy. I liked it. Back in the day, Detroit had seen its fair share of drug dealers. Yet the most memorable of names were the infamous "YBI" or Young Boys Incorporated, as well as the "BMF" better known as Black Mafia Family. Those men mastered the game. It may sound crazy but I was proud to be among the list. Never had a female been able to do what we did. This was only the beginning.

"This place is the truth," Tamia said into my ear. I nodded in agreement. The club was packed with people dressed to the nines. The disc jockey was bumping the jams. Our bottle service kept the bottles of Cîroc and Grey Goose on deck. The funny thing about it was none of us were old enough to drink. All the same, when you had money, people did whatever you asked in hopes that you would look out for them.

"Ain't that Chucky over there? What's his old ass doing up in the club?" Alicia laughed and beckoned for the waitress. "Here's five hundred dollars. Send that old nigga in the Kangol hat the best bottle of champagne you have in the building."

"No, please don't send that bottle." I stood and tried to stop the transaction between Ali and the waitress.

"Sweetheart, take this money and get his ass the most extravagant bottle you have at the bar," Ali slurred. She was already lit and we hadn't been here for an hour. "Keep this hundred for your trouble." She slapped the girl's butt. Keisha saw her but didn't say anything.

"Girl, why are you starting stuff?" I yelled at Ali. I hadn't seen Chucky since he refused my deal. Presently, there was no bad blood between us and I wanted to keep it that way.

"That nigga will be all right." She brushed me off then went back to slow grinding on Keisha. I sat back in the cut and watched with a side-eye how Chucky was going to react to Alicia's gift. If he accepted it, I knew we were cool. Unfortunately, if he sent it back, then we had problems.

"Grab your glass, Jane." Tyra held hers up along with everyone else while Alicia's drunken ass made a toast.

"To AFM and fuck everybody else!" she slurred. With the exception of me, the entire crew repeated her toast. I was too busy trying to see what Chucky was going to do about the bottle, but I had lost sight of him in the dark room full of people. Maybe he left? I relaxed a bit and sipped from the glass. Usually, I wasn't a drinker. I didn't like being in an altered state of mind, but tonight was a celebration. Besides, I needed to take my mind off of Ace. He was still behind bars, but Richard assured me he would be home soon.

"What's wrong?" Keisha came over to where I was sitting.

"I miss Ace, that's all." I offered her a smile although it wasn't authentic. My man had been gone for way too long. Every day he was missing out on Ju's big moments, which caused me to be despondent.

"He'll be home soon. His lawyer said it was looking good for him, right?"

"Well, yeah, he did say that, but they still haven't set a trial date." As we conversed, I noticed Chucky entering our VIP area, heading in my direction. My stomach hit the ground but my game face remained unchanged. "Keisha, give me a minute please." I excused her and motioned for him to take a seat. Back in the day, I would've stood to greet him, except he no longer deserved that kind of respect.

"Look at you all grown up, sending bottles and shit. What's this all about?" He was offended. "Are you trying to make me look bad or something?" He placed the bottle of Ace of Spades on top of the cocktail table before me.

"First off, I didn't send the bottle. Nevertheless, it was sent as a peace offering." I grabbed the bottle and poured myself a glass. There was no need to let a good bottle go to waste.

"Peace offering for what? I didn't know there was an issue." He was mind fucking me and I knew it.

"Look, Chucky, we just came here to have a good time. Sorry if the bottle offended you, but it really was intended to be a generous gesture."

"Well, I won't stop your good time. I just came over here to return the bottle and to give you a piece of advice." He smiled.

"And what's that?" I sincerely wanted to hear what he had to say.

Leaning down close to my ear, he said, "Watch your back."

"What's that supposed to mean?"

"It means you may think just because you've won the battle, the war is over. But not so. The streets are always watching." With those words, he excused himself from our region and vanished into the crowd of people on the dance floor. To say his words had me feeling some sort of way would've been an understatement.

"What was that all about?" Ali wrapped her arm around my neck.

"Chucky didn't like your gift." I sipped from my glass.

"Fuck that old nigga! He's just mad because we're young boss bitches." Alicia turned her attention back to the crowd then went back to partying, leaving me in the corner contemplating how to clean up this mess.


Outside of the club, there was a line for valet parking. We waited good-naturedly along with a few other party-goers. "Baby, I love you so much." Keisha wrapped her arms around Alicia from the back and kissed her neck.

"I love you more with your fine ass." She palmed her ass like a basketball.

"Why don't you bitches get a room?" I teased.

"Yeah, don't nobody wanna see that shit!" Tyra cracked up laughing. Alicia flipped her the bird. At last, my car was pulled in front of the door. I tossed my girls the deuces and went to retrieve my ride.

As I made it around to the driver's side, I heard the sound of screeching tires and then gunfire. Having no other choice, I dropped to the ground and lay flat. I heard screaming and saw everyone dispersing in one direction or another. The barrage of bullets appeared to go on forever. The moment it stopped, I was back on my feet, trying to make heads or tails of what had just occurred.

"She's been hit!" I heard someone say, so I checked myself for wounds but there weren't any. "Call 911. She's been hit!" This time I looked around to see who was hurt and if there was anything I could do to help. My heart skipped three beats when I looked over to see Alicia covered in blood. She was cradling Keisha like a baby. I knew this was bad. Leaving my car and purse right on the ground where I'd dropped them, I raced toward my friends.

"She can't die, J. Please make the bleeding stop." Alicia cried uncontrollably. Looking down at Keisha, I knew there was nothing I could do. Only God could change this outcome.

"Hold on, Keish, the ambulance is on the way." Tyra kneeled down beside them.

"Baby, please don't die." Alicia relentlessly rocked back and forth. "I love you, Keish. Don't do this to me."

It broke my heart to watch this scene unfold. Alicia was a mess and Keisha had already started to make that final transition. Her body began to shiver, her lips were practically blue, and her eyes kept rolling to the back of her head. We all heard the sirens approaching from a few blocks away. Even so, everyone knew it was too late. Keisha was gone in a flash. She died in Alicia's arms with her eyes wide open. While Ali was rocking her lifeless body, I reached down and closed her eyes.

"We promised each other forever, J, so she can't be dead."

"Baby, she's gone." Sniffing back my own tears, I tried to be strong for my friend. This disaster was definitely a hit below the belt. The person responsible had taken one of our own. For that, this shit had to be rectified pronto.

# Chapter Sixty-one

The days following Keisha's death were unnerving. My entire crew was on edge. Conversely, Alicia was a train wreck. I invited her to stay with me and Ju on the night of the shooting, but she refused. Not wanting to press the issue, I decided to give her time. However, days turned into a week. I still hadn't heard from her. I burned several tanks of gas going to her condo. She was either not at home or refusing to answer the door. I would've blown the locks off but I wanted to respect her space. Everyone grieved differently. Therefore, before I put out an all-points bulletin for her, I decided to see if she would show up at Keisha's funeral today.

"Thank you so much for coming, Janelle." Keisha's cousin Brandy walked over to hug me.

"I wouldn't have missed it for the world."

"Is Alicia with you?" She looked behind me. "I haven't heard from her since Keisha passed. I just wanted to make sure she was okay."

"Neither have I, but I'm sure she'll be here." I grabbed an obituary from the table and proceeded into the church. Keisha was very popular and loved by many people. Although the place was small, it was filled to the brim with nearly 100 people. At first glance, all of the seats were taken. Then I spotted Tyra and Tamia waving me over.

"Girl, we got here early to save you and Alicia a spot." Tamia slid down so I could scoot in.

"Where's Ju?" Tyra asked.

"With Gran. I couldn't have her crying and disrupting the service." I opened the obituary and began to read about Keisha's life.

"The question should have been where's Alicia?" Tamia whispered as the service was beginning. I shrugged then turned my attention toward the processional of family members going to view the body. We were in the third row. I could see just fine from my seat. Because I preferred to remember Keisha the way she was, I didn't want to see her up close and personal in that casket.

As the minister delivered his sermon on life and death, I periodically scanned the room for Alicia. She was still missing in action. A few people got up to say kind words about Keisha, causing me to wipe a few tears. Damn, my girl had her whole life in front of her. She didn't have to go out like that.

When the minister announced the final viewing of the body, my heart sank as I noticed Alicia standing in the aisle. For what seemed like an eternity, she stood there frozen before the tears began falling. She dropped to her knees. I was instantly out of my seat and consoling my friend.

"Why did she have to die, Jane?" She looked up at me with eyes that needed an explanation. I felt horrible for Ali as I pulled her up from the floor and ushered her toward the back of the church. "Keisha, I will get that nigga for you, baby. I promise!" she screamed.


The murder of Keisha had undoubtedly started a war between my squad and Chucky's crew. Alicia was on beast mode, and I could do nothing to tame her. "So what are we gonna do, Jane?" She paced my kitchen floor. "Somebody's gon' pay for this shit, no lie!"

"It's your call, fam. Whatever you decide, I'm riding with you." After the funeral, I'd called an emergency meeting at my house that same afternoon.

"I say we hit that nigga in his pockets," Tyra spoke from her seat at the stone kitchen table.

"Fuck his pockets. After what he did to Keisha, I want that man dead!" Alicia slapped the counter, which caused Juliana to cry. She was sitting next to me in her highchair, so I picked her up and rocked her gently.

"Since they know we're coming for Chucky, he'll be under heavy protection for a while. I say we go after his crew one by one until he's all alone and has no one to protect him." I handed Ju a Cheetos Puff and watched her chew with four little teeth the size of cooked rice.

"I'm with that! Let's brainstorm and make this shit happen." Alicia rubbed her bloodshot eyes.

For hours, we plotted on Chucky's crew and strategically calculated every move needed to make this shit successful. Our goal was to target his right-hand man, Perry, his son, Vito, and eventually Chucky himself. Frankly, I was to some extent apprehensive about what was getting ready to go down. Beefing with someone as big as Chucky didn't have the propensity to work out in the underdog's favor. Nevertheless, for Alicia I would've gone to hell with gasoline panties on. She had had my back on more occasions than I could remember. At this juncture it was time for me to have hers. I just hoped we didn't mess up!

# Notes